Praise for

Alan DeNiro's *Skinny Dipping in the Lake of the Dead*

"DeNiro blows his own distinctly different sounding whistle, and once you've heard it, you can't help but stop and take real notice."　　　　—JONATHAN CARROLL, author of *Glass Soup*

"Argues for DeNiro as a writer to watch."　　—*Publishers Weekly*

"Finding stories for *Fence* magazine was always a guilty pleasure. Now here's Alan DeNiro, whose *Skinny Dipping in the Lake of the Dead* was always my favorite. I'm thrilled to see him in bookstores at last."　　　　—JONATHAN LETHEM, author of *Chronic City*

"Refreshing, imaginative, funny-scary stuff."　　　　—*Booklist*

"The wholly original tales that comprise Alan DeNiro's *Skinny Dipping in the Lake of the Dead* are like colorful pinatas full of live scorpions—playful, unexpected, and deadly serious."
　　　　　　—JEFFREY FORD, author of *The Girl in the Glass*

Also by Alan DeNiro

Skinny Dipping in the Lake of the Dead

TOTAL OBLIVION,
MORE OR LESS

TOTAL

OBLIVION,
MORE OR LESS

A Novel

ALAN DeNIRO

SPECTRA

BALLANTINE BOOKS / NEW YORK

A Spectra Trade Paperback Original

Copyright © 2009 by Alan DeNiro

Published in the United States by Spectra,
an imprint of The Random House Publishing Group,
a division of Random House, Inc., New York.

SPECTRA and the portrayal of a boxed "s"
are trademarks of Random House, Inc.

Library of Congress Cataloging-in-Publication Data

DeNiro, Alan.
Total oblivion, more or less : a novel / Alan DeNiro.
p.   cm.
ISBN 978-0-553-59254-2 (pbk.)
1. Regression (Civilization)—Fiction.   2. Teenage
girls—Fiction.   3. Families—Minnesota—Fiction.
4. Survival skills—Fiction.   I. Title.
PS3554.E5325T67 2009
813'.54—dc22   2009036101

Printed in the United States of America

www.ballantinebooks.com

123456789

Book design by Elizabeth A. D. Eno

To Kristin

"*There is prairie behind prairie, forest behind forest, sites of nations, no nations.*"

—Ralph Waldo Emerson

PART
ONE

CHAPTER 1
Coal Miner's Devil

I KEEP FORGETTING HOW LITTLE I KNEW IN THE BEGINNING. How little everyone knew. It's not as if I'm *that* much older now—is there that much difference between sixteen and seventeen? And it's not as if I have a lot of answers now. I don't kid myself about things like *answers* anymore.

But when we started downriver—even after all the chaos in the refugee camp—I kind of prided myself on how I had my act together. Nothing could have been further from the truth.

No one had their acts together, at least in my family. I kept thinking, well, maybe all of this trouble will pass over, and electricity will start working again, and the Scythians will retreat to wherever they came from, and the Empire will give back their land, too, and people will be able to use their cars again and drive wherever they want to, and the government will find a cure for the plague, and we'll go back to St. Paul and I'll start my senior year, none the worse for wear. And everyone would have stories after coming back—crazy stories, to be sure. But stories that couldn't hurt people anymore.

Of course, some people wouldn't have come back. But a lot of people would! And then life would resume more or less where it left off. There would be a lot of memorials and speeches about "healing" and "averting disaster."

That was how I thought things would happen, in the back of my mind, for a while. But each day downriver, that hope—or maybe something halfway between hope and fear—became fainter and fainter. And I remember the first time I began to understand that things might not be the same again. It was when my dad told me this story. I was still clutching my old life, but for the first time I started to catch the drift. What made it odd was that my dad wasn't good at telling stories. But I think he was trying to tell me something important—something that he didn't quite understand himself.

Our boat, the *Prairie Chicken,* was bivouacked on the muddy banks of the Mississippi, near what used to be Red Wing. We were eating dinner in a run-down public park alongside the river. At that point in the journey no one was starving, and we were stopping overnight. It was almost like a picnic, except for the wannabe snipers on the boat, boys my age, watching out for roving bands of horsemen or just ruffians. There were refugees shacked up in the old rail station on the other side of the broken dock. I could see their little cooking fires through the oilskin windows. I felt sorry for them, stuck there like that. I didn't go and offer them food, though.

If I'd known about what we were all going to go through later, I might have tried to tell them: It's not safe anywhere, so you might as well hole up where you are, you're doing the right thing.

There were sandwiches with rye bread and ham for everyone. I had no idea how those were scored, or by whom. I raised a fuss. I didn't want to eat it.

Macy, eat, my father said, as we all sat down on the grass and unwrapped the sandwiches from the butcher paper.

I shrugged. I knew that I was being juvenile, but couldn't help it. The bread was soggy and the ham had these mottled spots and I honestly thought that this was the worst thing in the world. We had these bottles of sugary iced tea to drink. The iced tea was warm and a knock-off brand I'd never heard of— SUNSHINE! I managed to sip it. I wanted Diet Coke. Every inconvenience seemed like a mortal threat. My dad stared at me, but no one else seemed to pay attention to my little psychodrama. Mother nibbled, patting my hand once.

Instead of eating, I watched the boys on the boat take their best shots on the remaining windows of Red Wing. Their only usable guns were these antique M1s from World War II that they got God knew where. The shattering startled me. The crew was a little giddy. They must have thought the plague and the war were in a lull. They shot at Fire Station #5, a bed-and-breakfast, a sports bar, a pottery factory. The sun had nearly set, and the moon was low and full. Then I saw them aim their guns toward the rail station, where the refugees were, but Dad stood up and waved his arms at them. I was embarrassed at the time, but looking back, it was a brave thing for him to do. He motioned his arms toward the main town, like he was trying to land a jumbo jet. After a few tense seconds—there was nothing keeping them from shooting my dad—they went back to shooting out the glass in abandoned buildings. Dad sunk back to the ground, breathing heavily.

That was stupid, Ciaran said, stuffing half his sandwich into his mouth.

They could have been hurt, Dad said.

Who are "they"? Sophia said. Do we know them?

Dad shook his head. Well . . . they would have been shot. Those kids with the guns . . . they're the stupid ones.

Listen to your father, Mother said, though her words didn't seem connected to the argument at hand.

Sophia shook her head back in reply. It was clear she agreed with Ciaran. I didn't think she wanted anyone hurt, but she wanted Dad hurt even less. She put her hair in a ponytail and ambled back to the boat to flirt with the marines. Mom went back to the boat to sleep—we knew she was sick then, we just didn't know *how* sick. She was mumbling while she did this, and I caught a pained look on my father's face as he watched her walk away. Ciaran—I didn't know where Ciaran went. He had gotten up when I wasn't paying attention. He disappeared a lot, often with Xerxes. Xerxes was our dog. And Ciaran was my younger brother. And since I'm on the subject, Sophia was my older sister. I think that covers it.

About a half-dozen black geese landed near us and I threw my sandwich at them. They pounced on it, ate the ham. I didn't expect carnivorous geese. I did expect, though, my father to get really pissed off at me. He didn't, though. He just stretched his legs and, waiting for the latest pane of glass to finish shattering, he started telling me the story:

Once there was a coal mine deep in the mountains of West Virginia. That place might as well not exist anymore. The coal mine was hard to find, but people kept looking for it, because the mine was deep, which meant work. People were desperate for work. They would travel for days through mountain fog to find the sloped shantytown that had grown around the mine's opening. One man who started working there decided to go into the mine after dark. He had no family and no real prospects. He never knew what his purpose in life was. He decided to go into the mine because he had heard stories from some of the miners who had traversed the deepest areas, that the mine connected to a maze of limestone caves that had no end. Also, he was spectacularly drunk—rye whiskey was the chief culprit, but the devil had slipped a little something extra into the miner's whiskey jug.

What do you mean, something? I asked my father. The geese were fighting over bits of ham.

He startled and took a swig of his iced tea. An intoxicant of some kind, he said.

Do you mean kef? I said.

No, not kef, he said. Christ. You haven't tried it, have you? Tell me you haven't—

I *haven't,* I said. I shifted on the log I was sitting on. I just heard about it in the camps. Why don't you finish the story?

Even then, I knew how to nudge my father. As much as I loved him—and maybe it was *out* of love that I manipulated him, or at least tried to—there was no way that I could have told him that I had tried kef with my friend Stacy, who I would never see again after leaving St. Paul. I didn't even *like* kef, but if my father had found out, he wouldn't have cared about my not liking it.

Okay, my dad said. The story then:

With only a lantern, a pick, and a burlap bag, the miner secreted into the mine. *His* mine. He claimed many times, to anyone who would listen to him by the whiskey still, that he knew it better than anyone. He could rarely make out faces in the constant fog, so he was never sure whether his arguments were persuasive. He snaked downward. His hands followed the grooves and pockmarks made by picks and crude dynamite. Down gangplanks over underground streams, down rope ladders to the deepest veins. Soon enough he had to crawl. Hearing roaring water, he stopped in a shaft that was difficult to fit through. Water rushed above him. His light gave out, but he kept going, feeling the texture of crags and juts. After what seemed like many days, he saw light ahead. His eyes adjusted and he moved closer. The light was from a giant diamond, cut and struck into a thousand hard points. When he reached the diamond, he saw a small head inside of it—

A head? I had to interrupt and ask. What kind of head? A human head?

There was lightning to the east, even though it was October and not hot. There was a lull in the target practice. Or maybe the boys had gotten drunk-sick and wandered to their straw beds on the keel of the *Prairie Chicken,* to have sour dreams of their old lives. The river bluffs were high above us, littered with burnt Cape Cods. My father was getting impatient. I had expected this, his crossness with me, and it became so familiar to me that I would often mistake it for warmth. He was proud of his outward disposition, like a nice watch, and I'm sure he saw it as a valuable quality on our flight. A kind of toughness. Its utility varied in practice, but I was too afraid, or ashamed, to tell him this.

Especially when it broke down.

I was starting to get hungry, but I didn't want to give him any satisfaction.

Yes, a head, he said. Now listen:

So the man touched the diamond and peered closer at the head. The surface of the diamond was brilliant and hot. The head was the devil's, and the miner recognized it as such from sepia illustrations: high cheekbones, rosy skin, tiny tusks in the forehead. The devil's features were pretty much the only thing he remembered from Sunday school. The devil's eyes were closed, but opened when the miner touched the diamond. The eyes themselves were small diamonds.

You found me, the devil said. You found me in a piece of coal.

That I did, the miner said. What do you want with me?

If you can carry me back to the surface, I'll give you anything you desire.

Anything? the miner said.

The devil closed his eyes and opened them again. Okay, one thing, he said. But that one thing can be anything.

The man had nothing else going for him. He agreed, and was never heard from again.

My father turned away and finished his iced tea. He looked up at the stars that were beginning to come out. He was an astronomer, before we had to flee.

Um, aren't you going to finish the story? I said.

That's all, he said. Shoo. He said this last part to the geese, who were edging closer to us. He kicked his foot out and the geese scattered. Now it's time for bed, Macy, he said.

That's not enough! I said, raising my voice a little. I was pouty, I admit, about the stupid story. Maybe it was the hunger pangs. The coxswain, who was stirring a fire a stone's throw from us, looked over in our direction.

My father didn't shush or scold me. He was past admonitions that night, which scared me. He peered at me like that miner looked at the giant diamond with the devil's head inside. Or maybe like the devil looked at the miner.

Not enough? he said. It's never enough.

Carson had heard that story in the refugee camp on Pike Island. Up the river, where the Minnesota River fed into the Mississippi. A lot of people were telling the story, and no one knew why. Macy needed to hear it. He worried about her more than his other two children, though he would never let anyone know this, not even his wife. And especially Macy, who was too self-conscious for words. He dreaded what she might find down the river—monsters of men who would prey on her idealism. He didn't know how she would react, whether he had prepared her for anything that would come. He was naïve, too, he knew that—the absentminded professor in full force—but worked hard to hide it.

He worried that she took after him.

Carson had actually heard the tale from a man claiming to be the man in the story. Carson didn't believe him. But who knew? They had been standing at one of the latrine stations on Pike Island. The Imperial troops weren't crazy about the home brew served nearby—a guy from Eden Prairie who used to brew beer in his garage started the venture to make a little extra money—but they weren't teetotalers by any means and had enough crises on their hands. Minnesota was the northern reach of their territory. Fort Snelling, which overlooked Pike Island, was the last redoubt, and no soldier wanted to be there.

Carson had intuited from a very early age not to trust people who told stories while they were pissing. But it was hard to turn away—not only because they were both using the latrine, but also because the man told the story of the devil and the diamond with utter certainty.

Where did you end up? Carson said afterward. Right after you disappeared?

The man looked at Carson. He was thin and wiry. He had a smudged face. Here, he said, and then he pulled his pants tight with a sash and walked to the makeshift bar.

But then, two days later, Carson heard the same story from a woman who doled out sugar and tea on the east end of Pike Island. She also claimed to be the miner. She was about Carson's age, ruddy in the face, crooked-nosed, but nonetheless attractive in a sunburnt way. She looked like a hippie but swore she was Scythian, working for some vague nonpolitical aid organization, to help the poor refugees. She hadn't switched sides in the war, per se—as if there were only two sides. At any rate, the sugar and tea were welcome, so Carson listened, again, to the story of the miner, the diamond, and the devil. Carson didn't bother asking her anything about her life: how she ended up in Minnesota, what she had wished for deep in the mine, and so on. It wasn't worth it. The miner's disappearance was almost a punch line. Everyone liked to tell that story, and break off the end of it, like a dead branch from a tree.

CHAPTER 2

The Pig's Eye Blinks

I DON'T KNOW IF IT'S WORTH SAYING MUCH ABOUT OUR OLD HOUSE. Or for that matter, much about our old life in St. Paul at all. The city was called St. Paul until the name got changed back to Pig's Eye when the troubles began. The city *used* to be called Pig's Eye hundreds of years ago, when it was founded by a one-eyed moonshiner. But back then, priests didn't like the name, I guess, and decided to change it, to better attract settlers. I don't blame them. It was a very nineteenth-century thing to do. Back then, settlers made their way to St. Paul on steamboats. They were seeking a better life upstream. In a way, nothing has changed; I saw a lot of refugees taking old passenger triremes upstream, but I think for them it wasn't about optimism. I think they were just trying not to die. And upstream really wasn't part of a master plan.

Anyway, we had a house on Summit Avenue, or rather shared it. It was pretty nice. My father was a professor at one of the local colleges. He taught astronomy. I shared a room with my sister, who had painted it bright yellow, which I hated. But I learned to pick my battles. My mother stayed at home for the most part after Ciaran was born. She almost died from the birth.

And from that point on, Ciaran managed to live up to the expectations of his catastrophic entrance. I didn't say that to anyone, though. My mother would stop clearing the table or vacuuming, just stop, and grab her lower back and wince. After seeing this for the hundredth time when I was twelve or thirteen, I promised myself that I would never have kids, ever. I thought it was just too risky. Who knows if I'll keep that promise, and besides, I was just twelve at the time, what did I know.

I wouldn't say things were perfect, but even with my mother's pains, my brother's weirdness, and so on, things were imperfect in ways that everyone could handle. We treated one another like family most of the time.

It's hard to pinpoint exactly when things started turning wrong. Bad things were happening in the world, like glaciers melting and terrorists blowing up rail stations, but even though these were *areas of concern,* we weren't freaking out on a minute-to-minute basis because of them. We thought we were safe for a long time. Everything was normal. I was passing my classes and wasn't either incredibly liked or disliked at St. Paul Central. My sister was about to start hospitality school at Inver Grove Community College, and my brother was in a "special" program for the gifted and troubled. Words like "school" and "program" and "hospitality" seemed distant and clumsy in short order.

While school was finishing up, we began to hear reports, on the edges of our hearing, about a plague and the armed men following in its wake. Up north, and in the Dakotas. We expected someone to tell us what to do about it. No one did. They were just rumors. Someone in my history class had a cousin up in Moorhead who sent her an email about armed gangs and sickness and wild horses. It was all hard to understand. None of my teachers seemed to be worried, and the same with the people on television. I was worried a little, but thought that I was being paranoid, as usual.

One day they announced on the radio that the post office would be closed for reinventory. I think it was on a Wednesday, nothing special. Then our Internet stopped working. I called our provider—no one else could be bothered in the household—and no one answered. Then it became harder to get cell phone signals in town. Fewer bars and then no bars. It was early June and the sky didn't have secrets. I saw fewer planes in the sky, fewer traffic helicopters. In the last week of school my history teacher, Ms. Roth, started speaking in a language that no one understood. It was harsh and guttural and she looked confused. By the third day of that week, most of my classmates and I stopped attending her class. She didn't seem to mind. Teachers disappeared. On the last day I went in, there was a Shetland pony in the disciplinarian's office, munching on the potted geraniums. I cut out. I felt bad for the graduating seniors. I would have been a senior in the next year, but I didn't miss the opportunity too much. Besides, summer was in full swing. My only concern was getting my license. No one in my family really wanted to teach me, but I begged my sister until she gave up. We went to the Driver's License Center, which was inside the Sears building downtown, to get my permit. The DMV was boarded up, with a handwritten sign that said: CLOSED FOR SEASON.

What season, motherfuckers? my sister asked no one in particular.

The Sears was in bad shape. I mean, it wasn't always the best store in the world, since it was downtown and not a lot of people shopped there; it had a tawdry, empty vibe to it. But this was worse than pretty bad—clothes in the aisles, feces smeared on tractors in the lawn-and-garden department. We hurried out.

My sister put her hands on her knees and breathed. Then she said she'd teach me to drive anyway, screw the DMV. She never did teach me, but I was happy that she promised, even though I knew she'd never keep it. Not that it was her fault.

I think people started to get scared when the first horsemen came into town, about three thousand or so. They came from the northwest, following I-94 more or less. They'd already made forays into Monticello and St. Cloud, torching farms, strip malls, and automobile dealerships. They had demands for the governor regarding territory. The news teams found the horsemen both threatening and absurd. They were terrorists, the newscasters said. How could they not be? But the horsemen had no apparent ideology or religious fervor.

The National Guard, Channel 4 reported, fought the horsemen and pulverized the invaders.

Bullshit, I said, while my sister was duct-taping the cable connection behind our TV. All of our nonlocal channels had disappeared. Ciaran had wanted to dig around the front yard to see whether the cable was severed, but Sophia and I managed to convince him of the stupidity of that idea.

What are you talking about? she said, biting her lip and plugging and unplugging the cord into the socket. By the way, how's the picture now?

Better, I said, clicking through on the remote. But still no Bravo. Look, I call bullshit. Do you really think those mouth-breathers on Channel 4 would report the truth? I don't know . . . there's just something odd about it.

Wow, you think? Sophia said, crossing her arms. After a second, her duct-tape configuration fell apart.

Shut up, I said. And nice job.

It was easier to snipe at each other than to pay attention to what was going on. I mean, I *thought* I was paying attention and all—I was in Model United Nations. (Last year our school was Angola, and we negotiated a settlement to end illegal diamond trafficking, which was funding a nasty civil war.) I couldn't vote but I could read and watch, dammit. But if I was *really* paying attention, I would have been a lot more scared.

After a few days, the horsemen received their meeting with the governor. Then they killed him. They beheaded him and trampled the remainder of the corpse on John Ireland Boulevard. They stayed at the Best Western near the capitol. The next day the newscasters had torches in their studios. The weatherman on Channel 4 had a long, sudden beard. The national weather report was skipped.

No one wondered out loud what the proper response should have been against this threat. In terms of actual, ordinary citizens and not the military. We weren't asked to conserve water or energy or anything. The radio told us cheerfully and firmly to stay home. We did, except for my brother, who pleaded to keep going to his special program. My parents gave in. It turned out he didn't go there at all after the horsemen—Scythians, we found out later—came. Instead he just wandered around. On the third day of the state emergency, he came back with a dog named Xerxes, a bristly mutt with reddish fur. He was about as big as a jackal. Sophia and I were playing the Dictionary Game with my dad in desultory fashion. We were both trying to come up with fake definitions of "meander" when I heard the barking.

They let him keep the dog.

Where did you find him? I asked.

In Lowertown, my brother said. Xerxes, already named, was

rangy and muddy, and left tracks. My sister started to get a rag from the kitchen, but turned around. It seemed pointless.

Lowertown! my father said. What were you doing there?

On the news, there was a sickness reported in the artists' lofts, and loft-by-loft firefights in Lowertown.

I was just kidding, Ciaran said, laughing. It was apparent that he wasn't, but no one called him on it.

Food became tricky until the Scythians were driven out. I'd hear tusk horns and shouts all night and couldn't sleep much. I was going out of my skin. We weren't rescued, as a city, by helicopters and fighter jets. In a way, people didn't expect help from above. Assistance instead came from pike-wielding infantry in red-and-bronze armor. Thousands of soldiers. They marched past our house on Summit. It wasn't clear where they had come from, exactly, but people were very happy to see them, on account of the Scythians, who had been razing the city the best they could. No National Guardsmen were part of this procession, this *coalition;* they must have been defeated up north, like I'd thought. These soldiers must have come from somewhere else. They had nice uniforms.

My father tried to buy a gun at Pawn America. He told me about this later. In a way I think he was trying to confess cowardice to me. Anyway, when he asked to see the gun selection at the pawnshop, the broker laughed and said that all the guns were broken, would my father like a watch.

Do the watches work? my father asked.

No, the pawnbroker said, but they're very beautiful.

What do you mean the watches don't work? Why not?

But he didn't receive a reply. A few days later, the brownouts began in earnest, and then the power died altogether. It was July, sweltering, deadly. Arrows landed in our yard. The shafts were burnt. There were hoofbeats at odd hours. One Sunday morning, I watched the house across the street from us burn. No one came to put it out. The old couple who lived there sat on the lawn during the burning with faraway looks on their faces. I'd never spoken to them. I watched their faces with one of my father's telescopes. My father had a lot of old telescopes in his study. A couple of soldiers, who we'd all started calling Imperials—though we didn't know for sure what empire they were from—came up and jostled them down the street: move along, move along, nothing to see here.

The Imperials were on our side, I guess, though we still couldn't get a straight story on where they came from. They fought the horsemen and reduced their sphere of influence to only a few neighborhoods—in Lowertown and Frogtown for the most part—so a lot of people didn't mind the Imperials. People wanted safety. I found out a lot of this through the paper, which still ran through the summer, though erratically, after the TV stopped working. The ink was smudgy and the articles took on a strange tone. It was hard to know what was going on elsewhere. Reports were pretty scattered, but things were bad in a lot of other places. There wasn't exactly a newswire anymore. The only parts of the paper that appeared pretty much the same as before were the gossip columns and comic strips.

My mother became even more reclusive. She stayed in the attic and ate more than her fair share of soda crackers. My sister scoured the neighborhood convenience stores for supplies. Slim pickings all around. We weren't sure just how long we were to stay in our houses. Maybe, we reasoned, things would get better. Maybe the dream we were stuck in would end suddenly, leaving us to start over where we left off. But we knew this wasn't going to happen when an Imperial soldier, one of the limitanei, as I learned later, knocked on our door. My father answered and the soldier let himself in. Brusquely, of course. He didn't smell, which was a bad sign—it meant we were rancid with stench. He said something I thought was Greek. But I couldn't be sure. My father leaned closer to him. The soldier was young, only a couple of years older than me. I could see that he had a Lakers jersey, untucked, poking from underneath his breastplate.

As it turned out, my dad knew a little Greek from college. My dad listened for a minute, then reported back to me—everyone else was upstairs, oblivious—that we had to leave the house. He turned back to the soldier and protested, raising his voice. The soldier whistled. After a few seconds, a few more soldiers, who must have been milling around our lawn, came in.

They surrounded my dad and started shouting at him, pushing him like high school bullies picking on a freshman. My dad covered his face and tried to break away, but they started hitting him with their sword hilts. I started screaming but they ignored me. My dad fell to the floor, purple ruptures on his face, his arm bleeding.

I couldn't believe what was happening. A bribe, maybe I could bribe them, I thought. My hands shaking, I took out a five I had in my pocket. I was bad and loose with money. I handed it to the first soldier. He laughed and then cocked his head, noticing me for the first time. I realized, then, that my stupidity had no bounds. I needed gold or silver. Maybe bronze. Olympic metal of some sort. Abe Lincoln wasn't cutting it. That soldier started moving toward me, but one of the others grabbed his shoulder and motioned toward the door. They must have had a lot of houses to cover.

When they left, the rest of the family came down. My mother

was worried sick. My father downplayed the soldiers' visit, giving a sheepish grin and wiping his face with a rag from the kitchen. No one was buying it. They heard my screaming. Outside, an SUV was being towed by six mules. The chassis was covered in vines.

When we were packing whatever we could reasonably carry—although nothing seemed reasonable anymore—I asked my dad whether the college would give us any protection. But he said that the college was already taken over and being used as a garrison complex. He didn't think he would be able to get back to his office.

What kinds of things do you need there anyway? Ciaran asked.

He shrugged. My papers, star charts, he said.

Ciaran snorted, and yeah, I was thinking the same thing. But I'd be upset too if a weird soldier in a Lakers jersey came by and forced me to abandon my life's work.

We'll be back, my mother said, when all of this passes over.

No one answered her.

The soldiers had left a blurry, mimeographed map with CAMP scrawled above the design. Pike Island, where the Minnesota and Mississippi rivers met. We were to go there. We tried to think about this as little as possible as we got ready. While I filled my suitcase, I was trying to trick myself that we were only going on a camping trip. When we had our luggage full, we stood in the vestibule. The matching blue vinyl of our suitcases seemed gaudy. I went downstairs to say good-bye to the couple in the duplex next to ours, but their door was painted red. That meant plague. I had read a public-service bulletin about it in the paper: BEWARE RED DOORS! Other details about the plague were insane but vague. There were only scattered, contradictory reports. The bulletin mentioned to stay away from stinging insects and their nests, as well as areas where they might congregate. And also people with extremely dry skin. These warnings were too cryptic to be considered part of any public-health initiative. At any rate, it was supposed to get worse the farther south we went.

As we were about to leave, my brother declared he didn't want to go. My sister agreed. She could still, she argued, find work in the city. Live somewhere else. Maybe work at McDonald's or Wendy's. For some reason both the Scythians and the Imperials liked fast food and kept those restaurants open.

But my dad told us we had to go, and my mother agreed with a sternness that surprised me. She had seen the bruises on Dad's face, and I could tell she didn't want that to happen again by disobeying the soldiers' orders. That left the final vote to me. We almost never voted as a family. I guess my father thought that democracy would give him added legitimacy here.

What do you think, Macy? my father asked, raising his eyebrows. Xerxes was circling around, trying to bite his tail. The air smelled like garlic and urine. I didn't know what to think. It seemed our goose was cooked no matter where we were. Home, camp—they were just locations. On the other hand, I was sick of the house, sick of being frozen in our lives like flies in amber. And if this were all a dream, why not abandon waking altogether? What good would waking do? Or not to swim with the current and leave everything we knew behind? It was going to happen anyway.

And I thought of my father's welts, like my mother must have. I knew he didn't want to show anyone how or why he'd been hurt. I'd never been beaten up in my life, though I came close a few times in grade school. Dad never had said if he had been growing up. Maybe he had. But this was different. He didn't want to get killed, or us killed. I could see that.

When I gave my choice—even though it didn't really feel like a choice—Ciaran and Sophia glowered at me. My father nodded, and we went to the street, to wait at the old #91 bus stop for one of the wagons to take us to Pike Island, as the map said they would. Before I stepped out the door, my mother stopped me. She ran her hands through my hair and smoothed out a wrinkle in my T-shirt. As if she were reminding herself to iron it out at some point in the future. She smiled. I managed to smile back.

Possessions

Grace and Carson had married at a peculiar time. They were considered old when they had their kids, in their thirties, but in a few years they were part of the happy median. And yet a few years later they were thought of as "young parents" by many of Carson's peers at the college. People started to enjoy marrying themselves to each other later and later in life. But of course, *those* people had their sex lives in alignment with the rest of their personalities and were much more balanced as people. Even the professors.

That was what Grace thought, at least.

Grace and Carson rarely made love. But on the last night before they were evicted to Pike Island, their last night of privacy in their own room, they made love among all of the material objects that they would not be able to take with them, the possessions that were already ghosts.

Grace? he said beforehand. There was no response, except for snoring on her part. He had his hand on her arm and remembered how they used to be, how he used to think of her as an unkempt—if introverted—spirit who was willing to try anything.

Then she sat up and put her hands on his bare chest. She

was half awake. Her hands moved lower, and then they coupled.

Afterward, unable to sleep, watching over his wife, Carson was astounded at how tranquil Grace looked as she slept. Considering how fitful she usually was, her deep sleep was almost a miracle.

CHAPTER 3

The Children's Book of Heroes

WHY WE ENDED UP GOING DOWNRIVER IN THE FIRST PLACE, EVEN though we technically had a reason, wasn't clear. I didn't mind the camp, except when the night raid started. But that only hastened our departure; it didn't decide it in the first place. No, after we'd been in the camp for two weeks, my father got a letter from a colleague in St. Louis. The postal system was spotty, to say the least, but letters could still get through with a little coin to speed them along. Anyway, the letter was offering him a post in the University of St. Louis science department. I guess they consolidated the departments due to lack of enrollment. When he told us, my dad didn't look happy so much as *relieved*—that there was some semblance of his old life that he could still tout. He made it clear through his glares that the authenticity of the letter wasn't to be questioned.

Jasper wouldn't have gone through all this trouble if it wasn't true, he said to us.

That was possible. It was equally possible, if not more so, that Jasper, while having the best intentions in the world, might have been crazy, writing a half-cocked letter to someone in his distant past. Maybe he was in a refugee camp of his own. The perils were endless. After all, a few weeks before, we had a house, jobs, school. And then we didn't. It was hard to trust possibilities. My father's stubbornness made me depressed and panicky. I couldn't tell what my mother was thinking. Her hair was grayer than I had remembered before, and it was getting wild.

When we threw out our protests all at once, Dad stood up, hitting his head on the moldy canvas, and shouted:

Stop it! Christ, shut up! Why can't you trust me? Jesus.

He stalked off. We were all stunned, though maybe we shouldn't have been.

I wondered, really, what *use* we had. Did a family have to have a use?

Like I said, camp wasn't all horrible. I actually did try to think of it as camping. Our family had a large tent, a little musty but pretty new. I wondered if the soldiers had raided army surplus stores in the area. Pike Island was pretty interesting, from a geographical standpoint. To the north was the Minnesota River and to the south was the Mississippi. At the eastern tip of the island, where our camp was set, the two rivers came together. The soldiers had clear-cut a lot of trees and brush to make room for everyone. It used to be part of Fort Snelling State Park, but I heard they had hung all the rangers from the trees. Fort Snelling itself wasn't a living museum anymore. I felt sad thinking about the historical reenactors coming across real soldiers. The fake voyageurs and the fake fur trappers, the fake butter churners, the fake American soldiers doing their inaccurate drills on parade grounds. Those rangers and those reenactors had families, too. Our family didn't have this monopoly on being devastated. But if I kept thinking about it, I would have spiraled further and further down into helplessness and hopelessness.

What could I have done? It was the big question, and I didn't have any answer.

Fort Snelling was the northernmost outpost of America for a long time; tribes from Canada and the Dakotas would come to the fort to trade. I learned a lot about it in American History class. Now the Empire used Fort Snelling as an outpost, flying the red and gold standards, mounting arquebuses on the high corners. The Imperials probably thought Scythians or Thracians—or whoever—could come sweeping toward the fort at any time. But it would be difficult to take. The island itself was cordoned off with palisades, topped with barbed wire. It felt less secure than the fort would have been, to say the least.

Of course, I felt like an idiot, halfway through my stay on Pike Island, when I tripped on an overturned plaque that was lying on the ground. The plaque, in that history-teacher tone, said that Pike Island was used for the internment of over a thousand Dakota Indians. It was miserable, and a lot of them died. I felt like a moron for never knowing that. My friend Stacy was Ojibwe; she grew up around Leech Lake, way up north. I imagined what she would have thought of my utter ignorance. Maybe she wouldn't have pushed it. Maybe she had to deal with stupid white people all the time so that she would just be too exhausted to correct everything we got wrong. Which was a lot.

We ate a lot of stews. For beverages we had bottled iced tea and pop. Fanta and Faygo. It was warm: they must have commandeered it by the truckloads. But I always kind of liked third-tier pops like Faygo, so I didn't mind. I knew this put me in the distinct minority. My brother would have rather drank river water, and I think he did.

In a way, our two weeks on the island were like a microcosm

of our lives before the incursions. At first everything was normal
and well-paced, and then it was not. Non-normality began to
leak in, and soon it was a flood. My brother tried to burn the island down. I know, I said that they had cut down all the trees.
But he still tried to burn it down—the tents, the mess halls, the
garrison. Everything. He didn't get very far in his mission. That
night, I woke up to a bell clang. We all sat up, some of us grog-
gier than others, and we saw in unison that Ciaran was not
among us.

Shit. Sophia, come on, my father said. We're going to find
your brother.

Why? she said, turning over. I'm tired. I'm sure he's fine.

I smelled smoke.

Something's burning, I said. The ringing stopped and there
was a lot of shouting. I could see my breath but I wasn't cold.

Okay, Dad said. Everyone has to get up. Come on, Grace.

My mother was pretty alert, and she put on her shawl, even
though the air was humid and warm. I never knew, until then,
why I never called my mother Mom. When she put on the
shawl, I understood. Moms weren't supposed to wear shawls at
all, much less in summer.

We all lurched out of the tent. I could see pillars of fire on the
other side of the island, and hear shouts in the Imperials' language. I realized then that the island made an excellent prison as
well as a camp. Maybe the two were the same. The smoke made
me sick, and I sat down on the ground after a few steps. My sister tugged at my sleeve. Get up, she said.

I looked at her face, which was kind of hazy. She had nice,
straight hair, while mine was always curly and frizzy.

Why? I said.

She hadn't considered why. I don't know, she said. In case they start shooting us. Or impaling us. Or whatever.

But if I'm sitting down, I said, doesn't that make me *less* likely to be shot?

Girls! our mother said. Sophia and I both startled. We hadn't heard anything angry or parental from our mother in quite a while. Anger required clarity of thought. God knew what possessed her, but Sophia and I were stunned into silence. And I stood up.

Okay, my father said, not noticing our exchange, too busy trying to hold it together. Sophia, stay with the tent. Grace and Macy and I will look for your brother and find out what's going on.

Sophia crossed her arms, but stayed. I thought she was lucky.

We wandered toward the loudest shouting, parallel to the fires and smoke. Which, upon further reflection, might not have been the smartest idea. But the chaos didn't exactly promote smart ideas. There were people standing next to their tents, gawking but trying not to show it. Dad tried the "have you seen a boy with a dog?" routine but no one wanted to talk to him. These were "our" people, from Minneapolis, Wayzata, Columbia Heights. If we'd asked them a few months ago in a Target for help finding Ciaran, I'm not sure they would have helped much more. Oh, they would have been more pleasant about it. But they wouldn't have helped. Talk about the breakdown of civilization.

We reached the banks of the Mississippi, or at least near the barbed-wire palisades along it. Closer to the pillars of fire, we saw a few people trying to climb over or under the fence. Maybe they were scared of the fire, maybe they thought it was an opportune time. A few succeeded. There were shouts from the guard tower, and then thuds. Then torchlit silhouettes fell, screaming, clutching limbs. Must have been crossbows. On instinct, we edged away from the river. My mother grabbed my hand and let go right away. Her skin was cold. I saw a slow bucket brigade, soldiers joking as they tried to douse the flames.

Then I heard Ciaran's laugh, not too far away.

I led my parents into the tent city again. My mother almost tripped on an ashen tree stump, and an old man squatting in front of his tent snickered. No time to punch his lights out. I heard my brother laugh again, turned a corner, and found him, sitting around a campfire with soldiers, playing dice. This should have been shocking to me but it wasn't. In a way, the incursions and changes in the world brought out the best in Ciaran, or rather, what he considered to be his best. Not only in that fourteen-year-old boy sort of way, but in that he was discovering how far he could push without anyone pushing back. He had a midnight mind.

Ciaran, my father said. Xerxes was at my brother's feet, chomping away at something. I leaned closer and saw it was a giant snout.

Hey, Dad, Ciaran said. Mom. Macy. Ciaran was spectacularly nonplussed. The soldiers kept playing their dice game, which I couldn't follow, shouting and slapping one another's backs. One used his sword to point at the dice.

For some reason my dad was powerless. He was just an astronomy professor. He stood there as if his parental work was complete, as if Ciaran would come back to the tent right away. A soldier with pockmarks on his face started staring at me. We weren't in our element.

Ciaran said: Did you see the fire? I hope no one got hurt.

For a second, his eyes flickered at me, and then a soldier handed him dice and he threw. It was then that I knew he started the fire. I could have been wrong, but I knew it. And I think he knew I knew, which only made me madder.

My mother broke the stalemate. She rushed to Ciaran and wrapped her arms around him and started crying. Ciaran stood up and the soldiers startled, never a good thing. They drew swords and tried to push our mother away from Ciaran, but she only clung harder. It was embarrassing, not only for my brother, but also for me, and even in a way for my dad, although he'd never admit it. The thought of dying then and there, or of being raped, didn't occur to me, although it should have. I guess that's what they call shock.

Oddly, after a few seconds of confusion, when we could have been run through, it worked, although it wasn't a grand plan by my mother by any means. Maybe the soldiers saw something melodramatic in my mother's teary embrace from their own pasts and homes, wherever those were. Maybe their mothers cried in such a way when they went to invade—sorry, protect—distant lands. At any rate, the soldiers started laughing again, laughing at my mother. The pockmarked one kept staring at me as he laughed. I backed away a few steps. My dad stood there. It would have been expecting too much for him to defend his wife's honor, in some small fashion. My expectations were both unbelievably high and abysmally low for him, and changed on a whim.

Ciaran started laughing, too, and kissed my mom on her forehead. He'd indulge his mother, just this once. In a weird way, I think this increased his standing among the soldiers even more, that he was a good son, or at least pretended to be, at opportune moments. But he wasn't, it was a sham, he burned the tents, I knew it. My face was flushed. As we were walking back, I thought: I'm the good daughter, aren't I?

The next morning, as I was washing our clothes—they set up some wooden tubs full of river water and powdered Cheer— someone tapped me on the back. I gave a cry of shock. I was still tense and tired from the previous night. They had already put up new tents where the old ones had burned, although they weren't as nice. The air still had that charred smell.

It was my brother.

Hey, he said. I have something for you.

Ciaran, I'm busy. I leaned toward the tub, scrubbing harder. I knew the clothes would still stink.

No, you'll like it, he said. He tapped me again until I had to turn around and he dropped a necklace into my soapy hands. It had silver links with alternating lapis lazuli and moonstone beads. It was beautiful. I dared not tell Ciaran this. Instead, I squinted at him.

Where did you get this? I asked.

He shuffled his feet. Some of my friends, he said. I noticed he had a book under his arm. *The Children's Book of Heroes.* He probably stole it and was trying to sell it.

Let me guess, I said. Your soldier friends.

He smiled. He thought he had an angle on me.

One in particular, actually, he said. One who likes you.

I just knew it. I almost threw the necklace at him. The pock-marked soldier. Wonderful. Worse, who knew what my brother was telling him? Embarrassing moments from early childhood, what foods I liked (not that those would be available much any-more), my trivial trivia. It was sickening. Still, I didn't tell Ciaran off. The necklace was valuable, in that it would be beautiful to others. I wanted to be crafty more than anything, think like a survivor.

Aren't you going to wear it? my brother asked.

I put it in my jeans pocket. Not now, I said. I don't want to lose it. Besides, what do you know about girls and what they wear? I have to wear the necklace *with* something.

Sometimes I forgot that my brother was just a kid, but he was, and on certain matters not involving goods trafficking and burning down refugee camps, he was hopelessly naïve.

Oh, okay, he said, nodding. He smiled again. He was enjoying his role as matchmaker way too much. See you, Macy.

Uh, see you.

I was red in the face but he didn't notice. I had a disfigured stalker with a sword. This made going stag to junior prom look like a joke.

After the necklace incident, I wanted nothing more than to leave Pike Island. I sat in the tent while Mother was sleeping in the corner, snoring away. I cascaded the necklace in my hands, and looked at the stones again. There were little shapes in the stones. I put my eye right next to them to get a better look. Animal outlines: an ox, a giraffe, a lion . . . I couldn't make them out for sure, and had no idea how they got there. I lay down, trying to nap, but couldn't. I hoped that Dad could get his act together enough to smuggle us out.

The hope seemed slim. Our father, I could tell, had made earnest stabs at finding passage to St. Louis, but he couldn't find the right people. I'm not sure he would have been able to find the right people if they were standing in front of him.

Much to my surprise it wasn't my brother who bailed my father out, but my sister. We were playing a game of euchre in the

tent—my brother was off gallivanting, of course—and Sophia
asked our father when we were going to leave the island, what
was our game plan.

He threw down a trump.

It's hard to say, Sophia. There aren't a lot of boat captains in
the camps. Much less with their own boats. No one has access to
boats except for the armies.

Couldn't we take I-35? I asked.

My father shook his head and nudged Mother, who played
her crappy card. Her cards were always crappy. She smiled at me.

The interstates are closed off, my father said. I don't think
any of the buses are running. Or trains. The river will get us
there faster.

I know someone who might be able to help, my sister said,
turning her face down, pretending to study her cards.

Who? Dad said. Some guy? Christ, it's some guy, isn't it?

Does Sophia have a suitor? my mother said. All of us ignored
her, except for Sophia, who rolled her eyes.

No, it's just a friend. One of the garrison guards. I'm teaching
him English. Anyway, he says there *are* passenger ships. They're
contracted by the Empire. They bring refugees upriver, because
of the plague, but are pretty empty going downriver.

Wait, my father said, what did you say about the plague?

I don't know, my sister said. No one knows. Not here at least.
Just that it gets worse the farther south you go.

But the newspapers said that it was *worse* up north, I said.

Do you believe what you read all the time? Sophia said.

God, Sophia, I said. I'm just saying.

This wasn't reassuring, to say the least. Reports were scattered and confusing. I overheard a few days before a few women
by the laundry say that the plague turned the limbs of the af-

flicted into common household objects. Like a wheel, or an iron, or a pestle. This was so beyond the earlier warnings about insects and dry skin that I had read. I was going to laugh it off, but everyone was serious and scared, and I started getting creeped out.

No, no, another woman said, slapping a blanket dry, it changes people into dogs, dogs with white fur and red eyes.

I heard, another woman said, one who was tall and had wispy hair, that it turns people into what they would least like to be.

Dead? I blurted out.

The women fell silent, and took to glaring at me, so I turned my head.

Macy, Sophia, will you calm down, my dad said.

All the same, Dad didn't shoot the idea down.

Sophia promised our father that she'd look into it. Two days later, she was late for our dinner of crackers and tomato soup. She had blood on her face, though no cuts. We all stood, even Ciaran, who didn't look happy to be there.

What happened? our father said, trying to hold Sophia by the shoulders. But she wiggled away.

Everyone pack, she said. There's a boat in town. The *Prairie Chicken*. It can take us down, but it's leaving in an hour. In the dark.

I started packing. I knew something bad was going to happen, but my father didn't, not yet.

That's great news, he said, smiling. He must have forgotten about her blood for a second. Then the smile died when he saw Sophia's stricken red face.

What? he said.

The Scythians are coming, she said, any hour. That's what Nikolai told me. They're going to sweep through.

Nikolai your boyfriend? Ciaran said, straightening up.

I'm sure my brother relished the Scythian arrival.

Yes, Sophia said, with a seriousness that our brother's teasing didn't warrant, yes he is.

Before our parents could jump in with anything about her love life, she said: Do you have any gold for a bribe?

Dad frisked his pockets.

I have dollars, he said. A gold card.

Christ, Dad! Sophia said. Gold, not gold cards.

Her tone of voice, if anything, mimicked our father's. We were both our father's daughters, but one more so than the other. I guess that made me more my mother's daughter: brooding, a little crazy.

You didn't liquefy it? she said. You don't have coin? Fucking gold card and American Express.

Dad was hurt, because he knew it was true. He might have even known it was true some time ago, but didn't want to admit it until someone called him on it. He started twisting his wedding ring. At first I thought he was playing with it, as a nervous tic, but then I saw he was trying to get it off. When he did, he handed it to Sophia. There's a diamond and ruby in there, he said. The gold is twenty-four karat. Your mother helped pick it out for me.

He looked back at Mother. She was rolling her bedroll, and wasn't paying attention. It was better that way.

Let's go, he said.

As it turned out, we weren't a moment too soon. We wandered through the tent city toward the makeshift docks. I started running, feeling panic, but my dad told me to slow down, we didn't want to look too conspicuous. It was funny, but neither the camp nor the fortress above looked ready for a Scythian on-slaught. A usual twilight. I realized that a lot of people I passed might not live through the night, might be decapitated or en-slaved or who knew what else.

When we reached the dock—still enclosed on either side by barbed wire—we saw the ship, which looked ready to fall apart. We didn't know that the *Prairie Chicken* would be far less ram-shackle than most of the boats on the Mississippi. Our father haggled with the dockmaster—who, luckily, knew a little English—for access. I saw my brother tense up and lean forward a little. I knew he was contemplating sprinting away, hiding until we gave up on ever finding him and left. I put my hand on his shoulder. Looking back, I don't know why I didn't let him go. It certainly would have solved certain problems that arose later on. Although, I guess, my parents would have been sad to lose him then. He looked up at me angrily and turned his shoul-der away.

Leave me alone, he said.

Xerxes came running behind. Ciaran was calm, as if he knew his dog—no pretense of the "family dog" here—needed no guidance, no goading, and would find him like an iron nail to a magnet.

Meanwhile, a tall man in—what else—a captain's hat came forward to speak to my father. The ring was given, as in a wed-ding. The captain nodded, looked our way for a second, and opened the gate. We were free, in our not-quite-free kind of way.

Almost as soon as we were on the boat, the Scythians at-tacked. The boat unmoored. I heard drumbeats and smelled horses. I heard the limitanei in the fortress begin to shout, and the soldiers in the camp clamoring up the steep steps to the fortress for safety. Abandoning, as it were, their posts—and their charge of protecting the refugees.

Which maybe wasn't their charge in the first place.

The boat lurched away. I had forgotten that, ever since I was little, I didn't like boats all that much.

Everyone inside, my father said. We hurried to the large cabin at the center of the boat. I was the last one; as I was about to enter, I heard someone call out from the bank. Turning around, I saw the pockmarked soldier. His sword was out, and he must have been running, because he was out of breath. He waved at me with his sword. Our eyes met. I considered, I don't know, telling him off or something, but I didn't. Because he looked sad, crushed even, that he would never see me again. That he gave a foreign girl a necklace that didn't mean anything in the end. Then again, maybe he thought I was a stupid barbarian. Before I could do anything, he started running again—whether for safety or to meet the enemy, I couldn't be sure—and we floated away.

When I was sure he wouldn't have been able to see, I put on the necklace.

THE PIG'S EYE PIONEER
MINNESOTA'S FIRST NEWSPAPER (FOUNDED 1846)

August 2
Dispatch from the Battle of Toledo
by Maura Wi (Embedded with the Bemidji
Irregulars)

The Plain Dealer fortress in Cleveland was under siege and the Empire had legions ready from the Southern Michigan Themata, Evanston–Lesser Chicago, Appleton (Thracian Zone), New Nineveh, and LaCrosse Zee to come to the garrison's aid. After three days of forced march, they had spent a night along the lakeshore bogs. Toledo holds little to no strategic importance to the Empire, and was not well fortified, but they had thought the city relatively safe. The ambush at dawn, however, was laid upon them at Toledo with great ferocity while they were ready to break camp.

A sudden hailstorm lasted two hours during the pitch of the battle. The hailstones were as large as eggs, and a few soldiers bruised by them had sworn that they contained more than ice: bone chips, amethyst, drift-glass. The scouts had noted impeded vision and sight lines in the river flats. But the skyscraper javelin snipers let fly against the slogging troops. Avars and associated tribes swept eastward through the mud-flats, making retreat impossible. To their west, the Avars tipped over tower cranes using acquired Engineer Corps dynamite, causing understandable panic.

On the front lines, a thin phalanx of Ohio state militia took the brunt of the first wave of attacks. They had been training/camping in Mud Hen Stadium for weeks—preferring such a locale compared to their plague-stricken suburbs—and were conscripted into the expedition to Cleveland only the day before. The Americans waited in ankle-deep mud for the charge, surplus bayonets affixed to their rifles, with no assurances that their weapons would discharge. But the Imperial Command had decided that these men and women would be more comfortable with rifles, as opposed to swords.

Many Michigander platoons, sensing no easy victory with any central authority, have aligned with Upper Peninsula militia groups that have proved, for the Avars, worthy proxies and allies for the ambush. The Michiganders saw Toledo as rightfully theirs to begin with, and had volunteered for the first charge. It was hard to say whether they were surprised to find Ohioans ready to meet them in the hail and fog.

The Avars brought with them hastily constructed tre-buchets, and from unseen positions let loose indiscriminately with metal and stone projectiles into the fray of the Ohioans and Michiganders. After the siege engines broke down, Avars themselves went among the people on foot, in groups of seven or eight, the ground too unsteady for their horses. Most Ohioans were slaughtered with impunity, hacked to bits, their bodies half-frozen in the mud. The other Imperial legions, including the Bemidji Irregulars, retreated southwest from the unfavorable terrain, toward Indiana. The fog, previously their greatest enemy, was now their greatest ally. The troops from Appleton, trained by Thracians, held a line against the bands of Avars during the retreat.

As the Bemidji Irregulars themselves escaped, they were given a new charge, to protect a mule convoy heading west along dangerous interstates, wagons loaded with Game Boys and their cartridges. Although their machinery didn't work, they were used as currency in the Janesville clanholds of what used to be southern Wisconsin. No word was ever given about the fate of the Appletonians mired in Toledo, to say nothing of those besieged in the Cleveland fortress, which seemed to all impossibly far away.

CHAPTER 4
My Materials

ON THE RIVER, WE DIDN'T HAVE MUCH. WE HAD TO LEAVE A LOT OF stuff behind. Once, past Lake Pepin, my father told us to take an inventory of our possessions. It seemed like a waste of perfectly good paper. But I complied, cataloging my meager belongings in the smallest handwriting possible in my notebook. While I was composing, the captain paced the deck, no doubt wondering what was going on with the strange family that was busy *writing*. The leaves were just beginning to turn colors: deep oranges and reds. Early for that time of the year. It was happening early. I tried to think of our journey as racing the leaves turning, racing winter.

Anyway, this was what I wrote:

1. The 5-Subject Notebook. This is all important. The plastic is half torn off, but still serviceable. I still have the same notebook from the beginning of junior year. It has the remnants of a few World of Warcraft stickers, before I stopped playing and started trying to be popular. Not that I succeeded. Besides my notes, the notebook contains an appropriate distillation of

Western Civilization: a ruler set into the side of one of the folders (English and metric), a map of the United States with time zones (something tells me that daylight saving time isn't going to be much of a concern in the future), a list of Easily Misspelled Words, and a Measurement Conversion Table. Just in case I ever need to figure out how many quarts are in a dram.

2. Six pens. Paper Mates. I hide the box under my pillow.

3. Clothes. Two rugby shirts, two sweaters (one gray, one black with a St. Paul Central logo), three T-shirts (one dark pink, one black, one from the MIA concert from last year), three pairs of jeans (two American Eagle, one Earl Jean knockoff my mother had gotten from Target), four panties, two bras. No dresses. I'm not sure why—I'm not a tomboy. I guess when I packed I'd been thinking about efficiency. Now I kind of wish I had something pretty, something useless.

4. Tampons. A box. I do not hide this under the bed. I think my sister has more.

5. Books. My father said we could bring only one book. I couldn't decide, so I took two: Sylvia Plath's *The Bell Jar* and *The Lord of the Rings* trilogy. Three, if you count the Bible. I don't. I don't really see it as a book as much as a potential item for trade down the river. It's not like I read it, so how can it be a book?

Anyway, it's just an old Gideon from a vacation to Niagara Falls ten years ago, so it's not taking up much space at all.

Okay, so with the trilogy, you might think that I have five books. But that's just not true.

(A week later, my father would find the trilogy. It slipped out of my bag when we were landing, after eluding the *Nadir*.

What the hell is this? he said, though rather quietly, since we were warned about prairie jackals and scouts. Do you plan to kill someone with this? Is this catapult shot?

I swiped the book back from him. It's really none of your business, I said. I liked the trilogy because the Fellowship of the Ring was as dysfunctional as my family—they were only able to get anything done apart and not together.)

6. Knife. I don't think anyone knows I have this. Long as a butter knife but much sharper and prettier. I found it in our basement on Summit Avenue, behind the washer when I was supposed to be washing clothes, but really was goofing around. I have no idea where it came from. We shared the basement with the old couple, so maybe it was theirs? The house was built in the 1880s, so it was pretty old, but the knife feels older. Like it was a fur trapper's knife. Its handle is smooth wood. I had my friend Janice sharpen the blade in shop class for me. This was about a week before things started getting weird. I know I could have been expelled and everything for bringing it to

school, and be taken to a therapist with bad hair im-
plants who'd want to know about all my problems.
Still, the risk was acceptable. And worth it. Look
where I ended up.

7. ChapStick. My lips are always dry. (This ran out
about a week later. I sold the empty canister for a few
coppers.)

8. My grandmother's comb. I never knew either of
my grandmothers. How sad is that? It was painted
blue, and made of bone, I think. My mother's mother
had long white hair and was a nurse in World War II.
How many dead bodies did she see?

I think that covers it.

When I was done, I folded the paper and put it at the bottom
of my backpack. I was on the boat's edge. I dipped my hand in
the water, which was cold. The water was high, which was surprising since we had a drought during the summer and I didn't
remember much rain. Maybe there was more rain south of
Pig's Eye.

The *Prairie Chicken* was a converted steamboat, except there
was no steam. It just floated. The young soldiers, when there
were shallows or rough water, would try to control the boat with
these long poles. It didn't always work. There was a giant rud-
der where the paddle wheels were to be, and lanterns on each
corner, and one skinny cannon on the bow, which I thought
would be useless, and it was. Before the invasions, it was just a
stupid pleasure cruiser, taking tourists from St. Paul to Wabasha
and back again.

My brother wandered by me, twirling his pen in his hand.

Did you make a list? I said.

Yep, he said, barely stopping.

I pulled my hand out of the water and rubbed it. My hand felt like a dead fish encased in ice.

Where's your list, then?

Ate it, he said. Then he wandered off, calling for Xerxes.

Passing Through

No one could pinpoint where the horsemen came from, but people had their theories. The theories were rarely good ones. But what most people failed to see in America, and to a lesser extent Canada and Mexico, was that the horsemen were only the beginning. Trailing a few days after the vanguard came planters, tinkers, blacksmiths, armorers, beggars, healers, attendant husbands and wives, and the like. There was no official capacity for their movement. They just came.

What did they want? Surely their lifelong ambitions did not involve spreading fear. They might not have thought out the path of their journey properly, or with great foresight, yet all the same—the new arrivals would have argued—it became necessary to protect oneself in an unforgiving landscape. They didn't entirely trust the farms or the strip malls. They looked askance on conveniences. Granted, there were idiosyncrasies from people to people. The Goths took to Massachusetts, and the stony farms there. During the winter, they built siege equipment for their allies. They also grew marijuana and made small-batch ketchup. Ketchup was what they got out of the American experience. The Alans, expert falconers, raided the chicken farms of Delaware and the turkey farms of Maryland, as well as other former states along the Eastern seaboard. They were a bit too spread out to formulate much of a sociopolitical movement. They bred turkeys for swiftness and predatory instincts. Gone, in short time, were the days when turkeys were too pliant and rotund to procreate on their own. The sleek, gray turkeys of the Delaware Princes would not have made good lunch meat.

And then there were the Scythians. One would think, from their name, that they would have come from a place called Scythia. But the Scythians consisted of about five or six tribes, each of which claiming to be the *new* Scythians, the rest being subjugated and assimilated somewhere along the way, into a kind of pan-Scythian confederation. Each subtribe was honor bound not to tell the others that they were, in fact, lesser Scythians, so it all worked out and no one looked at the lineage too closely. There were about four Scythian kings, but they were too busy moving across the conquered territories to slow down for a civil war. That was, perhaps, why they always kept moving—to stop and look around at their brethren might have involved not liking what they saw.

Even the invaders themselves didn't seem to know where they had come from. It was difficult for them to remember their past communities, their connections with their ancestors (except the ones they had brought with them in the form of amulets, combs, knives, and ashes), their lasting contributions in other places. Their world became the one they found, not the one they left behind. Like the people in the towns and cities they swept through, their stories moved only in one direction—forward.

CHAPTER 5
Wasp and Worm

IT WASN'T UNTIL WABASHA, A DAY AFTER OUR LIST-WRITING, THAT we saw the first signs of plague. As we moved farther south, the high moraine ridges began to flatten, and the river widened. It was quiet, serene even, but the changing geography made me nervous.

Because *everything* was changing. There was so much change, in fact, that I wasn't even sure whether it was just my ignorance about the landscape of America, or whether the world itself was being remolded day by day. Were the cliffs crumbling? I wondered. Was the river getting deeper or shallower? (Deeper, I later found out for certain, but I wouldn't know that for a while.) Everything was an open book.

At first we didn't see much river traffic. Small-town docks were emptied of boats. This included Lake City, which a sign along the shore proclaimed as the BIRTHPLACE OF WATER-SKIING. I could almost hear the footsteps of people running down the docks, kids bouncing around and laughing with their life preservers on. But not quite. Along a few of the docks, the speedboats and pontoons were sunk, their hulls punctured in the duckweed shallows, still tethered to posts with nylon cords.

Black eagles soared above us. We passed under bridges, railroad and road. Some were intact and some were blown in two, iron beams twisted like pipe cleaners. I wondered if there were any working trains. Probably not. But some of the railroad bridges looked old and rusty, touched up with graffiti everywhere, and hadn't been used for decades anyway. It must have been too expensive to tear these down.

We didn't travel at night. The captain told us it was too dangerous.

But you're under contract from the military, my father said. Aren't you protected?

The captain laughed. You still think that countries are four-colored and on maps, that everything is neatly defined in terms of who controls things? No one controls anything here. No one even pretends to try. Armies are moved, people shuffled around, towns razed, provocations made. But it doesn't mean anything. Do you understand? The dromons—those are the Empire's ships, see—they go up the river, or down the river, but what enemies do they see? There's too much space. You see?

My father nodded and touched his chin. But I'm not sure he ever did understand. The teaching position waiting for him was his way to find permanence, the safety of a world map in a non-burning classroom.

We were on the tip of Minnesota and Wisconsin, or what was left of it, going into the prairie and slowness of Illinois and Iowa. The river kept widening, getting muddier. We were to stay overnight in Galena. I asked my dad if I could borrow his telescope.

Why? he said. He was in our cabin, putting a cool cloth on my mother's head. She was lying on a bed of straw in the corner and had a fever, which I didn't think much about. If anything, considering the last few months, it was surprising that more of us didn't fall ill. We didn't have antibiotics, and although our father brought a bottle of vitamin C tablets, they went fast.

I want to have a look around, I said.

My mother had a crossword puzzle book on her lap. My father was kneeling next to her, but stood up when he was done and folded the washcloth. The crosswords in the book were almost all done, and she didn't have a pencil. She was studying the answers, trying to keep her mind occupied with the patterns, I guess.

No, Macy, Dad said. The telescope is too fragile. We're not in our backyard anymore.

I know! Sorry. Sorry I asked.

I stalked away, and went to the upper deck of the boat to sulk. The wind was fast and I kept having to push my hair out of my eyes. I had my mother's eyes, everyone always said. Hazel and set deep in my face. Our faces. I looked at Iowa. Moss-covered, windowless pickup trucks were marooned on the highway running alongside the river. A skinned, headless deer hung from a tree in a flooded backyard, next to a swing set. A trio of hide tents were set up on the flat roof of a strip mall's bait shop. A small, skinny dog, smothered in mud, foraged along the banks. The dog might have been a poodle. I heard Xerxes barking at it from the lower deck.

On the horizon, I thought I saw massive silos, four of them. But they were made of flinty rock. I squinted. They were actually giant faces. I wished I had pushed Dad harder to lend me the telescope. I would have been very, very careful with it. My naked eye was kind of crappy. The faces looked male, stern, and identical. They were a bit like a cross between the Easter Island heads and the Mount Rushmore heads.

Really pretty, aren't they? a man said behind me. He had an accent. A soldier accent, I thought. I turned around. There was this guy in the corner of the deck, where there was a little nook. I hadn't seen him.

Sorry, I didn't see you, I said.

He was pretty cute and was eating out of a pot. Rice mixed with bread and gravy. But smelling like fish. He looked about Sophia's age—although who could tell anymore—and had dull black hair that was almost cobalt.

He shrugged. It's okay, he said, you were enjoying the scenery.

I wondered a bit how he had learned English. Maybe he was a fast learner.

I pointed at the heads in the distance. I saw that there was a farmhouse in their shadow. It was dwarfed. Do you know any-thing about them? I asked. Did Mount Rushmore migrate?

What? he said, waving away a wasp that was attracted to his head.

Mount Rushmore, I repeated.

He scraped the side of his pot with his wooden spoon, took a bite of, well, whatever it was, and said: No one I know has ever been to the heads. Someday I want to load up a wind wagon, see what I'd find there. Or mules, if I can't afford a wind wagon. It's not as if I get paid much—

Your hair, I said, leaning toward him.

Blackberry dye! he said.

No, there's a wasp in it—

But he had already run his hand through it. The few boys who ever wanted to impress me were hopelessly cursed. The wasp buzzed and stung his scalp, his blackberry hair. He shrieked and swatted his hair more, but it didn't help. He fell to his side and started seizing up. I wondered if he was allergic or epileptic, whether I should put his wooden spoon in his mouth so he wouldn't bite off his tongue. Instead I started shouting—Doctor, is there a doctor—like a useless girl and everything. Christ! No doubt I could have been more composed if things didn't happen so fast. But they always happened fast.

I heard footsteps from below, and soon a ring of people was around us.

Nikolai! Sophia shouted, kneeling next to me.

My heart plummeted.

Nikolai, can you hear me?

Then she turned to me, and managed to spit out: You little shit, what did you do to Nikolai?

Nothing, I said. He got stung by a wasp.

I stood up, shaking. My ubiquitous father and a short man who I was pretty sure was the first mate bent toward him.

Look on the head, I said, my voice croaking.

Are you a doctor? the first mate said to my father.

He's a doctor of astronomy, I said.

That didn't register. Sophia stroked Nikolai's hands, which were getting pale. It didn't take long before his skin was moon white.

The first mate found the wound. It was a bulge. And the wasp was still attached to Nikolai's head. The wasp was turning pale, too.

The first mate whistled, and then covered his mouth.

This doesn't look good, he said. He must have the plague.

Even Sophia stiffened, inched away. There was a murmur behind us. My curiosity was killing me.

You mean the wasps carry the plague? I asked.

The first mate stood up, still covering his mouth. No, he said, the wasps are attracted to people carrying the plague. There's something about the vapors they give off. The wasp eggs speed the plague along.

Eggs? I said. Wasps don't lay eggs. I also wanted to say: people don't emit vapors, like geysers. But that would have been getting ahead of myself.

I could tell that my father was growing impatient with me, but I didn't care. He didn't want me to catch anything, but also he wanted to be more in control of the situation than he was. Sophia, with her dying boyfriend, was making him nervous. Mom was probably making him nervous, too, down below.

Macy, he said. Why don't you go back downstairs. But not in our cabin.

Why not?

Your mother. She shouldn't be disturbed.

Oh, as if I'm more likely—

It would be bad luck to leave just yet, the first mate interrupted. He didn't elaborate. He had X's scarred into both of his cheeks, and I couldn't look him in the eye, but he reminded me, from the way he talked, of the "cool uncles" some of my friends at Central had. I wasn't sure if I was more freaked out by the fact that I could have been exposed to the plague, or that I had a tenminute crush on my sister's boyfriend before he went under.

Okay, I said, still shaking, I'm just going to sit here.

I sat on the floor of the deck. From there I saw the giant heads fade into the distance behind the *Prairie Chicken.* I would never find out their story. Nikolai started screaming.

Can you do anything? my father asked the first mate.

I was going to ask you the same thing, *Doctor,* he replied. So I guess that means no. The wasp is dead.

Nikolai writhed, like a drowning man coming up for air but finding the air poisoned. I could see, where the wasp had stung

him, a white husk fall off and blow away. The bump on his head
was papery, like fancy stationery, or a wasp's nest.

Sophia moved her hand toward his head. I wasn't sure she
even realized what she was doing.

Don't touch it! my father said, amazingly helpful as usual.

It doesn't matter, the first mate said. If she's going to catch the
plague, it's already happened. If he dies then we're all going to
die. Well, most of us.

My sister retracted her hand. I could tell that she was barely
holding it together.

What's happening to him? I asked. How much longer?

The first mate didn't look at me. He gave eyes only to Sophia.
They were not pleasant eyes.

Not long, the first mate said.

One thing that I liked, in our new world, was that being sixteen meant you were an adult for all intents and purposes (which
I always thought, until very recently, was actually "intensive
purposes," which worked, too). Of course, that probably meant
you were going to die younger. Die sooner. But as horrible and
hard as things became, especially later on, I had to acknowledge
the existence of a perk or two. There wasn't the hand-wringing
about overprotecting me from a lot of people I ran into. I wished
that my dad would get the message. He had enough to worry
about besides me.

Nikolai clutched his chest and then ripped his tunic off. The
skin below his collarbone was tattooed with a bird. A sparrow of
some kind, with three circles above the wings. But in other
places on his chest, there were hard, black lumps. Inside the
lumps I could see shapes moving around. Then the black bub-
bles turned gray and dull, like backsides of slugs, and the shapes
became clearer. They were little sepia pictographs. On Nikolai I

could see a cathedral with a sun over it, the sun's jagged rays falling on the cathedral's roof; and a bird that mimicked his tattoo. There were a couple of others that I couldn't see clearly.

Should they be lanced? my father asked.

The first mate shook his head, curt. That would be unwise, he said. If he's going to live, he's going to live.

He then turned to my sister, who was crying.

What I want to know, however, he said, is why a deserter from the Imperial Army is on this ship pretending to be a wooder. And more than that, a plague-carrying deserter. That's what I want to know.

He's—he's not from the army! Sophia said.

The first mate pointed to the tattoo of the bird and circles. His legion insignia, he said. Then he squinted at Sophia.

What are you trying to say? Sophia said.

You could have killed us all, he said. You still might.

Look, I don't know, Sophia said. I don't.

Sophia might have been trying to apologize, or she might have been trying to deny any wrongdoing. It was hard to tell with her.

Let's discuss this more practically later, my father said.

Practically? the first mate said.

He's dead, I said. I stood up.

And he was. He had died while everyone was bickering. The pustules continued to pale. I couldn't figure out why his head was turning into paper, on the one hand, and on the other, why the pustules were dioramas. With everything that had happened, it was just one more thing. Another line on a map that didn't exist. I ran my hands through my hair a few times. I never had an insect phobia, but now was as good a time to start as any.

Sophia stood and took a few steps back, resolute. She was

strange like that. I didn't know whether she loved Nikolai for real, or knew she was risking so much—aiding a deserter from an army that didn't exactly believe in due process and clemency. Nikolai seemed nice, but I was angry at him a little, too, because I knew I would have never been able to steal him away from my sister. And it was stupid, but I might have tried. Just to have one thing of my own. But he was dead and Sophia was going to be a wreck. Was I going to be a wreck, too? I didn't feel torn apart. But why not? I felt bad for Sophia, but I braced myself for whatever shit storm that was going to come from her.

We need to throw him in the river, the first mate said, as soon as possible. He closed Nikolai's eyes. Who will help me?

Silence. Everyone was afraid to touch the body, or just too exhausted.

I will, I said.

The first mate didn't look surprised, or disdainful, and for that I was grateful. I'm stronger than I look, I said, as a way of explanation.

I hadn't used a mirror in three weeks, so I had no idea how I looked, so it could have been a lie. But I felt strong enough.

Take his feet, the first mate said.

I took his feet. They were pretty cold, even with his ragged shoes.

As we heaved him up, Xerxes came bounding up the steps and started barking. He had been getting skinnier. Our scraps weren't enough, and he wasn't able to forage on the boat like he had on Pike Island.

Not now, Xerxes, I called to him.

We hauled Nikolai down the stairs. I almost tripped a couple of times but I gritted my teeth and kept my balance. The pustules on his chest started getting mushy, unreadable. When we reached the bottom of the stairs, we edged toward the side of the boat. The first mate nodded and said, Okay, on the count of three. On two and a half, pus came out of the buboes. No, not pus. I take that back. Small white maggots. The worms were mewling like kittens. I wanted to stop the tossing—not only because they were gross, but also to study them.

Three!

We tossed. The first mate's hand slipped, and Nikolai's head, going down, smashed against the side of the boat. It sounded, well, like someone hit a wasp's nest with a ball of earthworms. Dryness, wetness, a one-two punch. Worms and wasps. I rubbed my arms and watched Nikolai sink into our undertow. I felt horrible that Nikolai's head had broken on our account.

I realized I was pretty numb. I didn't like the feeling—or rather, the lack of feeling. The first mate was rubbing his hands on his smock—he no doubt had already spent too much valuable time on us passengers—when his eyes widened.

Get down, he said.

What? I said.

Then I heard a buzzing roar. I got down. Before I closed my eyes, I saw dozens of wasps descend on him. Only then did I start crying, screaming. I just wanted to go fucking home, sleep in my bed in St. Paul. *St. Paul,* not Pig's Eye.

No stings came for me.

I didn't catch his name.

Later that night, I had a dream about an airplane. I was living on a jumbo jet with my family. I was curled up in one of the back seats next to the bathroom, trying to sleep. My family was somewhere near the front of the plane. I think the pilot was showing Ciaran how to fly the plane. Whoever was in the bathroom kept rattling around, fumbling with the toilet seat and the paper-towel dispenser. I couldn't settle down and sleep. Exasperated, I got up and knocked on the door. Hello? I said. But the person kept slamming around. I tried to open the door but it was locked. I knocked louder.

Leave me alone! a voice shrieked from the other side of the door. It was my voice. I was on both sides of the door. I woke up shouting:

Leave me the fuck alone!

"THE FUNCTION OF DIS-EASE, AND HOW TO SOLVE IT"

Where does dis-ease come from? Medicine is a function of botany. Sunlight provides for botany. These arts and theorems are mostly lost. However, both gardens and the stockpiles preserve what memory does not. The gardens, even the wild ones, prove to be far more reliable than the old stockpiles, which die as people die.

Dis-ease is an accelerant, much like the forceful flow of water.

Look for aspirins in gas stations, but do not trust loose or bagged pills, unless there is reasonable written explanation as to why they aren't sealed away from children.

However, aspirins only dull pain and do not cure. For cure, look to berries in the cloud gardens of Nueva Roma. Do not trust the medicinal value of elderberry, fig, Liar's Wort, etc., of any garden below the twenty-fifth floor. Circular hedges protect the most precious balms, as well as the airy, antibiotic humors of those elevations. Check for pustules in the earthworms of this soil—you may have to use a lens.

Replicants of these cloud gardens occur naturally in Saskatchewan, but in inverse; that is to say, the gardens are deep underground because of the glaciers there. It is believed bird and bat droppings with Nueva Roman seeds left by migrants are interred by tunneling Canadian mammals. Everything is reversed in Saskatchewan, except for death.

Above all with plague, do not fear, provided you are truly who you are. In that case, the cure itself can slay.

(written with permanent marker on granite flagstone, five-meter height, one-meter width, at the confluence of the St. Croix and the Mississippi Rivers)

CHAPTER 6

What News

AS IT TURNED OUT, I'D DODGED THE PLAGUE. IT WAS A CLOSE CALL. The first mate, however, died the next morning. It was a long night for everyone.

I didn't get stung once. It was a miracle, I guess. I didn't feel miraculous. People were going to die all around me, and besides, all that the wasps avoiding me meant was that I didn't have plague *yet*. I didn't have papier-mâché skin or weird pustules *yet*. I wondered that night what my buboes would contain. Probably something stupid, like a heart or a cat.

As I was waking up the next morning—a couple of hours of fitful sleep after my nightmare—I heard people making breakfast on the upper deck, clattering pots. People still had to eat, and guard the boat from downed trees blocking the river and Scythian patrols. I coughed as I sat up in bed. My father tensed.

Are you okay? he said. Do you feel faint? He had covered every crack of our cabin with newspaper or fast-food wrappers, and tried to mend the oilskin window.

I'm *fine,* I said. It's just a cough.

Sophia glowered at me from the corner. It was dawn, but everyone was too burnt out to see what they were cooking above.

My brother was still sleeping, and Xerxes was curled up next to him, snoring. I had a brief impulse to throw Xerxes overboard, and then my brother. I wondered what it would have been like to do that. But then I felt ashamed for even thinking it. As our father paced, our mother was in her own corner, trying to wake from a bad dream. I could tell. I had a knack for detecting other people's nightmares. The claustrophobia was beginning to get to me, and anyway, I had my own bad dreams to worry about.

Wake up, I said to my mother, touching her shoulder.

Her eyes opened and she took in a deep breath. She grabbed my arm and twisted it, which hurt. She didn't know where she was.

Where am I? she said. God, where am I?

I pried her hand off my arm. It wasn't easy. She left marks.

On the boat, I said. Everyone's here.

Her eyes were glassy. Staring off into the distance, she said: I think I'm going to throw up.

Then she did. The vomit was black and thick and got all over her blankets. I was afraid for her. Sophia gave a look of distaste, and Ciaran startled out of sleep, no doubt when the stench reached him. He stood and went to the door. He had slept in something resembling an army surplus uniform.

Where are you going? my dad said to him, searching around for a rag to clean up with.

Out, Ciaran said. It smells in here. And I don't care about the fucking plague. We're not animals in pens.

Dad, let me get that, I said, trying to get the rag from him. But he didn't let go, and he kept staring at Ciaran, a hard look on his face. Ciaran kicked Xerxes, but gently. Come on, boy, he said. Xerxes sat up and stretched. They left. Dad probably knew cursing Ciaran out wouldn't do much good anyway; he was slipping away from all of us at a rapid clip.

Girls, our father said to us in a quiet voice, help your mother.

He let go of the rag.

It was clear he was at the end of his rope, if he ever had a rope. A trail of vomit fell down from our mother's chin.

I'm going to get water, Dad said. His hands were shaking.

The tanks are near the captain's quarters, I said.

He nodded and took off.

My mother started coughing. I found a corner of that rag that wasn't too dirty and wiped my mother's chin, cradling her head. I checked her scalp for wasp bites, and her arms for icons underneath the skin. I didn't find anything. Once I got going, it wasn't too bad. Except for the smell. My dad came back with water in a red plastic pail, what kids would take to the beach to build sand castles with. He knelt down by Mother, trying not to spill water.

My sister remained motionless in the corner.

Sophia, our father said. Please.

At last, Sophia stood, her hands limp at her sides. What can I do? she said, without much conviction.

Find Ciaran. Make sure that he's not getting into too much trouble.

She nodded and left our cabin. I was going to ask her how she was holding up, would I be able to do anything to help her, but she left. Plus anything I could say would have sounded stupid.

Dad put his hand over mine.

Thanks, Macy.

I shrugged. It's okay, I said.

It wasn't, but I didn't know what else to say.

Dubuque! the captain shouted from the top deck, ringing a brass bell. Dubuque in one hour!

My mother's head sank back down. I don't feel so hot, she said. But then she was out cold. Dad and I stood over her for a half minute, listening to her shallow, slow breathing.

Maybe we can buy some supplies for your mother in Dubuque, Dad whispered between his teeth, trying not to wake her up.

Dad, I don't think she—

Dad motioned for me to keep my voice down.

I don't think, I said more quietly, she has the plague. She's not showing marks.

My father shook his head. We have to act *as if* she does, he said. We have to take every precaution.

All right, I said, unsure that any precaution would work. How many on the boat do you think have died?

Too many. I don't know, he said. I don't know anything anymore, Macy.

Sophia came back.

Did you see your brother? Dad asked her. She shook her head.

I heard his stupid dog, though.

Doing what? I asked.

I don't know. Eating something.

All that dog does is eat, our mother said, sitting up. And then: God.

Waking, sleeping, Mother was all over the place.

Grace, Dad said, taking the towel from me and wiping her forehead with a clean corner. Grace, how do you feel?

She looked at all of us, and said: Pregnant. I feel pregnant.

Then she retched again.

None of us, least of all Mother, had any idea of what to say next. We didn't say anything at all for a while. Dad sat down, letting his rag fall, even though my mother didn't look like she was done with the vomiting.

Are you sure? he said.

Pretty sure, she said. I feel miserable.

She raised her head and lowered it again.

We weren't home anymore, far from it. But I would have had the same reaction if we were home; namely, that my parents' lives were predicated on a series of unfortunate accidents. They ought to have been more thoughtful of our situation, our mutual exile! I tried not to think of all the sitcoms that tried to keep cancellation away by introducing a baby into the fold. The names of those shows, which I watched on TV Land, and loved for some reason as a kid, were both sickening and prophetic. *Family Ties. Growing Pains.* The shows brought the babies in because they knew they were going to die.

My mother fell asleep again, and when she did, I tried, for the love of God, tried not to think of my parents having unprotected sex. It wasn't working very well, so I touched my mother's neck.

What are you doing? my father asked. The wind shifted, opened the cabin door, bringing the bite of little black flecks against my skin. Cinders from the shore? It soon passed.

Looking for pustules again, I whispered, in the calmest voice I could muster. Her skin was cold and lumpy, like leftover potatoes that weren't microwaved long enough. My mother fed us a lot of boiled potatoes growing up, along with tough cube steak. She was a horrible cook.

Macy, my father said. She doesn't have the plague. She said so. You said so.

Come on, Dad, Sophia said. Do you believe that if Mom is pregnant, she's somehow immune to the plague? I know a little about this from my classes and, well, it's illogical.

You took one obstetrics class at Concordia while you were a senior, Dad said.

Sophia shrugged. I'd been reading a lot on my own. What, you think I'm incapable of that?

Continual triangulation had its benefits. I *wanted* my sister to stick up for me for so long that I was surprised when she actually did.

We should just let her rest, Dad said. I'm not that naïve. But would it kill you girls to show some *happiness* about the news?

What news? Ciaran said, slipping into the cabin and shutting the door behind him.

Our mother's pregnant, I said.

Ciaran took a long, hard look at our mother. Then, shocking all of us I think, he knelt next to her and kissed her forehead. There were shouts and curses from the riverbank, and healthy retorts from the crew of the *Prairie Chicken,* involving goats and mothers.

Sophia sighed. I'm going to take a walk. You want to come, Macy?

Sure, I said.

The plague— Dad started to say.

Sophia rapped on the cabin walls with her knuckles.

The plague isn't going to be stopped by imitation plywood, she said.

We went outside. The cooking smoke had dissipated and gray-blue jays darted in the air. I blinked out the creepers. No plague moanings to be heard, but on the riverbank, there was a man standing on an unlit funeral pyre, made of heavy sticks and about as tall as he was. The boat had passed him already; he was still shouting at us. I couldn't make out what he was trying to say, or what he wanted with us. The river smelled a little, but not too bad. I put on the St. Paul Central sweater tied around my waist. When I was done, Sophia grabbed my hand. She was trembling as we walked toward the bow and the captain's quarters.

I'm sorry, she said, when we reached the bow.

Sorry for?

You had nothing to do with Nikolai dying. I was just pissed.

She let go of my hand and wiped away tears that weren't there.

Listen— I began to say.

I did love him, she continued. I think he loved me.

Where . . . where did he come from? I asked.

It doesn't matter, she said. All that mattered to me was that he wanted to leave with me. I couldn't help the plague. Away from that fucking prison island.

Did you *really* love him? I blurted out without thinking. I was such a doubter.

She looked out to the shore, and didn't say anything for a while.

No, she said. Probably not. But close enough, here.

The door to the captain's quarters opened and the captain stumbled out. He fell forward onto his knees. Even from some distance I could smell the alcohol on him. The two of us stood there in shock.

What are you two looking at? he growled and slurred.

We had a sense of foreboding that if we assisted him or said anything he would have become even more upset.

Jaco was the best first mate one could have hoped for, he said. He was a dear friend in uncertain times.

The captain waited for a response from us. Sophia stared at me. This type of damage control was apparently my job, since I had helped Jaco throw Nikolai's body into the river.

He seemed like a good guy, I said.

The captain nodded in wild fashion. That's right, he said, a good man. He knew this river better than I do, or ever will. Every cranny, every eddy. Did he die in vain? Is there some larger purpose to his death besides hauling your sorry asses to St. Louis?

We kept silent.

Well? he said. Spittle ran down his chin. Is there any reason?

No, I said. I guess not.

For some reason, my response seemed to satisfy the captain. At that exact moment, he seemed to realize he was quite drunk, and tried to regain a measure of decorum. All of us, including the captain, knew the task was hopeless, but the attempt itself was not pointless. It showed us that we could rely on him, in a strange way. Drunk or sober, he would be able to prevent the *Prairie Chicken* from crashing into shoals, or thread the needle of an ambush.

Dubuque is not far, he said. Perhaps we will be able to find succor there.

The captain waddled away, hunched over.

Medicine, I thought. Medicine for Mother.

Sophia had other ideas. The reason I brought you out here, she said, was to clear the air with you. Because I'm leaving the boat in Dubuque.

What? Why? I said.

What's left? she said. I'm nineteen, Macy. I would be starting college by now. I wanted to be a certified midwife.

That's gone, I said. There aren't any more certifications.

I know. But how is this a replacement?

You could go to school in St. Louis, I said. Where Dad will teach. I'm sure there's some kind of nursing program you could enroll in.

She gave a quick laugh. I don't trust that, she said. Do *you* trust that? Is anywhere safe on the river anymore? Can any learning and *higher education* take place on the banks of this fucking river? With Avars and Scythians and the plague?

She had a point. But one thought and one thought only was rushing through my brain: *Don't leave me alone with Ciaran. I can't control him. No one can control him. Our parents can't and I don't want to.*

But what about Mother? I said. Don't you want to look after her when she's pregnant?

She turned away from me. Don't make this any harder on me than it already is, she said in a low voice.

I was going to protest more, but I saw she was holding back tears.

Instead, I said: I'll miss you, Sophia.

Sophia gave me a brief hug. I didn't want to let her go. In her mind she had already moved past the boat, and toward Dubuque and whatever was past that. Who knew. I need to get my things, she said. You need to tell everyone else. If you could. They . . . they wouldn't understand.

Ciaran would, in a way, I said.

Sophia laughed. Yeah, she said. You're probably right.

Dubuque, however, was far from easy. All of us were on the deck when the port came into view. Dad had found our mother a plastic chair—a mutated lawn chair that looked like it had survived a few mortar rounds—and we were eager for land. Some of us for different reasons than others. Sophia must have hidden her backpack somewhere close by, ready to throw on. The air was a little rancid close to the port, but it wasn't horrible. But there was smoke from the docks and locks. A public park was alongside the banks, now not so public. Palisades enclosed it and catapults filled it. From the deck I could see the gleaming, copper dome of City Hall being disassembled. Crews up there had a makeshift array of cables and pulleys, but no safety lines. The world was in the process of disassembly. Our soldiers lined the perimeter of the boat, and laughed uneasily. Those that had them hoisted their rifles. They loved their rifles. I worried about that. It took me a few minutes to realize that the docks themselves were silent. Sophia was drumming her fingers on the railing. The *Prairie Chicken* lurched toward one of the unbroken landings, but a man in a trenchcoat came out from a little shed on the edge of the dock.

You can't anchor here! he shouted, his face red. You need to go on.

The captain gave the controls to his second mate and called out from the bridge: We need wood and supplies and medicine.

Medicine, the man said. Exactly. You have the plague on your boat. We can't let you dock.

One of the boys from the upper deck tittered and aimed his rifle at the dockmaster, who said, without looking up: Your guns won't work. And pointing is rude.

Wait, the captain said, what do you mean our guns won't work?

Guns don't work here. Things in general don't work down here. Now. I have authorization from Nueva Roma itself to prevent the docking of all ships except for specific and preordained military purposes. We're in quarantine. We can't let you get too close to us.

That was when my sister jumped into the water.

Wow, I thought. She's really doing it.

She'd forgotten her backpack; I wanted to call her back to remind her but figured it would make things too complicated.

Things were complicated enough. I realized, during her doggy paddle toward Dubuque, that Sophia wasn't a great swimmer. She wouldn't drown, I reasoned, but she wasn't as strong of a swimmer as I was, practiced by long laps across Tanner's Lake during my summers. That was where my great aunt Susie lived, right on the shore. It was a shitty lake, in a way, right next to the interstate, surrounded by way too many houses, but I still liked swimming there, even after Susie died and the lake house was sold.

Sophia must have really, really wanted to leave.

As it turned out, she didn't get very far. Her minute in the water was a blur. Our mother started screaming, the captain wasn't sure whether the whole thing was some kind of weird accident, and the dockmaster began citing ancient naval law in angry tones.

When Sophia reached the dock's edge, and the dockmaster tried to push her away with his foot, one of the mercenaries on the *Prairie Chicken* decided to take a potshot at the Dubuquean. Maybe he had a secret crush on Sophia, who knew. Nothing came out of the gun, however, except for singing. Or rather, a deep intonation of a chant. I watched the whole sequence with a mix of freakout and glee: the aiming, the trigger pull, the expected recoil that almost made the shooting boy fall forward, and then the chanting coming from the gun's barrel. It hung in the air like an echo.

Everyone stopped, except for Sophia, who was still flailing around. The dockmaster only laughed.

Keep doubting me about your armaments, he said. Truly. I implore you.

After ten minutes of negotiation, what ended up happening was the following: the captain threw a life preserver to Sophia, who reluctantly accepted it. I'm not sure if she ever considered drowning as an option. Our mother turned calm throughout the negotiations. That might have been a product of her not knowing what was happening. In fact, after a few minutes she lost her energy or interest and went back to the cabin. Which was good, because she was the only person I could think of who might have actually had the plague, or at least looked sick. Dad hauled Sophia up, and in short order the *Prairie Chicken* unmoored its anchor and was moving between the broken buoys.

Throughout the whole ordeal, Ciaran took it all in as if he was daydreaming. Sometimes I wondered if he was adopted.

Sometimes I wondered if *I* was adopted.

All in all Dubuque was bad, but it could have been worse. Sophia could have left.

I hoped the baby was a girl. One brother was enough.

What Does a Couple Want

When the Palmers were on the river, Grace had developed a secret theory that the problems—the invasions, the disease,
everything—were her fault, that she had tipped the natural balance in an unnatural way. She scoured her own face for tells, and
also her husband's. Maybe it began at the yoga class they took together, a few weeks before the Scythians arrived. They thought
it would help them grow closer. No other community-college
extension class could have been more catastrophic. Their in-
structor considered the two of them to be special projects. They
kept falling down and couldn't relax into a crane position. In the
car ride back home, the two of them got into a fight about the
crane position that neither of them could do. Grace had kept
flopping over. For the first time in a long time, Carson was embarrassed by his wife in public—much as he imagined their children would be—and this filled him with deep shame. So he took
it out on her. Grace, in turn, just wanted to be left alone in the
class—for her, the flopping was a *kind* of yoga, because she was
trying to concentrate on her body. That mattered to her. She
didn't want to hear his pecking voice. She screamed at him in the
car and forgot she was driving, and drifted to a stop on Grand
Avenue. The water-bottle truck behind them came within an
inch of their bumper, and perhaps their lives. They pulled over

and in the din of the thirty seconds of truck honking, they began crying. I want another baby, Grace said. All right, Carson said, holding her, looking at the shoppers on Grand gawking at the near accident.

We'll try.

CHAPTER 7

The Nadir of the M

CIARAN THREW SOMETHING SLIMY AT ME. THE THING FLOPPED IN my lap, like a wet sock. We both squealed, for entirely different reasons.

What the hell is this? I asked, grabbing it by the tip and holding it away from me.

Dinner, he said. Well, it's a river cucumber. Markos caught a bunch. I'm sure it would work in a sandwich. Not that we have bread or anything.

I let it flop onto the deck.

Is our food situation really this bad? I asked. *River cucumber* bad?

That's what they say, Ciaran said. Although, is the captain going to eat these? I'm sure he's got plenty of moon pies or something stashed away.

My brother was probably on the mark with that one. I looked at the "cucumber," which seemed halfway between a fish and a plant.

Why don't you try to steal some, then? I said. Some real food.

He leaned forward on the railing, which creaked. Believe me,

Macy. I've tried. But the bastard has them in a safe in his quarters. He has to.

I supposed this was what passed for a normal, sibling-like conversation for us.

Anyway, I said, I'm not hungry. But hey, thanks.

I pushed the cucumber away with my foot. Xerxes came bounding toward us from God knew where. He sniffed the cucumber, made something of a face, and spun around toward Ciaran, sinking down at his feet. Ciaran bent down and scratched behind his dog's ear. The cucumber wasn't even edible for the Dog That Would Eat Anything.

But you know what I don't understand, I said, aware and annoyed that, for Ciaran, the dog took precedence over me—is where the hell these come from. Because I'm pretty sure these are deep-sea creatures.

The river's deep, he said. Standing up again, he found a stone in his pocket—maybe from home—and skipped it on the water.

Right, but not *that* deep, I said. I was thinking of all the nature specials I watched on those weekday afternoons when I pretended to be sick. The cucumbers, I said, they're like the ones in the Marianas Trench. They live near geysers and never see sunlight. In saltwater, not freshwater. And Markos just caught one with a net?

Ciaran threw an angry look my way. Chill out, Macy, why don't you. Markos was just trying to do a favor. Maybe the river's getting deeper. Fuck, I don't know.

I was about to say: This has nothing to do with Markos, whoever he is, is he one of your new friends? But he stalked off. As he passed by, he kicked the river cucumber into the corner.

I felt bad, a little. It was theoretically possible that Ciaran was trying to be helpful, to feed me, although he always had a knack for snatching selfishness from the jaws of altruism, or something like that.

Alone on the deck, I realized how cold the air had become. The next port was Fortune City, which I had never heard of before. Halloween, my least favorite holiday ever, was coming up. It could be argued that every day was now Halloween for us, except without the fun-size candy and the plastic costumes. The river was wide and slow. It was hard to see the shore. Instead of trying to, I leaned over the railing and tried to peer down as far as I could, into the depths. No such luck; the water was murky and uncooperative. I sighed. I was hungry. But not, I thought, hungry enough to eat a river cucumber, even though I ate worse not so much later.

I also had a canker sore on my upper lip, which I couldn't help but rub. I tried to ignore the sore, but my conscious brain didn't win out in these types of situations.

I heard giggling below me in the boiler room. Men never giggled well. I went down the stairs on a whim. In the wood-fire light, I saw my father in the corner with two of the wooders, smoking kef. I could tell it was kef right away. It didn't have the fruity smell of weed; instead, it smelled like someone used a sawed-open skull as a container to burn trash. Before we left St. Paul—sorry, Pig's Eye—a few kids at school were smoking it. They weren't even stoners. I think the stoners were afraid of it. No, these were the kids who liked cough syrup with codeine and listened to hip-hop with the lyrics slowed way down. Those kids creeped me out, but also a small part of me wanted to be like them. I tried kef once, at a party. Only it wasn't really a party, since it wasn't fun or festive per se. More like a semirandom assortment of semilosers from high school who decided to get high. As one could guess, it was lame. I didn't know who brought the drugs. Probably Stacy, whose brother dealt. Stacy was one of my friends for a long time from the Episcopal Church and summer camp. We'd drifted apart over the years, but she still invited me, because we were in the same social never-never land. The gathering was a kind of last hurrah; we were on Pike Island just two weeks later.

Anyway, we were in Stacy's basement, and no one wanted to try the kef, so I did. They were cowards, but my hands were shaking as I took it. The kef made me feel like someone a long time dead was stroking my hair. I know that sounds a little creepy. Stacy took some, too, then. The basement had a lot of moss on the walls. And spiders. Wolf spiders, which weren't as scary as they sounded. A few of the boys were playing old-school Nintendo on a small TV that must have been from the eighties. They were playing Mario Party or some other game like that. Racing to put coins or fruit or mushrooms in a basket. I was slouched on the couch, watching the TV in a daze, and saw that the Mario character, while a plumber of some sort, was dressed in a black version of his suit, and had red eyes. He pointed and tapped on the screen, and started shouting this guttural stream of slurs that I couldn't make out.

The two boys playing the game put down their controllers very slowly. Then the TV shorted out.

None of the boys were interesting. I laughed at them, even though I was scared, too. That was the first time that anyone really thought me dangerous. I felt bad, afterward, about laughing at them. Being popular meant being dangerous—but so the fuck what. So other kids were scared of you and wanted to be your friend. What did that mean?

All those social equations changed soon enough anyway. The boy I was going to ask to homecoming, I heard in the camps on

Pike Island, was shot in the head with an arrow when he was in the Minnesota Irregulars, making a sweep through Bemidji. The other irregulars left him behind. His name was Trevor McLaughlin and he was captain of the cross-country team. I said "head" when I should have said "left eye." The Scythians probably defiled his corpse. (It wasn't like I lusted after the captain of the *football* team or anything. I thought my desire was *reasonable*.)

I was sick for days afterward from the kef. I vowed never to use it again, but it was a constructive experience, as far as experiences went. Stacy said that her brother said that the Thracians had built up a tolerance to kef, over many years. In fact they started smoking it at a very young age, like Italians would give wine to their toddlers. I didn't think my dad had any tolerance whatsoever, but there he was, laughing with the boys my age. I didn't want to disturb them, not in the slightest. I wanted to be a little rat in the wall, but then one of the boys—the ugliest, of *course*—ratted me out with a sidelong glance. My father turned to me. His eyes couldn't focus on mine. And I didn't want to give him the chance, I was so embarrassed—so I turned away.

Macy, he said, his face getting red. I thought back to when he told me the story about the devil and the giant diamond—and how horrified he had been by the slightest *hint* that I had smoked kef at one point. How the mighty had fallen.

What are you doing? I asked.

One of the boys held out a pipe. Dinner, he said.

I never once thought that kef's use as an appetite suppressant would come into play. Maybe that was why my father was doing it, I thought, but he looked like he was enjoying it too much.

I was hungry but didn't feel like eating. (Really on account of the canker sore, which I kept rubbing with my tongue. Which was bad, I knew, but I couldn't help it.)

Want any? the boy said. I scanned their skinny hips for guns and saw they had none, which didn't surprise me, after the humiliation in Dubuque.

She doesn't want any, my dad said, suddenly parental and everything. Nothing could have made me more angry. The boys cooled. The old guy was turning on them. It was as if they realized, only then, that he was taller than them. I was trying to formulate some dashing witticism to devastate my dad, even if it would have been lost on him, when I heard a bell from above.

The boys changed from boys to killers. I wasn't sure how they could tell, right away, that this was an urgent plea from above, and they perhaps would have to risk their lives over God knew what.

My dad blew out the pipe and set it on a ledge next to his head.

Don't tell your mother about this, he said, in a spasm of coughing.

You mean your pregnant wife? I said, raising my voice to be heard over the bell.

Macy! This isn't the time.

I heard a volley of shouts from above. We both looked up.

Okay, he said. Back to our cabin.

I nodded. I could see that Dad was afraid, which made me afraid. It might have been because of the kef.

On the deck, we both stopped when we saw what was downriver. It was an iron bridge, once used for automobiles, about a quarter mile ahead. The fact that there was an intact bridge, in and of itself, was pretty unusual. However, pouring over the bridge from west to east were hundreds of horsemen with their wagons. I could tell from their style of armor and the colors painted on their wagons—just a feeling I had—that these weren't Imperial forces. Dad must have had the same feeling.

Where are the defenses? my father asked, almost shrieking. Where is the Empire?

You would think there would be some, I said, almost nonchalant, or faking it. Huh. Maybe they're all dead. Maybe it's the plague.

Leave, the captain shouted to us from above. Hide.

But as we were going into the cabin—even though I didn't want to hide, my father gripped my elbow and wouldn't let go—Ciaran crashed into us. He was hefting a crossbow.

What are you doing? my dad said, switching his death grip from me to him, which was more than welcome.

I got conscripted, he said. I mean, I wanted to be conscripted.

Absolutely not! our father said. And what do you mean, you wanted to be?

It's what I want, he said. We're probably going to die anyways. So let me shoot something before I die, dammit.

Ciaran wasn't asking permission. It was more a tic than anything. I could smell smoke that was on the edge of incense, as if someone had thrown potpourri onto a burning body.

Carson! the captain shouted to my father, leaning over the railing right above our cabin. I need your telescope! And let your son go!

Ciaran's and Dad's eyes met, and my dad let go.

Well, I said to myself, maybe that will be a good way for my brother to let off some steam. I mean, that we were floating into the midst of hundreds of barbarians filled me with dread, but somehow maybe my brother would prosper from it.

I heard the captain shout orders as I entered the cabin with my father and closed the door. My dad was fumbling for his tele-scope. I think he was thrilled that he could be of some use. Sophia was there kneeling with my mother. My sister was trying not to freak out, because my mother was passed out.

It's started, Sophia said. I could tell that she was trying to re-main calm, let the training that she had guide her. But I could tell how hard it was for her.

What's started? I asked, though I already had an idea.

My sister lifted up my mother's shirt. My mother's eyes began to flutter. Ringing her belly button, like planets to a sun, were a half-dozen pustules. Sophia was crying. The pustules looked ready to break. They had, inside of them, little fingers and toes. The baby shouldn't have been that big yet.

It couldn't have been.

She's not waking, Sophia said. And then: What's happening outside?

Scythians, I said. We're pretty much fucked.

My sister's eyes clouded and I could see, I think, that she was torn between caring for our mother and having her own free-dom, her own life. The failure of her escape was hanging on her, but I could also imagine she was feeling guilty for wanting to es-cape in the first place. And I don't know what I would have done in her position.

Does Dad know? I asked.

Sophia shook her head, stroking our mother's brittle hair. They just came up, she said. Do you think we'd be able to find any doctors on the river? In port? If we dock anywhere?

I don't know, Sophia. I'm going to tell Dad, I said.

Yeah, he needs to know, my sister agreed. Good luck.

Her good luck sounded like a good-bye.

I grabbed her hand. She was a little surprised, but held my hand tight for a few seconds before letting go.

I burst out the cabin door. We weren't far from the Scythians. Some of them on the bridge had noticed us. They were pointing at our little *Prairie Chicken*. Their war wagons were painted with circles, in bright glittering colors, as if they used spray paint with a paintbrush. Fortunately, Scythians weren't crazy about boats, and thought it was bad luck to get a little wet. So that was good. Just pretend we're not here, I thought, closing my eyes for a few seconds. I had to do something to help my father out. I opened my eyes and ran up the stairs.

Macy! my father shouted as he saw me. Get back with your mother and sister.

Then I saw that his hands were tied, and the captain was wrapping the telescope in a vellum pouch, and everything dawned on me. My father gave me a helpless look. After that look, a few things happened all at once. A man behind the captain, a bodyguard, moved in front of my dad. He was holding a pike, or a halberd of some sort. I saw elephants—elephants!—at the base of the bridge, bringing water to their mouths with their trunks, stepping around slabs of broken concrete. They still had their circus refinements around their large heads, and they had useless-looking bands of leather armor on their legs. I felt bad for them. Maybe they thought that war was just another circus, albeit one without a big top. The man with the pike glared, and leveled his pole arm at me. It almost reached my chest.

We had only a few more minutes at most until we reached the Scythians. I had my knife in my boot. I don't know, I thought it was good protection. I ran back to the foot of the stairs and reached for the knife. I thought that if I could get Dad free, it would be better, just on a psychological level, and that maybe differences with the captain could be resolved. His whole selling my father into slavery in exchange for free passage—that *was* the only explanation, wasn't it?—could be excused as a cultural misunderstanding; even though no one would have believed it, it still would have been a diplomatic way to end things. Hell, the captain could have kept the telescope to smooth things over. A gift.

I guess my plan wasn't meant to be. The pikeman lunged at me, and got his sharp end nearly caught on my shoulder sleeve. He was off balance to begin with. I counted on that, but I realized then how outmatched I was and how I wasn't thinking straight. I was terrified and sluggish. I felt like I was moving in slow motion. I tried to fall back to the stairs. But then he eased the attack on me. Because my brother shot him in the eye with a crossbow.

One of the others, the second mate, approached the captain with a sword. The captain was very drunk and smiling, not knowing how out of control his little plan was getting. I went to my father and cut him free. He was shaking.

It's okay, I said. It's okay.

The second mate punched the captain in the face with his sword hilt. When the captain was down, the second mate kicked him on the base of the spine. Then he looked at my father and me.

Get down, he said. Go with your family. For some reason I knew this didn't mean Ciaran anymore, if it ever did. I tried to figure out, for a few seconds, how I felt about the fact that Ciaran saved our lives. I wanted to thank him, but there wasn't any time. The attacker with the pike was still screaming, flailing around. The second mate went behind him and kicked him in the back a few times, until he was still. I was glad about this, in a way, but also a little creeped out.

We went down the stairs. I tried not to trip. My shoulder hurt even though it wasn't touched. A preemptive wound. I could hear the Scythians shout at us. They were laughing hard. Bows were cocked. I saw a McDonald's past the bridge, in a strip mall along the river, which looked open for business. Horses and wagons surrounded it. I was about to go back in the cabin but my father held me. I hadn't noticed that he had picked up the pike. He held it like a sword.

Do you know how to use that thing? I asked him.

He half-turned it. Not really, he said.

You hold it two-handed, here, and here, I said. I showed him where to grip. My time playing Warcraft came in handy after all. At the very least it was the impetus to research all kinds of medieval weapons one boring summer. What I didn't tell my father was that the pike was an anticavalry weapon, so it was pretty stupid for anyone to have on a boat in the first place. After all, it didn't kill me. I bet that the soldier just thought that it looked cool, which was a stupid way to go about things. If he'd had a sword, I would have been dead.

It was when I got Dad to hold the weapon right, kind of, and the crew *finally* started to do some makeshift rowing from the lower holds to go back upstream—too late already, in my book—that the submarine arose from the depths of the river.

It was rather strange.

A huge wave from its ascent sloshed water across the deck of the *Prairie Chicken*. I wiped the spray out of my eyes. Some of the crew was crying. The submarine was black alloy, all business. The U.S. flag had been painted over in several places. In the flag's place, it was written: NADIR OF THE M.

The Scythians, who up to that point had been intent on volleying fire arrows at our ship from their bridge, were skittish.

They had good reason to be, as just then the submarine started shooting ceramic jars at them. Unpainted china. I had no idea how turrets and torpedo bays could have been retrofitted for this purpose, but I saw it. The jars shattered against helmets and horses' kneecaps. As our boat heaved away from the battle, my father told me to hold the pike. He ran up to retrieve his precious telescope. When he came back, he said that he had a looksee with the telescope. The jars were filled with scorpions.

Huh, I said. I then remembered that Dad didn't know about Mother's plague-catching. But I didn't have the heart to tell him quite yet. He was happy he was alive. I didn't want to dampen that.

The crash from the kef would dampen him plenty without my help.

Later that night—after he found out about Mother's plague— he kept to himself down in the bowels of the *Prairie Chicken,* smoking, no doubt. One of the crew boys baked a river cucumber for me. He put it in a kind of curry sauce, but since my canker sore was still bothering me, I had to scrape most of the sauce off. The night was cold and foggy; we were all hungry on account of still being alive and all. The dead don't have appetites. The cucumber tasted what I imagined sea snake to taste like, with maybe a little eggplant thrown in. A little chewy.

But it wasn't bad. I had eaten *much* worse in Central's cafeteria.

I saved some for my dad, but he didn't take it when he came back. He slunk right to bed.

I tried to feed Mother some of my river cucumber. But she wasn't interested, either. She turned her head toward some vision I couldn't see. Away from me.

Cartographic Nightmares

For a time, the oil industry did suffer from the developments in the geopolitical landscape. The shipping lanes were fraught with peril—aside from the massive spike in sea storms, offshore hurricanes, and the like, scattered reports from faint short-wave signals indicated that "sea serpents" had taken to attacking oil tankers. And there were pirates that seemed to be in collusion with the "sea serpents." At the multinational headquarters of one company, surrounded by palisades and mercenaries on the flood plains of Houston, these reports were attributed to a spoliation of clean water and scurvy. The executives were less sanguine about the GPS failures of the navigation systems; it took about three cases of electrum bullion—smelted from antiquities from the Houston Museum of Technology—to pay for the retrofitting of the tankers for cartomancy, paper charts, astrolabes, and the training of navigators. Most of those tankers disappeared around the Azores anyway.

The usual global hotspots were farther away than ever and yet the world—their world, rather—became a riskier proposition.

And even if they were able to retain the status quo, continue the free exchange of petroleum, and open markets with a distinct lack of ocean monsters, it became clear soon enough that demand was going to be a problem. With the invasion, counter-invasion, and the drop in automobile travel, the petroleum in the country sat unused in the strategic reserves, and most of the refineries were blown up—by accident or design, no one could say. The Empire—and to a lesser extent some of the ancillary tribes skilled in chemistry and allied with the Scythians—took over small batches of oil to use for Greek fire and other concoctions. But these were in such tiny proportions in comparison to the vast infrastructure of the American consumer that the petroleum wasn't worth brokering on a macroeconomic scale; and besides, the Empire pretty much took what it wanted anyway.

With the low demand for energy, the oil industry found itself at a crossroads. But the CEOs of these great companies comforted themselves in couriered messages between their headquarter fortresses: *at every crossroads is an opportunity.*

How could they prove themselves to be useful? They assayed their assets, which consisted of a robust shipping fleet with lots of cargo space, and a large workforce still looking for work. With this in mind, the industry as a whole had a collective revelation and decided to enter the slave trade. And not just enter it—to become global (be that as it may) leaders in the industry. The six largest American petro companies allied in a consortium, performed a cost-benefit analysis on their human assets in the form of workforces, and negotiated a bulk price with the Empire for their workforces' services. The employees signed contracts, and were sent in company tankers from the Gulf of Nueva Roma, and up the Mississippi, the Missouri, the Ohio—anywhere labor was needed. The employees who didn't sign the contracts were sent anyway. The casualty rate, on account of the plague—and to a lesser extent, the environmental side effects of transport in the mostly drained tankers' holds—was on the high side, but the oilmen knew about surplus and excess, and they had more than enough human capital from their own work-forces to meet the rather large demands of the Empire for public-works laborers, army irregulars, and manning the state-controlled fast-food restaurants throughout the Empire's reach.

The slaves were not called slaves, of course. That would have ruined the spirit of the endeavor. The oilmen knew themselves to be, through thick and thin, defenders of free enterprise and the happiness that came from it. The slaves were instead called "partners." The partners, it was explained to them, had a lot going for them. At the same time, their lives would become more difficult and more strange than their old lives, as it was for everyone. Their managers shared their pain. The partnership would provide for them. One had to roll with the punches. A lucky percentage of former employees—never more than 2 percent, and those with a thuggish, upper-managerial skill set—kept on with the company as overseers of the new partnership. People needed to pilot the boats, and broker the sale of DINKs and empty nesters, after all. And the supervisory workforce was peppered with those of a peculiar brutality. After a time, petro-leum seemed only a vestigal means to this end. Once the original partners were more or less depleted, no small amount was in-vested into the acquisition of new resources—first from allies in the big-box retail industry, who were late and eager to get into the game, and then . . . then whoever they could find. The net always had to be cast wider, the drill pushed deeper. With the near-continual warring between the Empire and its enemies, there would always be displaced people. There would always be enough people willing—or at least finding themselves in—a partnership.

CHAPTER 8

The Nadir of the M (II)

THESE WERE A FEW OF THE STORIES THAT I OVERHEARD ABOUT THE *Nadir,* the submarine that most on the *Prairie Chicken* had never seen until our encounter with the Scythians on the bridge. Our progress, once the Scythians were driven off, was edgy, cautious, and dazed for lack of proper nutrients. Fortune City, the second mate kept incanting. Fortune City will take any ship. That remained to be seen. We saw Scythian patrols, few in number, on both sides of the river. They watched us but didn't try anything on us.

So we essentially were waiting to port safely. As we went downriver, we listened to the stories. Ciaran didn't much, since I think he had heard a lot of these before. But the crew and marines on board were eager for a captive audience, and my family was eager to take breaks from caretaking Mother.

Listening was cake compared to having my heart broken with her.

Its Tithe

It was easy to listen to the first one, because it was about love. Of a sort. I wasn't sure if it was love of a man or a really cool submarine.

The captain, you see, was a woman named Em. But that was an abbreviation. Her name before was Emma, or Emily, or something like that. It really didn't matter. She enlisted in the navy at a young age, and worked in the boiler room of a nuclear submarine. I wanted to interrupt and say that nuclear submarines didn't have boiler rooms, but the storyteller, I could see, wasn't in the mood for facts. And after a while it did seem sensible for nuclear submarines to have boiler rooms. I rolled with it.

At any rate, Em's first commanding officer was noble and gallant. A little cruel, perhaps. He had his eye on her, but soon realized that she knew this, and wanted him, and wouldn't take any BS. They made love for the first time under the Ross Ice Shelf. None of the crew suspected anything for a long time. The submarine sank whales it mistook for enemy submarines. But who was counting, in those days, for the days were peaceful, full of long silences under the water. And even the furtive shore leaves in Norfolk were serene for her, unselfish and lonely, which was a good quality for a sub hunter to have. Killing whales made one lonely.

What did Em see in him? A gravity, a sense that it would be impossible for him to lose at cards or chess, which he rarely did. The trouble was that she was headstrong, even more than him, and considered herself to have qualities that he did not, such as patience and clemency.

This wasn't in the story per se.

For unclear reasons—which might have involved some falling-out—he left his command. Or was discharged. Again, unclear. Em stayed on the sub. Having fallen apart from each other, from command, he moved to Louisville. This was right before everything started to happen. He was recruited as a spy by the Avars. He offered them nuclear secrets but they weren't interested in those.

The Avars don't have spies, my sister said.

Yes they do, my brother said, coming into our little hold. He had stamped out his cigarette on the deck. His smoking didn't surprise me. In a way, the surprising thing was that he hadn't started sooner. Everyone has spies, he said. They're not as common as apologists and cowards, he continued—and here he kicked the captain in the stomach. The captain's hands were tied, next to the fire. The captain, not having had a drop of alcohol in two days, was mumbling to himself.

Em didn't know—the storyteller went on—that the sub captain was now a spy, and living on the banks of the Ohio in an old schoolhouse, and brushing up on his swordplay. The submarine had a new captain, who wore whaling dungarees and smoked a corncob pipe. He claimed Dorchester Central Command had sent him there. No one had any idea what he was talking about. He would often trail off while giving an order. No one met him in the eye. After a week in the North Atlantic, deep under quiet storms, Em led a mutiny. Even the new captain wasn't surprised as they jettisoned him. Immediately Em turned the submarine around, toward New Orleans. She didn't know New Orleans didn't really exist anymore. She figured her old captain was there, or close to there. But he wasn't, and would evade her for many years. The Ohio River hadn't crossed her mind, yet.

Many years? I blurted out.

Everyone ignored me.

That was around the time they began building Nueva Roma, the storyteller continued. Em evaded the construction in the Gulf.

That was only the second time I'd ever heard about Nueva Roma—the dockmaster in Dubuque had mentioned it in passing, but I'd thought nothing much of it. I let it slide this time, too, for future investigation.

Em found no luck on the lower Mississippi. From ravaged city to city she roamed with her sub. Hints came. Interrogations led to leads. She heard he was a double agent for the Scythians, and soon she began attacking, well, pretty much everybody.

Except us, I said.

The storyteller looked at me. We are unimportant to her, he said. And I imagine she could sense how vulnerable we were.

Isn't she under contract with the Empire now? another man said.

That's not important! the man said. But whether she is or isn't—she tithes. She runs orphanages up and down the river. We haven't passed any. We will soon.

Why orphanages? I asked, although I already knew the answer.

Because of the orphans she leaves, the storyteller said.

The Nadir Proper

The Nadir of the M was originally made of wood. In fact, it was the planned vessel to escape the final, fatal siege of Constantinople. The design of the "sub-marine-ship" came to a monk, Maderus, in a dream. It was a brilliant dream, filled with angelfish and cuttlefish and diaphanous squid large as cathedrals, and Brother Maderus floated among them in a cylindrical wooden craft that was sealed with resin to keep the water out. Although Maderus was in a monastery some distance away from Constantinople—in one of the few fiefdoms the Byzantines had left in the early fifteenth century—he saw this as no object of dispersuasion. He decided in the morning that he had to tell the Emperor about the craft he dreamed, at all costs. He left the mountain monastery for the first time in twenty years—this itself took a careful day—and coaxed a fisherman to take him to Constantinople.

It took a while, though.

There are sharks, the fisherman said. And the Turkish navy.

How can that be any of my concern! Maderus said.

The fisherman was cowed to comply. A little hellfire never hurt anyone in the long run.

For three days they sailed. The winds were not with them. Sharks talked to them, not at all kindly. The sharks promised the hidden bounties of the seas, and also the love of mermaids, if only Maderus would turn back! He chided the sharks with Scripture. Though their boat was far from land and nests, a swarm of hornets landed in the Brother's voluminous beard, and whispered of the tortures that would descend upon his soul— not to mention his head—if he presented the Emperor with such a *heretical* plan for underwater travel. It was Papal. Frankish, even. Didn't he know that the devil's abode was in fact the sea's abyss, where no human mind could travel, where Satan schemed to crack the ocean floor with the miasmic hellfire deeper below?

Maderus did not. But he let them settle in his beard, and told the wasps that *they* were, in fact, the demonic agents.

Of course we are, the wasps said. Otherwise we would have

no knowledge of what we speak. However, it would grieve us, truly, to have you lose your soul to us over such a little trifle. For we sent that dream to you as a lark. A mere lark.

There are no such things as larks, Maderus said, and with that, the wasps departed, though not without stinging the fisherman three times, out of pure spite.

In rain, they landed at Constantinople to zero fanfare. The dockmasters were underpaid Illyrians, who were indifferent to Maderus's charge. He thought he had a few strings to pull—the most gossamer threads—in the political weave of the court. But after a little sleuthing, he discovered that his former patrons and teachers were dead or imprisoned, or had converted to Islam.

Luckily, that night, the Emperor himself had a dream. It was much less complicated than the monk's, involving a fisherman's head encased in a diamond, which revolved in a starscape. The Emperor woke up to blue stars at a fever pitch, and left his bed to stare out the window. Below him in the palatial courtyard, Maderus and the fisherman were attempting to break into the palace by use of a rope and skeleton key. They weren't very good at it. After many tries, the fisherman managed to hook the rope to one of the jutting cornices at the top of the wall. When the Emperor saw the fisherman—who was, in fact, the one from his dream—he was tremulous, and pointed, but couldn't say anything. He put down his finger.

My Emperor! Maderus said when he entered the high window, kneeling. But the Emperor ignored him and gave deference to the fisherman. This confused Maderus, who began blurting plans about his "sub-marine" boat. But the Emperor waved Maderus away, and beckoned the fisherman forward, who became very afraid, although the Emperor didn't look at all like an emperor *should*—rather doughy in the face and fingers, actually. The fisherman still had drooping welts on his face from the hornets.

Tell me your story, the Emperor said, for I dreamed of you, just minutes ago. Like Constantine, he thought, although he didn't say this, because he didn't want to appear vain.

I was born to a drowning woman, the fisherman said. She delivered me on a sinking trireme. I was the only survivor, and was adopted by an old couple who raised me on a fishing boat that rarely came ashore. I know what it is like to grow up hungry, to never know a bed, only waves. I had an older sister who disappeared, and a younger brother who lived beneath the waves as a kind of ghost merman. Eventually, I—

Maderus pushed the fisherman out the window. The fisherman's neck broke and the body contorted. Maderus explained to his Emperor that the fisherman was, with all certainty, an agent of Satan, *and the holy monk's last temptation,* but since the monk had succeeded in vanquishing the dark lord, the path was clear for the Emperor to understand why Maderus was before him.

The Emperor gulped. He wasn't sure whether this was the case, but he decided that a man of the cloth deserved at least a hearing, however brief.

In that garbled span, Maderus not only described his submarine boat, but also the series of tribulations that he faced in his journey to the Emperor, so that the two were of the same narrative thread, the same dream. The geopolitical and tactical uses of a submarine were of little importance to Maderus, but the Emperor saw that one day, perhaps soon, he or one of his descendants would have to flee the second Rome, and it was better to be prepared than surprised, since surprises were the norm in those days.

And so the submarine was built, although it was never used

by the Byzantines. Though seaworthy by 1453, the last emperor insisted on painting the submarine painfully specific colors—rosehip, butternut foal, scorched apricot—that weren't available during the siege. And so the submarine rested in a hidden cave below the city for many years. The fisherman was buried in an obsidian coffin set into the eastern city wall. A Turkish cannon blew open that wall during the fall of Constantinople.

The coffin was empty.

There was silence for about a minute before I realized the story was over.

How did Em get the submarine, then? I asked.

The storyteller turned to me but didn't meet me in the eye. How the fuck should I know? he said.

The Nadir's Hesitant Apex

Enough, the final storyteller said. Even if these stories are true, that doesn't mean that they are not false. Everyone is born false. Everyone in the womb, even with just a thousand cells, looks like a frog, a fish, a dog. We are indistinguishable from what we fear most. Everyone is a corsair. Everyone gets murdered one day. Most people murder themselves long before they die. People are good at self-smelting, taking everything whole and melting it all down, like rare coins and statues into gold bullion, for ease of transaction and anonymity. Em, because she hides from plain sight, shies from anonymity. She might ply the river, but she's not like us, with our sad little cargo of mail and passengers. She *is* the river. She couldn't leave the river as much as she could leave her own body. So why did she attack the Scythians and not the *Prairie Chicken*? No one will know. Perhaps if one of you drown, you can ask her, and she will tell you a story about lost empires and amethyst-skinned sea snakes, pristine forests immolated into ashen craters.

The storyteller stopped and, stretching, stood up and wandered away, to do night chores no doubt. The boat creaked. I never did catch his face. I could hear my mother moaning.

Well, that wasn't much of a story, Ciaran muttered. He spat. I couldn't have agreed more, and yet the last story had exhausted me, left me on edge, which had to have counted for something, some impact on my life.

I bit my upper lip and my entire head was filled with a sharp pain.

Sophia leaned closer to me. Oh God, Macy, what's that on your lip? she said. Is that a blackhead?

Ciaran giggled. I touched my lip, my hands shaking, and knew at once that it was a plague buboe. I wondered what the pustule had inside of it, what secret trinket, like a toy at the bottom of a cereal box. I ducked my head underneath my arms. More than anything, I was mortified that the pustule was on my face, on such public skin. I could have just died.

A Family that Plays Together

Carson Palmer was born twenty-five years before the Cincinnati Bengals quarterback of the same name, outside Columbus, Ohio. He was the fifth of six children and received about a sixth of the attention in the family. He had four sisters and one brother, none of whom finished college. He was the first. They all dropped out to help with the stores except for Maya, his oldest sister, who died in a caving accident in her freshman year at Carleton, way up in Minnesota. He was closest to her out of anyone in the entire world. Growing up, she would tell him stories about space travel and Martians and unexplained phenomena, like petroglyphs in the Chilean deserts. Her eyes, he remembered, were always moist. And she laughed a lot. He was thirteen when she died. Even at that age he was planning where he wanted to go to college, but he had to cross Carleton off his list. He just had to.

His father owned the third largest chain of sports equipment stores in Ohio, USED TO PLAY. Carson's interest in his family business was minor, to say the least. USED TO PLAY sucked in everyone in the family, but he resisted as much as he could. He was rarely in the mood for the sporting life. Even Maya played outside all the time, and played golf. The school didn't have any girls' teams, but that didn't stop her from fighting to play. Carson admired this stubbornness of hers on one level, but he wanted nothing to do with it. Carson was never stubborn. He let events come to him, and then pass over. At the same time, he didn't like to stand still. He ran a lot, through the oak-lined streets of their suburb. Especially at night. He didn't consider running like this a sport. He would run either closing his eyes or looking up at the sky. At that time, a person could still see a lot of stars, arrangements of minor constellations. The strip malls hadn't drowned out the light yet. When he came back, with his own family, for his mother's funeral, he sat on the back porch of the old house one night with a beer and cigarette and couldn't see anything. The sky was a gray rust. Sophia was only five—she was inside watching TV and asking questions about where Grandma went. Grace was upstairs, trying, without much success, to get a shrieking Macy to bed. Macy was having nightmares, even during the day. Ciaran would be born in two months. There were a lot of employees of USED TO PLAY at the funeral. A lot of those employees were cousins or spouses of cousins. He worked in the store one summer, right out of high school, and it was a disaster. There was no getting around the fact that Carson was horrible with money, and everything that involved money: salesmanship, a winning attitude, enunciation. After a few weeks on the sales floor, his father moved him to the warehouse. On the first day he broke his foot when a box of hockey masks tipped. He got to go home, and he never went back. Carson was embarrassed by his own freedom, and doubled his effort to avoid the family stores whenever possible. His parents drank a lot. They hated the fact that he went to college. But they said they would pay for it. They didn't need to, on account of his scholarship.

The coroner's report indicated that Maya had been trapped in the small air space for about eight hours. During the summer when Carson had broken his foot, he forced himself to look up the report at the County Administration Building. The county in Minnesota where she died had transferred over the death record. Maya's fingernails had been ripped off, from clawing at the rock pile. The other three girls had concussions and fractures, and died from the impact. The coroner also said that there were some shapes on the limestone cave wall, which could have been letters or pictures. But authorities couldn't be sure whether Maya was trying to say something, and if so, what.

In a couple of months, Carson took the bus to Northfield, Minnesota. To St. Olaf, the college on the other side of Northfield from Carleton. He had been accepted there. He was seventeen, having skipped fourth grade.

He didn't pack enough winter clothes, needing room for his telescope, and a rather large book called *Cave Systems of Southern Minnesota*. He still wasn't sure if he could live without the former, or whether he'd find the courage to use the latter.

CHAPTER 9
Fortune City Pharmakologica

MY FATHER PUT ME IN QUARANTINE WITH MY MOTHER. I SAW MY future in her face. She was deteriorating, like an apple in a compost bin. With time, there would only be a core and dead seeds. I guess I was feeling histrionic because, you know, I had the plague. It sounds like a stupid thing to say, but I never thought I would catch it. For a long time growing up I thought that car crashes only happened to other people, families unlucky enough to be news.

That was, until I was eleven or twelve and our dad crashed the minivan when we were all inside. It was only somewhat his fault, but we all blamed him, even our mother, even though she didn't say anything. We were all on vacation in Wisconsin, in the Dells. It wasn't very interesting, but it was a place where families were supposed to have vacations, so we went.

Anyway, we were pulling out of a water park's parking lot (Safari Island, or Sahara Adventure, or something like that), and Dad crept in front of an oncoming delivery truck that was barreling down fast. It was also raining, I think. No one was hurt, not really. I had some glass embedded in my elbow. But it didn't hurt too bad. We were lucky. We all emptied out of the minivan and sat on a grassy knoll near the entrance of the water park until the Wisconsin state troopers came. We were shocked into calm, all except for my mom, who started screaming at the truck driver, over and over again, You nearly killed my babies, you nearly killed my babies. Us kids were too dazed and angry at Dad to be embarrassed. Dad sat on the knoll with us.

I remembered that helplessness as I was lying down next to our mother in the shoddy, smelly cabin. The plague cabin.

I was scared out of my mind.

Sophia visited on my first night there. She wasn't supposed to be there, but I was glad she was.

Christ, Macy, she said, I'm sorry.

I was thirsty but knew we were low on water and wasn't sure whether to ask for it. The floorboards were harder than I'd remembered from before.

Thanks, I managed. I was glad she hadn't ditched us in Dubuque.

Then everyone else crowded into the cabin, even Ciaran and Xerxes. So, not much of a quarantine. Probably everyone figured if they were going to catch the plague, they already would have caught it. Or maybe they didn't want to take their chances sleeping on the deck. Our mother moaned. My lip hurt, but the itching was worse. I had to lie on my hands to keep from touching my face. My body and mind were in a vicious civil war.

They were all looking at me as if I was already dead. I finally said, Does anyone have a mirror?

Oh, my dad said. I'm not sure that's a good idea, Macy.

I'm not a vampire, I snapped. I can handle it.

My sister fumbled for a mirror in her purse. Wow, she

brought her purse along, I didn't know that, I thought to myself. When she handed me the mirror, it took me a few seconds to focus. I wanted to drop the mirror but didn't. The pustule on my face almost stretched to the base of my nose.

Inside the translucent pustule was a little image of a dog.

A dog, I said. I looked at Xerxes, who was scratching himself and wasn't paying any attention to the dying going on around him.

When no one said anything, I said: Fuck, it *hurts*. One of the advantages of dying of plague was that you could swear as many times as you wanted and no one would call you on it.

Good news, Macy, my father said. He was almost whispering it, so Mother wouldn't wake up. We're going to land by the end of the day. In Fortune City. We can get some medicine for you and your mother.

Fortune City, I said. Never heard of it.

The captain might have mentioned it once, but I doubted it was on any map.

It's new, Ciaran said. Well, it sort of existed before. But not really.

My head sank down on the hard pillow. I could smell the trees and the ashes in the air—I knew it was there—more clearly. I wanted to know why I had a dog on my face. I could almost feel it churning there, like a pineapple tidbit or cherry inside a Jell-O mold. God, I hated Jell-O. God, I would have given anything for a spoonful of Jell-O.

How's the baby? I asked, turning over a little bit. The pain was beginning to make me a little delirious. I kept waiting to get used to the pain, to move past it. But it wasn't happening and I was starting to feel panicky.

Stop talking and save your strength, Dad said. Ciaran wandered off and Sophia went with him. Their fear of catching what Mother and I had floating in our bloodstreams probably caught up to them. Dad would have bolted, too, given the chance or permission, and I wouldn't have blamed him.

How's the baby? I said again.

The baby doesn't matter. My father gritted this through his teeth, so Mother wouldn't hear. She was sleeping.

Of course—I started to say, raising my voice. But then I whispered, too: Of course it matters.

It's going to die, Macy, Dad said.

How do you know what's going to live and die? I said, feverish and indignant. The two emotions fed off each other. Dark clouds blotted out the sun—I could see that from the open door. I didn't know where my father got off treating *his* child like a *thing,* even if it—no, he or she—died.

When my father didn't say anything, I said: No one's dead yet. Maybe, I continued, that means something, that we're strong, or lucky, or whatever.

My dad seized up and his eyes widened.

What the fuck, I said, trying to sit up. Dad, what the fuck—

He then slapped the wall with the flat of his palm, hard enough that Mother startled. Dad gritted his teeth and then fell to his knees.

What is it? I said, stumbling to my feet.

He held out his hand. In his palm was the crushed body of a wasp. His hand was already beginning to swell. The wasp had fur along its stinger. If it had stung me or my mother, our bodies would have crumbled like Nikolai's.

I didn't have time to look for a newspaper, he said.

Oh my God, I said.

He wiped his hand in a nearby rag. Too bad we don't have steak, he said.

Steak? I asked.

For the swelling. Haven't you ever heard that?

I leaned forward and hugged my stupid and brave father. I was crying and everything. In a few minutes I passed out from the bravado and shock of it all. And the plague, of course. As I fell asleep again, I heard my mother talking to my father, completely lucid, like I remembered from when I was really young. They would just talk about things. Constellations and gardens a lot of the time. Some nights I would pretend to sleep as they talked over coffee—both were willing insomniacs for years— late at night, and then there'd be that laugh of my mother's, clear and clumsy, like a woman tripping over a bell that someone left on a cathedral floor by accident. I missed that laugh, but I heard it again that night on the *Prairie Chicken,* just once.

It was twilight and raining when I woke up. I startled when I thought about more wasps coming, but it turned out I didn't have much to worry about, at least on that front. The cold was slowing and then killing the wasps. If it had been hot and sunny, like upriver, then I doubt my father would have been able to hit the wasp at all.

The beddings were damp from the air and my sweat. The boat had stopped. So we'd found a harbor after all. Fortune City, here we come. Ciaran was helping me up. He wore black gloves.

Get up, get up, Macy, he said. Mom's already up. Get up.

Okay, okay, I said, but it was hard to get the words out, my throat was so dry. My head both pounded and burned, which was a nice trick. Outside the cabin, through the oil-paper window, I could see red and orange lights, and bodies rushing around.

What's going on? I asked. What are we doing?

I managed to stand up with Ciaran's help, although I teetered. He had grown stronger on the river, I could feel it in his hands.

We're going to get you to a doctor. You and Mom both.

How's Dad's hand? I asked.

He helped me out of the cabin, taking his time.

His hand? Ciaran said, cocking his head. Oh, right. It's fine. One of my friends had chrysanthemums. I wrapped his hand with the flowers in an Ace bandage. Seems to be working okay.

I stopped and at last focused on the city where we had docked. Fortune City was built on a swamp. An undrained swamp. A lot of the streets were flooded out. Some people were in rowboats and some were wading in knee-high water to get from place to place. There weren't searchlights like in the refugee camps, only lanterns hung on tall poles. Everyone looked tired in the shadows. Or in the chiaroscuro. I learned about that in art-appreciation class.

Why are we all going? I said.

We all had to leave the boat, except for a skeleton crew, Ciaran said. The captain—by this he meant the second mate, the acting captain—is going to find a priest to cleanse the boat.

What about the captain? I said.

When he raised an eyebrow at me, I added: I mean, the old captain.

Oh. Him. Ciaran laughed and the old Ciaran was back, if he had ever left. We dumped that little bitch in the middle of a school of leeches that was swimming under the boat.

He paused and then added: The leeches were pretty big.

. I supposed I should have been cold and unmoving about this, as if the captain's execution was all but inevitable, since he tried to kill us and everything. But I had a little twinge of remorse that I couldn't explain away. Surely there was some Imperial judicial system that could have condemned him. Granted, Miranda rights and a trial by peers would have been stretching it, but any halfhearted stab in the dark would have been better than drowning while being eaten by leeches.

Ciaran read my look. He was going to die anyway, he said. Now come on, it's the plague speaking, not you. He led me off the gangplank.

Do you see Carson and Grace and Sophia over there? he asked.

Only Ciaran could get away with calling our parents by their first names.

What? I said. I drifted and then managed to focus again. I saw a few passersby stare at me, crossing themselves in the light rain.

Ciaran must have noticed this, too. Shit, he said, I almost forgot.

While we were still walking in cold, ankle-deep water toward the rest of our family, he got a ski mask out of his pocket. Then he put it on my head, and pulled it down to my chin. I was too tired to protest. There were, luckily, eyeholes, although one of them wasn't aligned right over my right eye. I wondered if that was what the captain had felt like.

So no one knows you have the plague, Ciaran said. It's for your own good. He said it in a tone like he was steeling himself for a big fuss out of me, which I couldn't have done even if I wanted to.

Yeah, but aren't the only people wearing these going to have the plague, too?

Not at all, he said. Criminals wear these. Spider-Man is very retro.

I'm a sixteen-year-old girl, I said. No way I could be a criminal.

I could catch out of the corner of my impeded eye that Ciaran shook his head. Uh, sure you could be, he said. Here, you could be anything.

Macy! my mother called out. She was happy. It must have been the fever. Everyone else looked miserable. Sophia came forward and took my other elbow.

The doctor's only a block or two away, she said.

I'm going, Ciaran said. Come on. Why do we always have to wait around?

Okay, Dad said, sighing. I saw an umbrella salesperson standing about a "block" from us. UMBRELLAS, his sign said. PRICE? DON'T ASK. GIVE ME SOMETHING. A little distance ahead of us, behind barbed-wire fencing, there were actual buildings—meaning, architectural structures made of space-age materials like vinyl. The vinyl was black. The buildings even had electricity inside and SUVs parked out in front! This must have been the postinvasion equivalent of a gated community. I squinted; there were tall obelisks of smooth obsidian between the SUVs and the houses. Through the window of a black house, I could just make out a family at a dinner table: mother, father, son, daughter. Their heads were bent down and their hands were in their laps, as if they were praying. I wanted to walk up to the fencing, ask for amnesty. Even if I couldn't find a way inside the barbed wire and the obelisks shot laser beams or something at me. Even if the SUVs were dead for the lack of gas, and were there just for show.

Instead, Dad took my arm and said: Okay, I'll take you and Grace to a doctor. Ciaran and Sophia . . . I think I saw a McDonald's over there.

I was sick of people taking my arm. My dad fumbled in his pocket, and started to give a few little silver coins to my brother and sister.

I've got my own money, Ciaran said, sounding a bit hurt.

Me too, Sophia said, although she was less indignant.

Fine, Dad said. Save something for us. Find a dry booth.

As they wandered off, Dad took my mother and me into an alley. We sloshed. The water was cold and there were dead fish floating in the avenue. Rowboaters catcalled to one another, offered rides to us. At least that was what I thought they were doing; I couldn't understand a word. Fortune City was kind of like Venice, except for the walkways. And the nice art. My head was burning up from the stupid Spider-Man mask, but I was also shivering from the God-awful water. Mother wasn't doing much better.

My dad's hand was bandaged up nicely, as Ciaran promised. He wouldn't die. From that.

Of course, that was when my father got us lost. Maybe it was the absentminded-tenured-astronomy-professor thing. He went around the corner and then doubled back.

They said it was around here somewhere, Dad said.

Come *on,* Dad, I said. Either choose a direction, or let me sit down.

I'm *trying,* Macy. I'm trying. The streets are confusing.

I saw a black blimp overhead, though it might have been my overactive imagination. I wondered if there were any *Nadir of the M* sightings in Fortune City or its environs. Em would have blown this pop stand to bits, I thought.

At long last, we reached a storefront made of moldy wood, with a sheen of semirecent yellow paint. There was a tiny, hand-painted sign outside that read HEALTHILYZER. From the window I could see a crooked ocher sofa, a gaslight, and a desk you'd buy at Goodwill, misuse for a couple of months, and then give back to Goodwill. There was no door. When we stepped inside, a man came out to greet us. He wore the blue pajamas of a hospital orderly, spattered with blood and what looked like mustard. He had his arms crossed.

Is this a robbery? he said. There's nothing to steal, really. Not really.

My father took off my mask, which hurt, and I blinked, which also hurt.

There's no place to sit down, I blurted out. The couch didn't look palatable.

The doctor, if he was indeed that, ignored me. He took my father by the shoulder and spoke to him in low tones. To arrange terms, no doubt. My mother and I were forced to look at each other, but her eyes were rolled back. I held her hand. It was dead cold. Her stomach grumbled; I couldn't tell whether it was from the baby or hunger. After a few minutes the doctor went to the back of his sad shop. And Dad came back to us.

He's going to have to get some supplies on the other side of town, he said.

Antibiotics? I asked.

Didn't say.

It was clear that my father forgot to ask.

I'm going to sit at the desk, I said. I sat at the desk, which had about fifty declarations of love carved into it. The carpeted floor had that rough, burlap texture I just abhorred. It probably came from a dollar store, way back when.

Don't you think your mother would want to sit there, Dad said.

I'm fine, my mother said. Macy can sit there. She needs the rest.

She said this with her eyes rolled back. Her moments of clarity almost always made me cry, because I knew they'd pass sooner rather than later.

It's okay, I said, I'll get up. But I tried to and couldn't move. I was embarrassed that I took the seat without asking my mother. I'm trying, I'm really trying, I thought. I set my head down on the desk, but I couldn't sleep. An hour passed. No one else came in. Dad started to doze. I wanted to pretty badly, but wasn't sure I'd wake up again. That sounded melodramatic, but it wasn't. The dog on my face was getting bigger, no doubt. I wondered how well Mother's baby—my sibling—was handling the stress of the plague. Sometimes I thought that it would be worth it to go back to the womb, at least for a little while, where you wouldn't have to worry about anything. I thought maybe dying was like a womb. But, who knew, maybe the womb was a crappy place to be—I didn't remember one way or another.

When the doctor returned, we were too exhausted to notice. Ciaran and Sophia hadn't come back to find us. They were probably busy stuffing their faces. The doctor gave a sheepish grin. He held out a generic aspirin bottle, which he offered to Dad, who looked at it as if it were a baby snake.

You fuck! Dad shouted, standing up. You're gone for an hour and you come back with fucking aspirin?

Well— the doctor began, but his English wasn't good and he was having trouble formulating proper words.

Dad snatched the bottle. And it's not even full, you fuck. The child-safety seal is broken.

I'd never seen my father like that. The flooded town and the plague were getting to him. This might have been the final straw.

Come on, he said to us. We're leaving.

Have we been forsaken? our mother said, rubbing her belly.

Not at all, Grace, my dad said, calming down a bit. But only a bit.

I'm wondering, would you be able to lance the pustule? I asked the doctor after I put the mask back on. I lifted up my mask a bit and let it down again. He was startled by the fact that someone was speaking to him in a somewhat rational tone.

Don't talk to him, Macy, Dad said. He's a charlatan.

I wouldn't advise it, the doctor said to me in a quiet voice. There's no telling what would come out.

And that was that. We left. The air was misty and smelled sour. Even with the mask, my head was freezing.

Fucking aspirin, my dad muttered, pulling his arm back to toss the bottle away. But I stopped him, taking the bottle and putting it in my pocket.

It might be . . . I started to say. I was trying to find the word "valuable" but it escaped me. Then I tripped, landing face-first in the water. If I wasn't wearing my dumb mask I would have been feeling even more worlds of hurt. But it was pretty bad. My face felt cut up by dull knives.

After I was helped up, and Dad wrung out my mask and put it back on again, I managed to say, I want to go back to the boat.

We need to get something to eat, my dad said. By "we," he meant "him," of course. Backtracking, we reached the McDonald's, which was packed. I was starting to hallucinate. Or perhaps not. In the front window there were unplucked wingless chickens on display, hanging upside down. Each was punctured with a half-dozen swizzle sticks. Inside the air smelled of meat steam. People of all stripes jostled at rickety tables, devouring livers, eyes, intestines, tongues, you name it. The floor had a film of sawdust and blood slop. My father led us to a corner table, where Sophia and Ciaran were stuffing themselves. They looked up for just a bit, but didn't say anything.

May I? Dad asked.

Sure, Ciaran said with a full mouth. We got extra for you. Did you get the medicine?

Not really, my father said before taking a jab at a cow's foot. I looked toward the counter, and the long lines in front of the counter. There were cows wandering around in the back kitchen, mottled and paunchy but alive and kicking.

Why is this place such a fucking dump? I said.

Ciaran shot me a dirty, offended look. Some Avars have picked up the franchises along the river, he said. They're popular. It's a little taste of home for everybody.

I wanted to know, would Ciaran have been so blithe if the Avars had a taste for dog, and caught dogs, and chopped up dogs, and cooked dogs, and encouraged people to eat dogs, which they would call McDogs?

I didn't think so. Ciaran loved Xerxes more than any of us, and you don't eat what you love.

Ciaran burped.

Gross, Sophia said. I think I've lost my appetite.

I'm out of here, I said, standing up, and I'm taking Mother with me. This is *ridiculous.*

I coughed, hunched over. The dull knives attacking my face were now extremely hot.

Dad put his hand on my shoulder. I had no bearings, and my eyes were watering, so I could barely see through the eyeholes. I had no idea what my mother was doing, whether she was taking this all in calmly, or whether she was past that. God, I hoped she wasn't past it. I wanted her to keep fighting. I wasn't sure if I had the strength to fight for both of us.

No, I'll go, too, Dad said.

My dad—that guy was always snatching redemption from the jaws of really, really bad parenting.

Excerpt from the *"Jack Anubis" Tidbits Newsletter,* Being an Apologia, of Sorts, Regarding Iowa–North Egypt.

. . . JACK ANUBIS recommends the Fortune City arts "scene" for the discerning river traveler through the Egyptian expanses of the River. There are many hidden treasures to be found among the common commercial traffic plied there. Your lifestyle will be enriched.

In particular, it is worth investigating the MUSEUM OF IOWANS, a canopic monument—and might I say elegy—to the Iowans departed on the land that was once Fortune City. The museum was erected by the founders of Fortune City, and speaks well to their civic compassions. During daylight hours, you can experience what life was like for prelapsarian Iowans: SIT within their black, horseless carriages, which they practically lived in more than their houses. KEENLY OBSERVE, within their houses, the lifelike, preserved remains of Iowans in a simulacra of a dinner ritual: saying their "Lord's Prayer." (Can you find the scrap-ravenous pet underneath the table?) Then, THRILL to their table-tennis crypt within the house's basement! For the SCIENTIFIC-MINDED, there is also a science room where the Iowans' belief in the electrical properties of household objects is expounded upon at some length—and with many talismanic objects on display.

DONATIONS from the itinerant for the up-keep of the museum are appreciated, and noted on the scrolls-of-living within the museum's administrative offices.

It must be noted that there is plenty of un-claimed, Scythian-safe farmland outside Fortune City. Know and observe the forthcoming red moon on the sixth day of the twelfth month. The water will rise. The silt will run. This winter omen will almost single-handedly birth a rich, fertile crop of legumes. Expect many new chil-dren.

CHAPTER 10

Moxie or Not

THE NEXT FEW DAYS BLURRED EVEN MORE THAN USUAL. THE PLAGUE began to assert itself in my body. I was worried about my lips' proximity to my brain. The dog on my face was a puppy no longer. Sometimes when I looked in the mirror I thought I saw it barking.

I didn't recall much of our departure from Fortune City. Which was fine by me. All I remember, really, was feeling grateful that Dad pulled through and rescued us from that awful fast-food restaurant. Mother was my roommate again. The rest of the family slept out on the decks for the time being. There was a sudden warm spell for a few days that everyone took advantage of.

We were going through Missouriland and Illinois. The territory was also known as Little Egypt, I was pretty sure. The Egypt name was an old one—the first white settlers in the area, way back in the nineteenth century, thought that the Mississippi River was exactly like the Nile, and would produce a civilization upon its banks as great and wondrous as that of the ancient Egyptians. I was taught that in American History class, and it always stuck with me for some reason. How those settlers—before they drove off the Indians, of course—were so *optimistic* about their chances, and how right they were.

I wished that Mother and I had used our fevered time together to bond, to have all those meaningful mother-and-daughter conversations like you see in the movies. We did have one. I guess you take whatever you can get.

Macy, she said, after a cough. I was all groggy, hallucinating about a hippopotamus wading in the gunky water of Fortune City. The hippo had a tiny black obelisk growing out of its forehead, and was trying to tell me something.

Macy, where are you?

Right here, I said, startling. I'm right here.

Do you . . . do you know how we ended up here? she said.

I felt a kicking on my face from my pustule.

I'm not sure, I managed to say. My throat was hot and dry, and I had trouble getting the words out. I haven't thought much about it.

That wasn't true. I thought about it all the time, and couldn't get a straight answer out of anyone.

Don't you want to go to college? she said. Maybe your father's new university will have . . . She searched for the right phrase.

Tuition reimbursement? I said.

Yes. Tuition reimbursement. Come look at my belly, Macy.

That's . . . okay, I said, as gently as I could.

Macy, you have to. I'm begging you. If I wasn't so weak I'd order you.

I sighed and rolled over next to her. I was deathly afraid of what I'd see, and what my mother would see on my face. She lifted up her tunic. I saw a baby, parts of it anyway, straining through translucent skin. The pustules created little stained-glass windows into her womb. It was freaking me out but was also weird and beautiful. The pieces didn't match, though. The little toes of the left foot were where the little fingers of the right hand should have been, and vice versa. And the baby seemed close to term, insofar as I knew anything about those things. I was surprised by how *advanced* my mother's pregnancy was, much more than it should have been. Time was sped up for her. I didn't ask her about this. I wasn't sure whether she would have been able to offer an explanation anyways, scientific or otherwise. I was scared that my pustule could develop at the same clip, whether—in a sick kind of way—I'd give birth as well. Whether that dog would burst out of my face and kill me in the process. There was no reason, at that point, to expect some kind of miracle for either of us. So, in my hazy state, I took the time to stare at Mother's baby, concentrate on what was going on inside of her. To try to slow down time on my end, force it to bend to my will, at least for a few seconds. I counted about a dozen breaths before I got exhausted again.

I tipped my head back and said: The baby's beautiful, Mother.

Satisfied at my answer—or maybe she didn't hear me—she went back to sleep. Before I did too—because I wasn't sure whether I would wake up again, I really wasn't—I pulled out the little bottle from my jacket that I was using as a pillow. It took me about ten minutes to manhandle the bottle open, even though there wasn't a child-safety seal. I was regressing. When I did open the cap, I popped two pills out and closed the bottle again. I didn't even look at the pills. I just decided that I wasn't going to let our entire visit to Fortune City go to waste. If they were cyanide, that was all right. It wouldn't bother me much, anyway.

I put the pills in my mouth and managed to choke them down dry.

Good night, Mother, I said. I love you.

She didn't say anything.

I slept. There wasn't much waking done, on my part, for quite a while. I wasn't sure if that was a sign of my moxie or not.

When I did wake up, I was in the cabin, but sitting up against the wall. Through the open door I saw a giraffe on the deck, and heard the sonic stylings of a tiny Casio keyboard. Dad was standing over me. I then heard my mother heaving beside me, like she did when I was last awake, but I wasn't able to think about that.

I wasn't in the afterlife. This was surprising. My mouth tasted sour.

Macy, you're awake, Dad said. He looked older, grayer, more tired—as tired as they come.

How long have I been out? I asked. The giraffe walked away, and the synthesizer music stopped. I wondered if I was still hallucinating a bit.

Three days, he said. Look at your face.

He held out Sophia's hand mirror.

I took the mirror from him and looked. I was afraid to. But the pustule on my face was crusted over, dry. There was no dog inside my face anymore.

I realized I was better. Still hazy, but better.

The pills, I said, trailing off. I fumbled for them in my jacket but couldn't find them. I must have searched my pockets three or four times. I didn't meant to be so pissed off, but there was no way to help it. The anger blew through me and out of my mouth.

Goddamn it, Dad, I said, where are the pills? I took two and went to bed. So these were in an aspirin bottle, so what. We can still save Mother. Where are they?

He didn't say anything at first, although his face flushed. It wasn't a pleasant way to awaken from a coma, with family politics as my alarm clock. Wake up, Macy, back into the swing of things! It was probably even less pleasant for Dad.

I don't know, he said. I didn't see them. I didn't take them.

Well, you should fucking know, I said, my voice cracking. Someone probably stole the pills from me while I slept.

We have bigger problems, he said.

I raised my eyebrows. What? I asked.

Maybe not . . . bigger. Just different. Dad took a deep breath. I don't know how to say this, he said, but Sophia's gone.

What?

I should have expected this, I thought. No, I *did* expect this. Just not in this way, without any good-byes.

My face must not have registered shock, or enough of it, because my father added: She's alive. She's not hurt. She just wanted to leave.

How do you know she's not hurt, I wanted to say. Instead, I said: Did she tell anyone?

From the shore, he said. About two days ago. But not beforehand. She waved good-bye.

My mother cried out a little louder. Her body was pale, her skin almost translucent. I was surprised she wasn't dead yet. I didn't mean to be mean—it was pure surprise. I thought we would be having our last breaths together. Besides, what we were living through couldn't be reduced to easy platitudes about being "nice" or "mean." People weren't exactly bowling over to help other people on the river, to further the aims of a Judeo-Christian society. People weren't planting community gardens, or having marathons to raise money for breast cancer cures, or joining the Scouts anymore. That was gone and my sister was gone and soon Mother would be gone, too, and I could have hit my dad for not doing everything he could to find the pills. To tear the boat up and down. Did he need *me* to figure this out?

I tried to be happy for my sister, I really did, but I didn't think personal choice and personal freedom—whatever that was— worked well as a survival tactic anymore. I needed Sophia. More than that—Mother needed Sophia. Cured, I was already going crazy. And getting judgmental.

I looked at my mother's belly for the first time since waking up. It was hidden under some ratty blankets, huge, ready to burst. I could see the baby's head in there. A boy's head. Larger than my head. Another boy in the family, then. The fetus probably had plague, too, but it seemed to suit him. Maybe he was the reason Mother was still alive; that he was processing the toxins through his own tiny body. To tell you the truth I couldn't trust the biology of the situation—what was real, what were the rules.

I turned my head away. I didn't want to startle the monster. My baby brother. I wondered where the giraffe went, or whether it was an afterimage of whatever dream I was having before I woke up.

Why don't you stand up? my father said. His jacket was tattered wool. It looked taken—commandeered—from a dead Imperial soldier.

Nice threads, I said.

I kind of blurted it out, but he managed to laugh. My stupidity was always good at breaking the ice.

My brother came in the room with a keyboard slung over his shoulder. Hi, Macy, he said. It looked like he had aged a year in three days. Everyone was aging: Dad, my brother, my baby brother. The keyboard's keys looked like coffee-stained bone, or the "before cleaning" dentures in a Fixodent commercial.

Hey, Ciaran, I said. You . . .

I saw a baby giraffe peek its head in the cabin behind Ciaran.

You have a giraffe.

Oh, you mean Carl, he said.

Carl had doelike eyes, but his legs were scarred and lashed.

So why is Carl . . . with you? I asked.

I found him on the banks, Ciaran said. I figured he'd fetch a good price in St. Louis.

Dad sighed. This must have been an argument that he'd lost. The lack of cash must have tipped the balance in Ciaran's favor.

Carl bleated. I became less and less sure that I was awake.

Did you find your synthesizer on the banks, too? I asked.

No, I won that at dice.

There was an awkward pause. Dad muttered something and went below deck. I wondered whether it was to smoke.

So, uh, where's Xerxes? I said.

I think on the top deck, he said. Are you going to ditch the boat like Sophia did?

I shivered. The boat felt like it was moving backwards.

I'm not leaving, I said.

But I can see in your eyes that you want to, he said.

God, Sophia, why did you leave me, I thought.

What do you know about eyes? I said.

He made a gun shape with his hand and pointed it at me.

The whites.

I snorted, trying to sound braver than I was. But Ciaran scared me. I'm going to take a walk, I said.

Don't jump off.

What would you care?

I needed to move my limbs, so I stood up. But before I did, I turned around to Ciaran.

Did you see those pills that were on me? I asked him.

Pills? he said, his hand on the base of Carl's neck.

The ones we got in Fortune City. I had them on me, but now they're gone.

He looked confused for a second, and then he looked at me. Aw, no, Macy. I didn't see them. Did you really lose them? I bet someone stole them from you. Shit, Macy. That's too bad. I'll keep an eye out for them.

I couldn't tell if he was being sincere about his concern or pulling my chain. I stalked off. The boat creaked. I worried about the poor giraffe in the cold air. Out of his element. But then again, we all were. Snowflakes landed on my shoulder and I brushed them off, only to discover it was really ash. The keyboard started up again. It was "Theme from *Beverly Hills Cop*," except the sound was that of a dulcimer. I did some sprints on the deck. Tried to get my heart rate up. Trying to be glad I was alive. I *was*, sure, but I didn't feel lucky.

It was hard to feel lucky when my mother was still dying.

After a few minutes I ran out of breath; my knees were sore. But all the same, the soreness felt good. One of the sharpshooters looked at me from above, shaking his head at my goofy exercise. I waved.

It appeared food was still scarce since Fortune City; all we had was a lentil and river cucumber gruel. My appetite still wasn't there, so while they were cooking on the top deck, I went back into our cabin. Standing in the doorway, I was surprised to find that Xerxes was visiting Mother. He was sniffing in her ear. She was out cold, her belly heaving. This wasn't a good sign.

Mother? I said.

She didn't respond. But Xerxes did. He looked up at me and gave a low, guttural growl. Throughout our journey, I had never thought of him as a pet as much as a canine hanger-on. Now he seemed like a true interloper, and dangerous as all hell. I tried not to make any sudden movements, and edged away. I took a quick scan of the *Prairie Chicken,* but couldn't find Ciaran or Dad anywhere. I imagined them taking off, leaving me alone with a mad dog and fading mother.

One of the sailors who had been kinder than most to me saw my creeping away on the deck and called out: Ciaran's on the bow with your father. When I spun around to go up the stairs, he said: That wouldn't be a good idea.

I can take care of myself, I said, trying to keep my voice kind of low, so I wouldn't startle the dog. But he didn't follow me.

No, no, the sailor said, indulging me a bit. Look downriver. Look what's coming toward us.

I leaned over the side of the railing and saw a rusty giant tanker, a giant red flag hoisted on its prow. Looked like a condemned oil tanker. Carl neighed. I didn't know giraffes neighed.

What the hell is it? I asked.

Looks like a gladiator ship. I think they're docking to us tonight. It's better you go below deck.

I didn't want to sleep in my mother's cabin anyway. I went downstairs and found a place next to the coal bin—where the storytellers had told us about the *Nadir.* In the back of my mind, I thought about warning Dad about Xerxes, but I didn't have the energy. I was pretty quickly asleep, even though it wasn't twilight. I still needed to recover a lot of strength.

I spent the night dreaming of sounds. Sounds that were both real and unreal. Sword clashes. Elephant trumpets. Guffaws of men. In English and Spanish and bizarre pidgin.

In actuality, the sounds were coming from the gladiator ship that had tethered to us in the night. Men were clubbing and slashing other men. At first, in a daze, I thought we were under attack, but then I heard our own soldiers laughing and calling out bets from our deck. They must have been able to see the action through the portholes on the gladiator ship. It didn't sound pretty. I would have counted sheep but I didn't want them to get slaughtered.

I was alone near the cold coal bin. More than that—I *felt* alone, and it wasn't a terrible feeling at all, no matter what terror was being inflicted on others on the next boat over. Being alone meant no one was near me that could hurt me. I didn't sleep as much as have a chain of fitful naps.

The solitude changed course soon enough, when fourteen tourists—yes, tourists—came aboard the *Prairie Chicken* from the gladiator ship. I woke up before they came, went up the stairs, and watched them board. Shivering, I knew we had a boat of trouble, a boat of crowds again. It turned out these people were from Minnesota, *our* people.

Plague would be nothing compared to them, I thought.

Before the gladiator ship kept churning upstream, Ciaran sold the giraffe to its captain. I tried to feel bad for Carl, tried not to feel cold.

Most of all, I tried to feel glad to be alive.

Then I thought of my helpless mother, and I felt nothing but guilt for trying to feel that way.

Travel Arrangements

What did Sophia want? All her life, people had been asking her that. What do you want, Sophia? Her heart, to them, was a Rubik's Cube. She blended in. Her grades were neither extraordinary nor poor.

When she left, she finally decided what she wanted. And it wasn't that different from her initial impulse, before the invasion and counterinvasion: to be a midwife. It seemed like a profession that would have a lot of staying power in the absence of hospitals. The bureaucracy of medicine, as far as she knew, was gone forever. She imagined herself as a wandering healer. Nikolai had told her about his homeland, the hanging vineyards and temples there. She had no idea how to get there, but there had to be *some way* to reach it, and deliver babies there.

Sophia missed his kisses. She didn't love him, in the end, but she missed those.

Plus she wanted a job. Starting at the bottom? No problem. Anything to get the ball rolling.

She reasoned to herself that she was, in actuality, no help to her mother with the tiny bit of training that she had. No medicines or herbal remedies to speak of, and the strange biology of the plague rendered any of her knowledge useless. She could have done something for Mother in Fortune City, perhaps. But she was so hungry in Fortune City that she couldn't think straight.

That was unfortunate, she admitted to herself. A bad-daughter type of unfortunate. She accepted that.

Sophia was the oldest, but always felt to be somewhere in the middle. She was the nucleus of the three siblings. Macy and Ciaran were electrons wildly swinging around. Sometimes Macy acted like the oldest and Ciaran the youngest, and sometimes it was vice versa. Sophia noticed these changes only after they happened, not the changes themselves.

What pushed Sophia to leave the boat was one sudden insight. This was what she assumed growing up involved, and what made her realize that she was actually the oldest. While Macy was out cold but healing, and her mother was fitful and not healing, she watched her father. She studied him, on the deck and in the cabin, and saw how his heartbreak was almost all centered on Grace. He could barely hold it together because of her, as if the culmination of their love had come down to this test, this disease. He would guard over her, keeping that stupid dog away—who for some reason wanted to guard over Grace, too—and talk to both himself and Grace. And when he wasn't doing that, he was smoking kef, to try to hold himself together. Sophia thought about asking him to stop, but didn't. He wouldn't have listened. He wouldn't have listened because of this:

He loved his children, of course, and cared and looked out for their well-being and happiness. But *that* love meant nothing to him without Grace—the two lives they shared became, over time, one life. And when he lost Grace (Sophia tried to make that *when* in her head an *if,* but it was hard, and she couldn't in the end), he would be half a person, and he would have to change into a different person altogether to become whole again.

And the three kids had little if anything to do with that.

Macy didn't understand this. It was dormant in her, but she couldn't see it.

Sophia knew she would, one day.

Right before she jumped overboard and swam for the shore, she kissed her little sister's and mother's foreheads, and said her good-byes, even though they wouldn't remember them. Then she threw her backpack over her shoulder and went to the outer railing. She looked at the reflection of her face in the water, wondering how she could be so happy and sad at exactly the same time. Her father was down below smoking, but he would rush up once he heard her hit the water.

I'm okay, she called out to him, once she reached the shore. I'll be just fine!

CHAPTER 11
The Pirates of Highland Park

THE FIRST THING THE RICH MINNESOTANS DID WAS TAKE OVER OUR cabin, and most of the other passenger space. Not good. Not good for my family. The boat had started feeling a bit like a home. Now it sagged, slogging low in the river through almost constant fog. That first morning and afternoon, I was always bumping into strangers on the decks and holds. Now my whole family and I all slept where I'd slept the night before, next to the coal bin. We had a fire going in the bin; at least it was warm. It made the newcomers feel better, no doubt, to consider us steerage. That was how I judged them—it wasn't fair, or pretty, but it might have been true.

Who were they? They were extended families from Highland Park, Wayzata, Woodbury. They were of a particular ruddy age, late teens to forties. That age when you—if you were of a particular social standing—participated in a lot of well-managed outdoor activities like rock climbing and crew. Nothing too dangerous, but certainly helpful in the wilderness. Even the eldest among them had an unnatural, healthy sheen. They had the glow of the old world on their skins, and in the brand names of their clothing, on fabrics that I had forgotten about:

Lycra, Gore-Tex. I saw them that morning pass out vitamins. They had a duffel bag full of them.

They were rude and well-meaning. They once had jobs in architecture, advertising. I hated them all. They paid little attention to us, and looking back, it has to be said that I barely remember them. They were not memorable. They had nice haircuts. They were tribal. The soldiers hated them even more than I did, if that was possible, and I know they complained about them to the new captain. But the newcomers must have paid the captain off well. To keep the crew happy, or at least tolerant, the captain had to have given out large bonuses. So they shut up, though they simmered. I had no idea what the Minnesotans' business was, besides "tourism," or why they were on the gladiator boat (though it couldn't have been good), or why they didn't continue upriver on that ship instead of downriver with us. I tried to keep a safe distance. Pretty hard, though. The *Prairie Chicken* wasn't meant for safe distances. I knew, also, that I was trying to distract myself from Mother's long, slow decline. The newcomers were an unpleasant reminder of what life used to be like for us—more casual and less survival oriented.

Maybe I was just jealous.

At first I seemed to be the one most distressed about their presence. Mother was in her dream haze and Xerxes kept wanting to be with Mother—or the baby. He hunkered down with her next to the coal bin.

Dad didn't even put up a fight when they burst into our quarters when he was tending to Mother's forehead, as if they already owned the cabin—and the ship and the river, too, for that matter.

Ciaran was staying with the soldiers, so no change there. And I was beginning to feel Sophia's absence. I would think of things to tell her—especially snark about the new arrivals—but then I'd stop myself, and my sarcasm would have nowhere to go, and I'd ache inside.

That night, though, I realized I hadn't given Dad enough credit. In our below-hold, as the newcomers were enjoying their supper upstairs—they brought marshmallows, graham crackers, and chocolate for s'mores, the bastards—Dad sank down next to the coal and next to me.

Two days, Dad gritted through his teeth. Two more damned days. He had some astronomical journal on his lap. He had crossed out a lot of the passages with a thick ink pen and had scribbled a bevy of mathematical formulas.

Till they leave or St. Louis? I asked.

St. Louis.

Thank fucking God, I said. I didn't care about swearing anymore, and apparently neither did my father.

I miss Sophia, he said all of the sudden. I miss your sister.

I grabbed his hand. He was shaking. He was barely holding it together. Mother was cooing something on the other side of the coal bin. Xerxes was curled next to her. That morning, after the interlopers settled in, more or less, I had asked Ciaran what the fuck we should do with his stupid dog, so that he wouldn't kill us all. And I saw, in a quick glint, that Ciaran was both bored with and afraid of Xerxes. It was that same look—except maybe for the fear part—he had when he begged and begged for a pet hamster when he was seven, and when Mother (not Dad) broke down and got him a hamster, which Ciaran named Lucy, even though Lucy was male. He loved that hamster to death for about, oh, two months, until he asked Mother if Lucy could be taken back to the shelter. Lucy wasn't fun anymore! I would have said, Tough shit, feed it, care for it, but Mother was exhausted and tried to stall for a few days, until Ciaran reported that Lucy "went missing." I was so angry with him, and yet I was afraid to ask him how Lucy had disappeared.

I suspected pretty much the same boredom with Xerxes, although on a much more dangerous scale. The bite of a hamster wouldn't kill anybody. Ciaran told us that as long as Xerxes was well fed, he wasn't going to kill anyone. So we kept him stuffed—gave him a double share, in fact—and he slept a lot. I still tried not to startle the dog in any way.

Late that night, being unable to sleep again, I went above deck to stretch my legs and get some air. A steam whistle sounded a fair distance away. There was moonlight, but still lots of fog, and I couldn't see either shore. Huge logs jutted out of the water like dead giants' arms. This debris greatly slowed our progress south.

Hey, someone said behind me.

I turned around. It was a girl, about my age, in Timberland boots and a Columbiawear parka. She might as well have worn a space suit. I had noticed her before, as part of the clan who had boarded from the gladiator ship. She had bright blond hair and a plastic baggie in her hand.

Hey, she said again. You. You have a light?

I squinted at her, trying to confirm she was real. What? I said. A light?

She startled. Oh, sorry, she said. I thought you were a helper.

I wondered if "helper" was a euphemism for "slave."

Um, I said. I don't have a light.

I looked at her little baggie. What do you have in there?

Pot, she said. One of the gladiators gave it to me. Do you want to smoke some?

Sure, I said. I don't know why I assented so quickly with a

total stranger, and moreover, one of *those* strangers. In high school I hated the blithe social ease of girls like her, the drugs, the inauthentic authentic whims and fashions. But high school was a long way upriver.

Her name was Lydia. She had turned twenty right before the invasions. She went to Mankato State and was undeclared. Her mother was long divorced from her dad, and she was in rehab somewhere along Lake Superior. I was afraid to suggest to her that her mom's cozy methadone retreat was probably a Vandal garrison. She had a stepmom who was drunk all the time and didn't like sunlight.

The gladiators, Lydia said, shuddering, as we sat down in a dark corner of the *Prairie Chicken*. My God, the gladiators. It was pretty . . . fucking . . . intense. They had a fight between an unarmed man and a guy with this giant axe.

She sat Indian style, and spread her materials on a flattened portion of her Gore-Tex vest: paper and pot.

Anyway, she continued as she rolled the joints, the axe man pretty much cleaved the other guy after a few seconds. Wasn't even close, right? After the cleanup, they took the axe from the winner and gave it to *another* gladiator, and told him to go to work. There were about five rounds of that. Jesus.

She took a lighter from her pocket—was she lying to me before about not having one, or had she forgotten?—and cupped the little flame. She lit a joint and took a hit. Her face, when she came up for air, was both frozen in place and fluid, like a flash flood beneath a sheet of translucent ice.

Who are they? I asked.

What? she said, slurring, handing me the joint. I don't know who those guys were. They were gladiators.

My hands trembled as I took it, and then I almost fumbled

it to the deck floor. Don't get it wet! she said in a tiny, distant voice.

I said: I mean, who runs the gladiator ship?

I don't know that either, she said. It was just arranged on our tour. Come on, smoke.

I guess that on some level this constituted a great choice on my part, that my life would *never be the same after smoking pot.* Histrionics from the old world, I wanted to believe. Hell, I'd survived kef. Opportunities to rebel on the boat were few—it was either jump overboard, play soldier, or . . . this.

I took a hit. My mouth felt a bit gummy. It smelled like extreme compost, like it was somehow beyond a mere smell and made a push into the other senses. I lifted my head after taking a massive whiff and handed the joint back to Lydia. She called it "pot," but what did that mean anymore? Where did this marijuana come from? How did it change, or was it combined with anything else? The smoke was neither calming nor unsettling, nor for that matter balancing. Instead, it seemed to have its own personality and intelligence, and was setting up shop in my head for a spell. Hard to describe but easy to stomach. The drug was less creepy than kef, but it felt like a form of puppetry. It pulled my strings in opposite directions.

Soon after passing around the pot, or "pot," we were talking about our deepest fears. Funny, I forgot almost right afterward what those secret fears of mine were. That might have been useful information.

I do remember Lydia's, though, in perfect detail. She hated her family and their friends, a fact that warmed me to her. She had pretty good reason to.

She leaned close as she told me this:

A few years before everything started changing, her father

and her stepmom enrolled her in an all-girls punk rock camp. It seemed like a good idea at the time, a way to allow her to rebel in a socially constructive and empowering way. Her father was in advertising, and did a lot of coke, but that was neither here nor there, because of his success and awards. He brought home metal statuettes. He thought he knew what young people wanted. Lydia had musical aptitude of just about zero. Which, in theory, wasn't a detriment at all at a punk rock camp, and might have even been a big plus. Lydia soon found out, though, that this wasn't a camp for artless abandon. Her camp peers had endlessly groomed pedigrees in indie rock: electric-guitar lessons at five, Pixies concerts at seven, anything they wanted to help them succeed at making it. At any cost. In the pine forests an hour northwest from Duluth, it wasn't a place for dawdlers, for tourists. The other campers were merciless to Lydia, because she really didn't give a fuck about their training to, one day, earn a contract on Sub Pop, or open for Yo La Tengo. The art-school grad counselors condoned and sometimes led in the anti-Lydia festivities. She was pranked daily. Food was also thrown at her daily: organic burritos and soy yogurt sailing through the air onto Lydia's back or arms. The final straw was when a senior counselor woke Lydia up one midnight with a scream and a rag of menstrual blood. Lydia immediately walked four miles in the middle of the night toward the nearest highway—bears be damned—until she was in cell phone range, and told her dad to pick her up, or she would kill herself then and there, and no, this wasn't some kind of punk prank.

Pack mentality, I said, my head spinning.

Assholes, she said. They're probably all dead anyway. She paused and said: But you're not like that, Macy.

Dead? I said.

No, she said, propping her head up, not wanting to look at me for some reason. I mean, you're not an asshole.

Thanks, I said. You're not one either.

I then got all nauseous—completely unrelated to the conversation—and threw up over the side of the boat. Some of it slopped on the hull. When I sat down again, legs and arms leaden all of the sudden, Lydia didn't seem the least bit fazed.

This batch isn't easy on the stomach, she said. The first time.

When was yours? I asked.

Right after we moved to Nueva Roma—

Wait, I said, trying to lean forward, not being able to. You live in Nueva Roma? What's it like?

I still had no idea why it was called Nueva Roma, and never found out whether it was a translation or a mistranslation.

It's okay, she said. Good, I guess. Except for the parties, it can be kind of slow. I live in this tower.

Her dad had been commissioned by the Empire to form the first advertising agency in the city, she told me. While she was talking, the boat passed a column of blue fire, giving it a wide berth. Natural gas burning? But it didn't smell. I turned my head back to Lydia.

I would give anything to live there, I said, and I meant it. I'm moving to, ugh, St. Louis.

Why there?

My dad got a job there. At a university. He teaches astronomy.

That's cool, she said. That's like predicting the future with stars, right?

Uh, that's astrology.

Oh. Listen, she said, changing the subject. Why don't you come with us? We're going back to Nueva Roma in a week.

Until then, we're just tooling around the river, looking at archaeological sites—

I froze. Are you kidding with me? I said.

Why would I kid with you? My dad is desperate for me to have friends who are American, and not ten years older than me. It would be fun. We have an extra room. You could, I don't know, intern for the new agency. Or something. I'm sure we could work something out.

This was my window, then. And it was a *great* fucking window.

Well, it was nice while it lasted. I got a few seconds of idyllic bliss from it.

I can't, I said. I really appreciate it. But my mother is pretty sick. I'm sorry.

She kept looking away from me. Look, don't apologize, she said. You don't have to be sorry for me. Just forget I mentioned it then, okay?

Okay, I said in a quiet voice. The boat was beginning to swirl. A vortex. After a few seconds I figured out it was *all in my head.*

Maybe I should go to bed, I said, although I didn't move.

Lydia wasn't paying attention to me. I thought she was still mad at me, but she had already moved on. I liked that about her. It was so different than how it was with my family.

Look at that sky up there, she said. Do you know your constellations?

A little, I said, looking up. Actually, none of the stars were *exactly* where they should have been.

Do you know that one? she said while pointing upward. That one with the kinda blue star, and the really faint three next to it.

I wondered if this was a test of some kind. I had no clue what I was looking at.

I think that's Cygnus, I lied. The Black Swan.

Yeah, she said. That's what I thought, too.

I heard my mother scream from below the hold. I felt weighted to the deck. Rather than rush to help her—Dad, I was sure, was already on the case—I started panicking about Lydia's offer, already vanishing in the night air.

But about your invitation. If I change my mind at some point, when my mother is better—I began.

She lowered her head toward me and whispered: Do you know that there's a spy traveling with us?

What? I said, a little pissed that she was ignoring what I was trying to say, my heart-opening.

A spy. I'm sure of it. He's the handler on the tour. The guy with the black hat; I'm sure you've seen him. He's like an albino. I think he's looking for something. He's been really friendly with my dad.

Looking for what? I said. I was uneasy all of a sudden, though I didn't know why.

Lydia shrugged. I think it's some package. I don't know. When we were on the gladiator boat, I bumped into him while he was going through the ship's parcels. I was looking for the bathroom, and he was tearing into all of this luggage. The captain's luggage, even. He's looking for *something*. It creeps me out.

And would your father say anything?

She snickered. As if. He's too high to notice most days. Holy shit, it's dawn.

It was. Well, not quite, but close enough. The sky was turning a light purple.

We're disembarking soon, she said. Up there. You can pretty much see it. She pointed ahead of us, but I couldn't see anything yet.

You're not going to St. Louis, then?

No, she said. Short ride, wasn't it?

To tell the truth, I was relieved. For one, the *Prairie Chicken* would be somewhat quiet for a couple of days before we reached St. Louis. And secondly, I was afraid Lydia would want to see where we lived. I had no idea where we would be living. The university? But what did that mean? It could have meant a hovel. It was shitty of me, but I would have been embarrassed.

Is that it ahead? I asked, seeing a collection of brown domes alongside the river.

I'm pretty sure. It's part of the itinerary. Inside the huts are these old bones. Scythians deposit gold-dipped bones there. And rugs. Or something like that. To tell you the truth I wasn't paying much attention.

In the near light, I saw her necklace for the first time: a wooden cell phone on a gold chain. The cell phone wasn't a flip-top; it looked carved with no small amount of care and attention to detail. There was a number in the "screen" with a Twin Cities area code. Was this Lydia's old number? I was too afraid to ask her about it, in case she was sensitive about the loss of her old life. And at any rate, she was getting up, getting ready to ease away. The rest of her party was milling about below, shouting, having breakfast sandwiches and granola bars, making ready for the rest of their adventure. They were at ease in their surroundings. I could never understand them. Lydia shook her head when she heard the noise of her family.

My God, she said. Look . . . if you ever change your mind . . . She gave me a small wooden chip with a random string of numbers, about eleven or twelve.

Use this in Nueva Roma, if you ever get there, she said.

Lydia must have forgotten my earlier pleading, which was just as well.

Is this a phone number?

Eh. Not exactly. You'll see.

Lydia didn't seem any worse for the wear after our smoke. I, on the other hand, not only had extreme time dilation, but also a nasty splitting headache, and a dehydrated mouth, and my ass was asleep from sitting in one position for way too long.

So, see you, Lydia said, as she made her way down the stairs. And thanks.

She then leaned forward and gave me a kiss on the cheek. Quick, but startling. Her lips were cold.

Bye, I managed.

She went down the stairs and I sank back down to the deck.

I tried to focus again on my surroundings, what needed to be done for Mother—or daydreaming about life in Nueva Roma— but all I could think about was that kiss. It might have been a family custom or she might have wanted me or was just stoned. In all likelihood I would never see her again. And I didn't want *her,* certainly. That wasn't what I wanted at all. But in extreme times, no one was looking gift horses in the mouth. And deep down I couldn't say what I wanted, where I would let myself go.

The *Prairie Chicken* veered toward the leeway shore and anchored, letting the tourists disembark. Peering down from the deck, I saw the man in the black hat that Lydia had talked about. He carried, in both of his hands, fine black luggage that must have been very expensive. His hat was a Texan, ten-gallon kind of hat. As he reached the shore, he turned around and looked at me. I couldn't see his eyes from that distance, but I did see him smile at me. It wasn't very pleasant. His teeth were silvery. I thought about waving at him, but checked myself. That could have been very, very dangerous.

I was freezing. Xerxes was barking below me. When the boat started going downriver again, I heard my father call out my name, wondering where the hell I was.

I looked back at the huts on the shore, the makeshift village probably built just for tourists, as I made my way down the stairs. The smoke from the huts was blue and the air smelled like kef and I wished I was with Lydia.

My dad kept yelling, though, and I knew something was wrong.

TRANSCRIPT OF TRIAL/CIARAN PALMER/JUSTICE LEVEL: AZURE (excerpt)

PRAETOR1: With this incident in question, what was the first moment you knew your mother was in trouble?

CIARAN: She was in a lot of trouble, a ton—a ton of trouble—

PRAETOR1: In this particular incident.

CIARAN: You mean right before she died.

PRAETOR1: Yes. The incident, please.

[EXPURGATED BY ORDERS FROM THE LEGION OF THE BRONZE CANOE]

CIARAN: . . . saw Macy coming toward the door. She started screaming. I heard Dad and the dog fighting.

PRAETOR1: What kind of fight were they having?

CIARAN: How the fuck would I have known?

PRAETOR2: This is enough out of you. Guards—

PRAETOR1: Not now. I understand my peer's frustration. But we need to give him time. If you would continue, after my rephrasing. When was the first time you saw your father and the dog fighting?

CIARAN: Right after I pushed past my sister into the room. I wasn't thinking. I think she hit her head or something. Xerxes was between my mother's legs.

PRAETOR1: Was she dead?

CIARAN: No, she was just knocked out—wait, do you mean my sister or my mother?

PRAETOR 2: This is foolish.

CIARAN: All right, all right. My mother. I . . . I think so. It was hard to . . . []

PRAETOR 1: Please continue, defendant.

CIARAN: []

PRAETOR 2: Defendant!

CIARAN: The dog was almost wrestling with Dad. That's what it looked like. Like they were playing almost. You know how dogs can play rough, play hard, but they don't really mean it? It kind of looked like that with Xerxes. Except Dad was hitting the dog against the floor, trying to get . . . get the dog away from him.

PRAETOR 1: Him? Do you mean "himself"?

CIARAN: No, I meant my brother.

PRAETOR 1: You mean the unborn child.

CIARAN: My brother. Mom had just given birth to him. But with the plague—

PRAETOR 2: Yes, what *about* the plague? That is why we are here, is it not?

CIARAN: Grace caught the plague, and my sister did, too, although she got better. But William had the plague, too—

PRAETOR 1: William?

CIARAN: My baby brother. Now, will you please let me fucking continue?

PRAETOR2: [ ] Do continue.

CIARAN: A lot of times I talked to William, when Grace wasn't paying attention. Which was a lot. I was his little window into the rest of the world. But all that didn't matter anymore. After the fight.

PRAETOR1: And why is that?

CIARAN: Xerxes . . . he . . . consumed . . . William. [ ] I don't know what else to say. What do you want me to say?

PRAETOR2: Was this a wild dog?

CIARAN: What? Um, sure. Wild. Sure he was wild acting, but he was mine, as much as a dog can be.

PRAETOR1: We see. So if he was "wild," as you say, and yet yours, then why weren't you in control of him? Why not a leash?

PRAETOR2: Yes, or a muzzle?

CIARAN: Are you serious? We were on a boat. He wasn't going anywhere until I pushed him off.

PRAETOR2: But legally, you had, as the dog's owner, a responsibility toward the crew, the other passengers, and your family—

CIARAN: The dog . . . attacked my family!

PRAETOR2: Precisely. You—

CIARAN: I don't like you or your tone. And I didn't expect this to happen. And I killed Xerxes as soon as I found out.

PRAETOR1: You killed him? How did you kill him?

CIARAN: I threw him overboard. And I cut him with my knife, too, before I threw him.

PRAETOR1: Why did you do that? Throw him overboard?

CIARAN: There were way too many bodies in that little room already. And I wanted to give Grace and William a little respect. Xerxes was still twitching and putting up a little fight when we pitched him.

PRAETOR1: Wait. What do you mean "we"?

CIARAN: Dad and me. I . . . I couldn't pick him up all by myself. I think I was screaming. Macy would have helped, too. She never liked Xerxes. I should have listened to her.

PRAETOR1: But the crew didn't want you or your family anymore. As passengers, I mean.

CIARAN: No, they voted us off the island.

PRAETOR2: The island?

PRAETOR1: We have no record of a vote being taken!

CIARAN: Nothing, never mind. The boat, they decided to kick us off the boat. So they jettisoned us on a riverbank in the middle of nowhere and kept going down the river. Macy was groggy still, but they didn't care. Some of the guys on that boat were good friends, but they didn't care anymore. They spat at us, fuckers, while we left. Called us cursed, no good. And they pitched Grace and William overboard after they escorted us off at swordpoint. Just heaved them into the water. Dad wanted to wade after her but I kept him back because Macy was coming to and—

PRAETOR1: That's enough. That's quite enough. [TO THE RECORD] As one can clearly see, the defendant, even at the most tender of ages, was imbued with both a malicious nature and a profound recklessness. . . .

[RECORD CONTINUES]

CHAPTER 12
Where

THE NEXT THING I REMEMBERED I WAS ON A COLD RIVERBANK PUK-
ing my guts out. Dad's hand was on my shoulder and Ciaran was
shouting into the river. It was coming on noon. The *Prairie
Chicken* was nowhere in sight. Farther down the river, I saw a
speck that might have been the *Prairie Chicken*. About a quarter
mile away there were three or four fishermen—fisherwomen,
too—and they did their best to ignore us. I didn't blame them.
We were sad sacks.

Since I didn't remember anything about what happened in
the cabin, later I was forced to rely on my remaining family's
memories. Those, too, were fraught with holes. Perhaps the
most complete—if not necessarily the most reliable—account
came from my brother, during the trial. And I didn't receive this
accounting until much, much later.

But the incident was only a minor thread in the great tapestry
of Ciaran's trial; they were merely using the death of our mother
as background corroboration for their case. I don't think I ever
forgave them for that. And I hated that an official transcript—
the words of my brother—had to stand in for memories.

I saw the fishers rowing toward us. We were numb and cold. Ciaran explained what happened the best he could. I sat down on the cold bank and started bawling. Shell-shocked, Dad was stamping his feet. Along with a few other paltry possessions, he had his telescope with him. He'd managed to save that. My knife was still on the boat—bastards—but I still had my comb. It was in the pocket of my hoodie. Dad had grabbed my 5-Subject notebook, although I didn't find that out until later.

How far to St. Louis? Dad muttered to himself, pacing. Six miles, less?

Perhaps the strangest thing, standing there on the bank with Mother dead and gone, was how it finally struck me, hard, how she had been gone more or less for weeks. And yet this was the first time I was able to miss her for all those times, too. Those times snapped back at me like a rubber band. I tried to stop crying, cover it up, but then I gave up and cried until the fishing boat came. I buried my head in my arms and tried not to pay attention to my dad talking to the fisherpeople when they came. People in general—the human race—were on my shit list. I couldn't handle them. (Dogs were a close second.)

Then I felt a hand on my shoulder. I flinched.

Dad, leave me alone, I said, because I couldn't think of anyone else who would do that.

But the hand didn't feel familiar, so I looked up, and saw one of the fisherwomen standing above me. She was wearing an orange, tattered commercial-fishing uniform, or maybe something from a fish-sticks processing plant. Her eyes were bloodshot and her fingers were, too, if that makes sense. The look on her face was one of concentration and confusion. She handed me a cigarette with a thick hand.

I took it.

Then she gave me a soft pretzel. It had green string cheese—that was what I thought, at least—baked on the outside crust.

Okay, I said, trying to wipe the snot running down my nose with my sleeve. Thank you.

I turned. I saw that the other fishers were giving my brother and father similar gifts. Ciaran was wolfing down his soft pretzel. Dad was beginning to fray, but he still wasn't to the point where he could acknowledge that his wife was dead. I wondered if he was going to come down hard on me for smoking. Because I was going to smoke. I really, really needed to smoke.

The woman was smiling. She had a bronze knife tucked into her boot. It was probably good for cleaning fish, but all the same I wouldn't want to mess with her. She said something to me in a language that was like a cross between French and German. I figured she wanted me to converse with her. All I could do was smile, forcing myself to move my face muscles.

But it helped.

Then I gave her the universal signal for "do you have a light," which I remembered from movies. But she cocked her head at me.

Here, Macy. Ciaran said that. He produced a lighter and tossed it to me. I managed to catch it. It took a couple of tries but soon enough I was taking deep draughts of the cigarette, which had small Phoenician letters around the circumference of the filter.

Thanks, I said to Ciaran.

He tipped an imaginary cap.

The cigarette was helping, too. I ate a bit of my pretzel and didn't realize until then how little food I'd had on the *Prairie Chicken*. Soon I had eaten the whole pretzel. It tasted like fish, but I wasn't complaining. The fisherwoman shouted something to the others, loud but not crazy sounding. My dad must have finished his negotiations, or conversation, or whatever, because he stood up and told us in a shaky voice that the fishers were going to take us downriver.

These kind people, I remember Dad saying—it was something Mother would have said.

He didn't say anything about his children smoking. His own cigarette was tucked behind his ear. I got up, walked over to the others, and handed the lighter back to Ciaran, too freaked out to offer a light to my father.

We piled in the fishing boat. Crowded for six, but I didn't care. I finished my cigarette while they were unmooring and extinguished it in the river water, leaning over the blue boat.

Don't litter, Dad said. That was all he had to say on the cigarette subject. I ended up putting the butt in my pocket.

Untied, we began to lurch into the current. The fishers were telling jokes to one another. I could see Ciaran trying to follow the hand gestures, which seemed to be of bats and groundhogs, but soon enough he gave up and turned to Dad.

What do they want for passage? he said to Dad.

Nothing, Dad said. They were going that way anyway.

They must want *something*. Maybe they weren't clear—

I grabbed Ciaran's hand.

Hey, maybe they're just being nice, I said.

It was clear he didn't entertain that possibility, not once. He kept quiet for a while as we drifted down the river. There were tall white birches lining the eastern shore, their bark like an albino's skin. They seemed like trees from a different place—but then I remembered that we *were* in a different place. And anyway, we'd never be going back to these birches. Few things from the journey would really be remembered. But maybe I would make a point of remembering the birches, because no one else would.

Then the fishers started passing out beers to us. They were in hard plastic bottles, kind of like the bottles they had at Twins and Vikings games, so that when the drunk idiots started throwing the bottles onto the field they would bounce instead of shatter. The beers didn't have labels of any kind, but rather Roman numerals—or something to that effect—written near the base in black Magic Marker. We all opened them up, in stereo. My bottle had an "LV" on it. I took a swig. Down the hatch. I never really had a taste for beer. My friends didn't drink, either. There were a few times in high school when I snuck beer into my room when everyone was asleep, and I didn't see what the big deal was, in terms of the taste.

This beer was a little vinegar tasting, but I didn't mind at all. Far from it. I tapped the fisherwoman on the shoulder, pointed at the beer, and made a little bow. That seemed appropriate.

She laughed and gave a thumbs-up.

A small part of me kept expecting these people to frisk us for money, ask for bribes, or slit our throats. I kept looking over to that woman's knife. But nothing like that happened. Smooth sailing. An hour of equilibrium, a quiet boat ride, which I was more than thankful for, as I was breaking up inside. I wondered what Dad's new university would be like, whether I'd be able to take classes there. I also wondered about Sophia—was she happy where she was? But I also worried about Dad, how he was going to make it. That seemed a little bit easier to contemplate than how *I* was going to make it.

As we made it to a wide bend, Ciaran stood up, lurching the boat.

The city! The city! he shouted.

I'd expected, closer to the city, suburbs of some sort. There were a few crumbling, suburblike buildings, but no people in them, and they were all covered in moss and vines.

I stood up, too, which nearly tipped over the whole damn boat. I saw the outline of taller buildings, skyscrapers, but it wasn't quite what I expected. One was broken in half and another had smoldering fires on its roof. There was a silence in the air.

Then the river turned into a kind of marshy lake. The banks were flooded for miles, and there were low, grayish reeds popping out of the water in a swampy thicket.

I sat back down. Ciaran did, too.

Passing by our boat, in the other direction, was a man in a black rowboat. He wore all black, and had one eye. The other socket was empty. He whistled as he rowed against the current.

Look, Ciaran said, as the rowboat was almost past. He pointed to the southwest, to the St. Louis Arch.

Only it wasn't quite an arch anymore. It was only half there, and looked like a giant question mark jammed into the ground.

Dad hailed the man in the black rowboat. I don't know if you speak English, he said.

The man stopped rowing. Sure, he said, smiling.

Great, Dad said. I was wondering if you could tell us how we can reach the University of St. Louis.

University, the man said, uncomprehending.

Yes, of the city of St. Louis, my dad said.

The man cracked his knuckles. He looked just about ready to get rowing again.

Where? he said.

PART
TWO

CHAPTER 13
Javelins

I WANT IT SHORT, I SAID, BUT NOT TOO SHORT.

The barber, a man named Jeremy, pretended he didn't hear me.

Did you hear me? I don't want it *too* short, I said.

He muttered something under his breath. His shop smelled good, like chamomile soap, but I couldn't relax. Every time I started to let my mind wander in peace, I would startle. My heart would start beating fast. It got to the point where I'd always keep my guard up because I didn't want to feel that panic. I had thought it was better to stay alert, even with a simple, allegedly therapeutic, haircut.

He promised that he was the best barber in Lou. A couple of years ago he had graduated from the Southern Missouri Hair Academy and worked at a Great Clips with no health insurance. Now, well, he didn't have health insurance, but no one else did either. On the other hand, there weren't any Great Clips either, so he could set up shop in an abandoned dentist's office and no one seemed to mind.

He was cutting my hair as an exchange. Dad had given him a "comet chart," whatever that was. Ciaran, Dad, and I had been living in Lou for about a month. That was what everyone called it. Most of old St. Louis was flooded out, including every university, community college, and charter school. I heard that some of the kids of the local elites—not that I met any—had a private academy behind well-guarded gates. That wasn't in my league, and I thought I was better than them, anyway.

He started snipping. I closed my eyes. From another part of town I could hear a trombone playing a slow, staccato dirge. The scissors dicing up my hair syncopated with the trombone sounds. Outside it was sunny and cold. Everyone stamped around town, with newspapers stuffed into their overcoats and hauberks.

Your brother . . . Jeremy began, once he got settled into the rhythm.

I blew a stray piece of hair out of my eyes. What about my brother? I said.

Have you seen him lately? Do you miss him?

I didn't say anything. In the four weeks or so we'd been in Lou, I'd seen my brother maybe four times. I thought, for a time, that our mother's death would have brought us closer together, that Ciaran would dial it down a notch and start acting more regular. But nothing of the sort happened. He pretty much disappeared after we had found a town house in the center of the old town. Disappeared like he had in Pig's Eye and Pike Island. He came for supper once in a great while. Dad had a lot of food at the ready after he started up his trade, and we cooked a lot of it together. I helped him chop a lot of vegetables, and I didn't mind being Dad's kitchen help. It didn't require much thought on my part.

And truth be told, I wasn't that happy when Ciaran came by and pulled off the prodigal-son routine. Dad didn't seem to care that much that Ciaran was living on his own, who knew where. Actually I did find out where, but not until a little later.

Jeremy kept clipping and my head kept getting lighter.

You're blond, he said, laughing.

My hair's dirty, I said.

Yes. I'd say so. This suits you. You never answered my questions, you know.

I sighed. I wasn't comfortable talking about Ciaran with a near stranger.

We've grown apart, I managed to say.

That's clear, he said. But your father worries about him.

I almost stood up.

How do you know? I asked, raising my voice. Are you spying?

He took a little step back. He was a little hurt that I'd lashed out at him. No, nothing of the sort, he said. People, in your father's meetings, can just tell.

He paused and continued: His aura.

As if that were obvious.

I managed to keep myself from groaning. The meetings. I knew a bit about them, although they were never held in our town house. Dad had started talking more and more about them, and he was finding more of a place—an internal place—with the ex-hippies and ex-gnostics and ex-chakra massage therapists who were strewn across the new Empire's lands and trying to reconnect with their spiritual grab-bag brethren. There might have even been some wayward Celts and Huns in their group—their horse worship and exotic mythologies (exotic, at least, to the Americans) would have blended right in.

I couldn't touch that place my dad retreated to. Which was all right, for a while. He'd lost his wife, a woman he loved more—

when it came right down to it—than I did. I didn't want to blame him or touch where his grief was. Because, for one, I had more than enough grief to deal with myself. But after a few weeks, his astrology seemed less like a grief phase and more like a final destination.

He wasn't quite the same.

Not that I was going to tell my hair stylist about any of this. What was strange was how deeply Jeremy *cared* about my dad's well-being. Caring, after the time on the river, still left me a little bewildered.

I know he appreciates you, he said. But he grieves about his son.

Sons, I wanted to say, thinking of dead William. Dad had to have grieved over that as well. But I didn't say anything.

He coughed, not sure what to do about my silence. Then, shifting gears: I'm done. See what you think but please don't kill me.

He handed me a mirror that used to be a toy, either for a baby or a parrot.

The hair was *short*. A bit spiky.

Holy shit, it's short, I said.

You can see your face, Jeremy said.

Yeah, great, I said. I wasn't super happy about that. I stopped looking at the mirror and handed it back to Jeremy.

It's nice, I muttered.

Then he grabbed my wrist, gentle but firm. Stop hiding who you are, he said.

I stared at him and then burst out laughing, which was the only thing I could think of doing besides hiding.

He let go of my wrist. I'm *serious,* Macy. And you look good, so shut up and enjoy it, won't you?

I shrugged. After being on the river, I didn't care about look-ing good. I only wanted to blend in and keep my head down. I figured Lou could be a place where that happened, but that didn't make it a utopia, either.

I gave Jeremy a hug—more for my dad's sake, because I knew Jeremy would report the whole conversation, including the hug—and stepped out into the bright sunlight. The city militia were doing drills as I was walking toward home, and I al-most ran right into them before I could get out of the way. About a hundred of them, looking pretty ragtag, a group cobbled to-gether from various conscriptions. Many of them weren't much older than Ciaran. I realized, with a quick shock, that maybe Ciaran was hiding out from the draft as much as his family. He was good with weapons. They might have been able to see that.

The militiamen's footwear was irregular—Pumas and Nikes and Skechers. A lot of the shoes didn't seem to fit quite right. The soldiers had knobby swords and pikes, a few maces. Lou was an important town on the confluence of two rivers, but its defense appeared, to my untrained eye, sketchy at best. People did their best to go on with their lives. Legions went into the fields of Illinois and Missouri in skirmishes, to protect farms, and a lot of kids didn't come back. If it wasn't for the river navy that was stationed at Lou, the city would be pretty much fucked.

As the boys walked past, I couldn't help but notice that most of them had horrible posture. And they weren't holding their weapons right at all. I expected such things from my father, but not from peers who had grown up playing video games requir-ing a great deal of sword wielding.

But maybe that in itself was the problem. Maybe they were untrainable.

I wasn't sure whether that was a quality or character defect.

Behind the irregulars, I was surprised to find about two or three dozen women marching in formation, maybe a little older than me. They were wearing leather breechings and were carrying javelins. The javelins looked like they were carbon fiber, but sharpened to war points. They also wore sweatshirts that said: IOWA STATE TRACK AND FIELD. Their faces were weatherworn, but they didn't slouch like the boys ahead of them. Their shoes had spikes and were in much better shape than those of their male counterparts. Watching them march past, it was no surprise that these women had been recruited—or conscripted—into the army. They would have had to learn to kill moving targets on horseback, but they were probably already deadly at that.

After they passed, I cut across Onion Alley—which smelled like raw garlic, go figure—to our town house. Dad had put up a weird garland in our doorway that looked like a long sausage that had been left in the cold for a couple of months, then pierced with pine branches and inscribed with star shapes. They were entrails of a goat, or something like that. According to Dad, it was our home's security system. I didn't want to delve too much into that matter.

We had squatted in our town house after we found ourselves in Lou—but after the first plague wave in town, which we only heard bits and pieces about, pretty much everyone was a squatter. There was no electricity or heat, of course, so we set up a fire pit in the living room, and opened up the windows to let out the smoke. That wasn't ideal. We were both hot and freezing at the same time. The cheap drywall was already cracking and breaking. A raccoon—or another creature of that ilk—had used the kitchen as its own personal playground during the early winter, and it took a long time to clean up. This was a building that would have gone for a couple hundred thousand dollars just a year ago, and would have housed a childless, young professional coven. Architects or interior designers, people wanting the convenience of city life without any sight lines to the wastelands of East St. Louis. Anyway, it was a gilded shithole. White rats snuck around corners at odd hours of the day. I wondered if there was a secret medical laboratory nearby that they had escaped from.

Dad had set up his telescope in the attic. Wearing his overcoat and gloves, at night he would search the stars, the constellations that were unfamiliar to us. The sky had changed. It was a whole new game for him. He had to start over with all of his astronomical knowledge. But he plunged into it, bought reams of industrial paper from a warehouse on the north side, and started plotting the sky. He became quiet, and less nervous. I thought that it was a way of working out his grief. But it was also something much more than that. He was changing. He was becoming more a part of the world we had found ourselves in.

I'm not sure who first noticed him from the attic window peering into his telescope, but his first customer was the woman who had saved us on the banks of the Mississippi, after the *Prairie Chicken* ditched us. She checked in on us once in a while, gave us fish and those fishy pretzels. At any rate, with the help of one of her downriver friends who spoke a little English and acted as translator, Mari (that was her name) asked for a star chart. Dad, once being a scientist, balked at first. But after some persistence and the promise of coin, he relented.

For a while I think he took the astrology as a kind of intellectual exercise, to see *how people thought of him* doing astrology. But the constellations of strange stars lured him in. Planets, too.

Mars isn't where it's supposed to be, I heard him shouting once from upstairs. Mars, Mars, Mars!

Then it took hold of him, all of him. Astrology caught fire. He raided the "Metaphysical Speculation" sections, what was left of them, of every Borders, Barnes & Noble, and Books-A-Million in a ten-mile radius, and stacked his loot in neat piles in the attic. He scribbled instead of slept.

Word had spread about the astrologer in the window.

Within a week, he had made enough from his star charts and consultations to get us a cooking stove, with a chimney, and have it all installed. Or maybe he did the barter for birth lines with an antique-stove specialist.

Dad had set up a shrine for Mother in the northeast corner of our house, and worked on it over the course of two whole days. He kept candles for her burning twenty-four hours a day. They were red tallow that smelled like cinnamon. He had managed to save, throughout all our travels, quite a few pictures of her throughout the years. Mother as a toddler standing next to a fallen oak tree, from the farm where she grew up, way up north. Her high school graduation picture, thick glasses and a goofy smile. Their wedding photo, where I'd never seen her happier. And so on. Tons of photos. The one I almost couldn't bear to look at was the most recent one—taken about a year before we headed downriver. It was a family portrait. Dad had decided to take us all to a portrait studio at the Mall of America, which wasn't a super-popular idea with us kids. Mother had frizzy hair and looked dazed, and Dad was the eye of the storm, trying to hold it all together with a forced smile. Ciaran had tried, the night before, to cut his own hair, to get a mohawk, and an emergency trip to the barber had to be made, with much kicking and screaming. So anyway, Ciaran had a buzz cut. Sophia's eyes were looking down at a text message she'd just received. And me? My eyes were closed. I'd blinked right before the flash. At any rate,

Ciaran had raised a huge tantrum, and the photographer at Sears wanted us out of her hair, so she gave us those pictures free and sent us on our way. The photo sucked, and it was never on our mantel in our house in St. Paul, nor in any wallets. But Dad had taken it with him, and saved it after all this time.

That picture hit me the hardest. Some nights when Dad was buried upstairs in his work I'd sit on the floor in front of the shrine and cry, putting my fist in my mouth so Dad wouldn't hear me.

Maybe Dad had tried to make a memorial not just for Mother, but for our entire family, what we used to be.

I was thinking about that shrine as I was unlocking the front door, underneath the hand-painted DOCTOR OF THE SKY sign. I heard someone walking on the street past our townhouse. Paranoid, I paused. I looked to my right. It was the man in black who had been traveling with Lydia's family. The creepy man searching the river towns for Something Very Important.

He squinted at me, and then gave me a fuck-you smile as he passed.

He recognized me.

Strapped to his back was an ivory-colored crossbow that looked like it was manufactured by giants.

As soon as he was out of sight, I finished unlocking the door with the heavy iron key. I scurried inside and bolted the door. Shaking, I found a chair next to the stove and slumped into it. I heard my father humming upstairs, something lilting.

Letters from Camp

[note: Transcriptions of letters from Leipoxis, crown prince of the Royal House of Scythia (one house of a tripartite system of government). Leipoxis was thirteen. He spends his summers in New Gelon (formerly Duluth) and the winters on the great plains of Kansas. These are the letters he sent to his mother in New Gelon during the summer, when he rode with his uncles, skirmishing with elk, buffalo, and the occasional Sarmatian. Leipoxis was illiterate. The first letter was transcribed orally from a captured Scythian courier, who had memorized the letter and ridden the eight hundred miles to Leipoxis's mother's estate at what used to be a ski resort. The courier was taken to Nueva Roma for questioning, and only revealed the contents of his "letter" after much tactile persuasion. The rest of the letters are from a wood-and-gold tape recorder hand-powered with a crank. The inventor remains unknown, although the prototype seemed to be a combination of a hesychastic solid-state drive and a JVC answering machine circa 1981.]

Letter 1

Dear Queen Mother:
   Your son is enjoying himself quite beautifully as we plan to kill more civilians. We are training on Sarmatians, at first. I thought you would be pleased at this.
   Your loving son,

Leipoxis

Letter 2

Dear Mother,

My uncles were talking about the plague-cure. Has it come yet? Uncle Mayvar is sick. His head has turned into a falcon. It tries to fly away. None of us feel safe and have taken to wearing masks. A loving word from you would be appreciated.

Your son,

Leipoxis

Letter 3

Kansas has a history of madness. Why did you send me here?

Mayvar flew away.

Your son,

Leipoxis

Letter 4

We raided a general store. It's pretty hot today. I killed my first man. Didn't like it much. I'm wondering whether this is what it's all about.

Best wishes,

L.

Letter 5

Mother:

Have not heard about the "vaccine" yet. Have you?
You are our lifeline. I want to come back.

I have discovered the soul music of the locals.

L.

Letter 6

Two weeks until I come back. It's been locusts all afternoon. Why have you abandoned your loving son?

At the same time, I have found pleasures in local
customs. How I long to see your face again—and yet
my duties to these people and their small lives will not
be sad duties. I want to learn to grow wise. Even
though we will, perhaps, move on from these lands before I rule.

Your son, as of this moment untouched by the
plague,

L.

[from *Espionage Report: Interceptions,* editor anonymous, presented to the Emperor, with preapproval by the Committee of
Geophysic Safety]

CHAPTER 14

Feinting a Family

CIARAN BURPED. I HAD ONLY NIBBLED MY BUFFALO FLANK. I DID A little better with the baby carrots, which were almost tart.

Where did you *get* this, Ciaran asked Dad while chewing. This is incredible. Ciaran was eating the tongue.

Dad leaned back on his chair and put his hands on his belly. He was getting a little pudgy. He wore a T-shirt that had a black ankh on it, which I didn't want to ask about.

One of my clients has a buffalo farm in East Lou, he said.

Organic, I assume, I muttered. Vegetarian fed.

Dad set down his fork. I guess so, he said. By default, these days.

I was still a bit shell-shocked about seeing the man with the crossbow, but did my best to push that down. It might have been nothing. It might have been a lot. I couldn't have said at the time.

I leaned toward Ciaran and said: So, Ciaran, when do I get to see your place?

It surprised me when I said this. I'm not sure why I wanted to. I was bored, mostly. I also wanted to know what secrets Ciaran was keeping from us. Because I knew he had them. And I wanted to yank his chain a little bit, too.

He was taken aback, I could tell, but he didn't snap back with some smart-ass answer. Sure, he said, I guess, if you want to. There's not a whole lot to see.

Is that okay, Dad? I asked. I wasn't sure why I was asking permission. I almost never bothered, and he was too wrapped up, most days, in his own work to take notice.

Sure, he said. You two need quality time, right?

I think he really believed that.

When the two of us were in the street, walking northwest, into the marshy slush, I craned my neck back for some reason—I thought I heard something—and saw that there was a man on top of the broken Arch. I saw his silhouette, at least. He was flapping his arms up and down.

I stopped Ciaran, pointed, and said: How the hell did he get up there?

He shrugged. I don't know. Don't they have elevators?

Yeah, but you wouldn't think they'd work anymore, would you.

How the hell should I know? Come on, stop goofing around. You're the one who wanted to see my place, weren't you?

He started walking again.

All right, all right, I muttered.

We went through a lot of flooded neighborhoods I didn't recognize. Most of the houses were dead and empty, with symbols—owls' faces, spirals—spray painted onto the front doors in fluorescent paint. There were dim fires in a few of the bungalows, and a bastardized canal/latrine in the middle of a street. The mud—and there was a lot of mud—was frozen here. It was like walking on a field of Fudgsicles. Ciaran was walking fast, and I struggled to keep up. I wasn't sure what was going through his head; sometimes I thought he was trying to ditch me and get me lost. We went through an alley strewn with fine pieces of black eggshells. The alley was lit by a random gas lantern on a pole (river whale oil?). Then an empty lot of slick weeds. Then down a smooth hill that would have been perfect for sledding if not for the toppled statues. Of civic leaders or new emperors, I could not say.

At last he stopped. I was running to keep up with him at that point and I almost slammed into his back.

What? I said. My voice sounded loud. After my eyes adjusted, I saw we were in a public square, with stone buildings five stories high around us. I could hear a river. It couldn't have been the Mississippi. The Missouri must have migrated.

Ciaran crouched, and lifted a flagstone with the edges of his fingers. There was a blast of moist air, and a metal ladder leading down.

So let me guess, you live in a sewer, I said. St. Louis's finest.

St. Louis hasn't existed in a long, long time, he said. I didn't ask him what he meant by that, because he told me to go down the ladder first.

Why me? I said.

I need to replace the stone, he said.

So I went down. The ladder was damp and rusty, but I didn't fall.

After a minute at the bottom, Ciaran was down with me. He took off fast in one direction.

Jesus! I called out. There were torches set in the walls. The corridor smelled like moths and dung.

I tried to warn you, he said, not bothering to look back.

Uh, not really, I said, more to myself.

Well, you didn't have to come.

You could have told me at least to wear better shoes, I said. My feet are killing me.

But he didn't even shrug about that, or have any type of response. I had no idea how I was going to get back home. What, call a cab?

The underground trip was pretty short, thank God. After a couple of minutes he opened a metal door to the side.

His place was not what I expected at all. It could have been a foreman's office or employee lounge at some point. I heard rushing water near one of the walls. There was an eighties-style vending machine in the corner, with grainy photographs of chocolate bars and coffee. There was a blue couch and a potbellied stove that had some coals in it. The walls were covered with rugs depicting hunts: stags, mammoths, wolves. I was a bit surprised by the hunting of wolves, though when I later learned of the company my brother kept, I shouldn't have been. I shouldn't have been at all. The room shone. Ciaran turned around and did a mock bow.

Well, here you go, he said.

Wow, I said. Where did you get all this stuff?

Friends, he said.

He then removed the field gear backpack from his back and took out *The Children's Book of Heroes* from it. *That book.*

What's with you and this book? I said, moving a hand toward it.

He was sullen, and nervous, I could tell. Which made *me* nervous. He moved in front of me, blocking my path to the book, and cracked a big smile. But I knew he was faking the smile. Or rather, he was *forcing* it. He was always faking it, one way or another.

Maybe I just find it inspirational, he said. Then he laughed.

He didn't want to arouse my suspicion, which aroused my suspicion. To continue with his forced ease, a double fake, he said: I have to take a piss. Don't get crazy and break anything.

He went to the back room, more of a curtained partition. When I heard him pissing—not exactly pleasant—I took a step toward the book. I was dying of curiosity and didn't care about his warnings. I paused for a second and opened the book.

The Children's Book of Heroes wasn't a book. It was a container designed to look like a book. It had a deep cavity with a vellum interior. Inside the cavity was a small vial of milky blue liquid, and underneath it in a separate, smaller compartment was a translucent, blue oval cylinder, like a large gelcap.

Inside the cylinder was a wasp.

My mind started churning, but it wasn't going anywhere.

Then I noticed Ciaran running toward me from the bathroom with his knife drawn.

You cunt! he shouted.

I grabbed the book. The vial and wasp jostled. I held it, still open, over my head.

Step off, I said. He kept moving toward me, shoulders lowered. I could see the bony handle and the curve of his blade and knew he wouldn't, at that instant, hesitate to slit my throat. He had that look about him. Whatever was in the book was that important to him.

He inched toward me. Just an inch.

I mean it, I said. I let my arms sag.

That made him stop at least.

Now back the fuck up, I said.

He took a couple of steps back.

Now, after you apologize for calling me—

I couldn't even spit the word out.

—what you called me, you're going to tell me what this is, you little shit.

Apologize for that, he said. He was still holding his knife out, which I didn't like.

Me? Apologize? Apologize for *what*? I said.

For calling me a little shit.

I almost shattered the book then and there, just on general principle.

You've got to be kidding me, I said.

But what you said hurt me, he said.

And he *actually looked hurt*.

I started laughing. I was losing it. Look, I said. Let's back up. Just tell me what the hell this is, and what you've been doing with it the last three months.

I can't do that, he said.

You better do it, I said, or it's gone.

You wouldn't do that if you knew what it was.

Then tell me! Jesus.

But. If you knew what it was, you'd do everything to protect it, and then I'd have to kill you. Because you'd be too busy protecting it.

I sighed. The book was pretty heavy and my arms were getting tired. I tried to tell whether my brother was bluffing or not. But I couldn't tell anything. He was a kid pretending to be a man pretending to be a cold-blooded killer, and he was so confused in his own head he didn't know *what* he wanted. All the same I knew he *could* kill me, just for that reason.

Try me, I said. If it's so important then I'll help you.

This time he snickered. You can't help me, he said, and he

had a look of panic and desperation on his face as he said this. You wouldn't know where to begin.

Try me, Ciaran, I said again, though deep down I didn't want to help him.

Should have never trusted you, he muttered. Stupid bitch.

Then I threw the book against the wall.

But for the Grace

Grace wasn't always off dreaming. She grew up on a pig farm, up north. She didn't move down to the Cities until she was twelve. By that time she had a sense she wasn't good with people. Better with pigs than people, even though she knew they all ended up getting slaughtered. But she still tried to talk to the pigs, in the barn on winter mornings, feeding them and cleaning the stalls. The hogs seemed to appreciate this, she thought. Don't worry, she told them. Don't worry. The pig smell never bothered her until she went to school. Her father had told Grace, when she was six, about a pig heaven, which was adjacent to people heaven. Like the house and the barn? she asked. Yes, her father said, exactly like the house and the barn. Her parents didn't say much in general, to her or other people. The farm was outside of Biwabik. Both of her parents were descended from Icelanders and were third cousins. Most of Grace's classmates in school were miners' children, working taconite. Her parents didn't smoke or drink, but neither were they strict Lutherans. For Grace, this meant the worst of both worlds, sliding into the limbo between virtue and vice. The miners' kids teased her, telling her she stank. Every night she would scour her body with the Lava soap her father used, imagining smell to be a kind of color on her body.

The summers were too hot for comfort and they also meant the disappearance of the hogs. Best, for her, was spring, which could still mean frost, snow, and mud—not like spring any-where else, she imagined. There would be shoots of green in the snow. She would wander the brown-gray fields and collect fos-sils. Old clear-cuts, aborted mines, streambeds, the water loose and rushing after winter, pine trees and wind. This was where she felt most at home. She looked up fossils in her field guide, knowing geologic eras better than recent history. I'm going to marry a scientist, she vowed to herself the year her father's legs were crushed loading a half-ton hog that got free. Her mother held her hand as the sheriff shot the crazed pig in the head. One thing she knew from fossils was that people wouldn't last. And yet this didn't make her sadder than usual. At the hospital in Duluth, her father wouldn't look at her. He talked about Iceland a lot. That was one thing he talked about, even growing up, even though he didn't know anything about it. He said that they were all descended from Vikings, and he was proud of that. But what did that mean? She wanted to know. Excusing herself from the hospital room, the other bed occupied by a wheezing man who would die the next afternoon, she went to the bathroom and locked herself in a stall. Then she started laughing. Tears ran down her cheeks. She bit her palms as she laughed. One of her greatest regrets as a mother was that her parents never met their grandchildren.

CHAPTER 15
We're Americans

I DIDN'T GET HOME UNTIL DAWN, A WEAK DAWN IN WHICH THE SUN didn't peek out of the gray clouds. Father was waiting outside for me in a great ermine coat and beaver pelt hat. He looked like an old Russian communist. With him were four men wearing Missouri Irregulars uniforms, iron pikes clutched in their hands.

My father opened his arms and I collapsed into them, sobbing.

Once we were inside, and I was bundled in a quilt next to the fire, the militiamen left my father after a brief conversation in low tones.

Who were they? I said when they left. My voice cracked. I felt dizzy.

I was worried about you, he said, kneeling next to me, rubbing my shoulders. I thought you were dead. The governor . . . I told the governor about you during my session with him. And he became worried, too. He gave me some of his troops on a loan.

The governor? Your session?

Yes. Do you want soup? It's lamb and lentil, which I know you don't like, but . . .

I knew Dad didn't want to upset me, to shake out of me what

the hell happened, but I needed to talk, to let my panicky, broken feelings come out.

Ciaran's been arrested, Dad, I said.

Dad stopped his dawdling and stared at me. And maybe he felt a tad guilty about not asking about his son.

Arrested? By whom? For what?

A man with a large crossbow who said he was working for the Imperial court itself. And for high treason and espionage.

What? That's insane, that's . . .

Then he saw the look on my face: anger, exhaustion, fear.

I decided to tell him everything. Except for the parts about me and Ciaran fighting after I threw down the book and the vial shattered. He chased after it anyways and I landed hard on his back. I pinned his arms. I wanted to fucking kill him. Instead, I hit his head on the floor a couple of times. All the pent-up anger from the last month—since our mother died—came out. He wasn't knocked out, but he was groggy and bloodied when I rolled off him.

He didn't even wait for me to grill him. He just started talking. This was where I picked it up with Dad, who was staring into space as I told him this stuff.

It was an antidote against the plague, Ciaran said. It was made in a lab way up in Canada. They shipped it down to Pig's Eye, and then gave it to me.

And you were going to do what with it? I asked.

He coughed. Take it up the Missouri River to the Scythian camp, he said.

To the Scythians.

Yeah.

Why, Ciaran? The vaccine could have done a lot more good here.

Ciaran spat blood. You really think that, don't you? he said. Who do you think bred the wasps and the plague?

I snorted. You can't be serious, can you? The Empire—God knows they're not saints—but the Empire couldn't create a plague if they wanted to. And they don't want to. Think of how many soldiers have been killed by the plague.

I thought of Sophia's boyfriend, Nikolai, then, and I wished I hadn't.

They thought they could control it, he said. Use it as a weapon. But they couldn't. They can't. The Scythians are starting to come together with other tribes. After winter, they'll be moving against the Empire again.

I sighed and considered hitting him again. And so you'll be welcomed by these barbarians too, I said. They hate us more than the Empire does.

He shook his head. Some do, he said. But we're our own tribe, too. We're Americans.

Oh, please, I said. I'm not going to respond to something so stupid.

Then something came to me, and I was tempted, more than any other time in my life, to kill Ciaran then and there. But I didn't even lay another hand on him. Instead I said, in a low voice: You had this when Mother and I had the plague. You could have saved her.

He didn't flinch—he just gave me a line. I hated him even more for it.

The serum needed to be produced in large quantities, he said. If I'd used it on Mom, it would have been gone for good.

Besides, he continued, you could have saved her, too. You took an antibiotic. Why didn't you give one to Grace?

I couldn't believe that little fuck was going on the offensive.

I didn't know it would work, I said.

But you took one. You figured *something* would happen.

I kept silent.

So no, Macy—he propped himself on his elbows as he said this—don't try to lay a guilt trip on me, or try to play the good and righteous sister on me. I was offered a lot of money to smuggle the vaccine. We could have used that money.

We don't need your money now, I said.

Then just let me go, he said. That's all I want. I don't belong with any of you anyway. I got all of you out of that hellhole of a refugee camp by forging that letter, and if I didn't, you'd all be dead. But don't thank me or anything.

Wait. What letter?

But as soon as I said it I knew which one he was talking about.

Do you mean the one from Dad's friend? I said. I couldn't believe what I was hearing. Everything was unraveling so fast. My head was spinning.

Yeah, he said. Ciaran was struggling to stand up. I mean, I had friends who forged it. Can you give me a hand up?

I was stunned. He said it in such a quiet way, in such an extinguished voice, that I thought I had beaten some sense into him. That after his bravado he had some change of heart. That he still wasn't fighting and clawing for his life, for whatever he thought he could do with his life.

It was one of the worst mistakes I'd ever made—and I don't know, whatever screwups I have in the future, whether I'll ever make a mistake as bad as that, ever again.

Sure, I said.

I leaned over and took his right hand. With his left hand he slid out a small knife he had been hiding, and slashed my leg. I crashed back into his kitchen table. There was a lot of blood. I tried not to look at it as he stood—no, lorded—over me, wiping his knife on his sleeve.

That's a nasty cut, he said.

I didn't say anything. I knew there would be more if he had his way. The pain didn't come, not yet.

I want you to know, Ciaran said, that I loved Mom more than you ever did. Don't ever pretend that you did.

I started screaming at him. I don't remember what I said. The shock and the blood loss set me free from any sense of caution.

That's when, I told my dad, trying not to shake, Ciaran got arrested.

I told Dad I fell into some broken glass while Ciaran and I were talking.

Let me see your cut, Dad said.

It's fine, I said, stiffening, not wanting him to see it. Hell, *I* didn't want to see it.

I had it mended, I said.

Dad's back straightened. By whom? he said.

Um, the man who arrested Ciaran.

So . . . what? Did he walk in and arrest him?

Yeah. Pretty much. He must have followed us, I said, taking a deep breath.

Also, I guess, I didn't tell Dad about the crossbow bolt that went through Ciaran's shoulder as he was threatening me, waving his knife around in my face. That was how I knew someone else was in the room. He came in quietly and then there was a thunk. When he was hit, Ciaran shrieked like a fourteen-year-old boy—which he was. Ciaran slumped over me, convulsing, and I rolled him off me.

Then the room was full of soldiers—Imperial soldiers. My rescuers. The man with the white hair—*him*—was recocking his crossbow, pulling back the drawstring with his foot. I just stood there, dazed and bleeding. Men swarmed over Ciaran and picked him up roughly. A field doctor of some kind touched my shoulder and had me sit down on the floor while he took a look at my leg. It was bloody but not life threatening. While he bandaged the cut, I kept my eyes on the man with the white hair. He finished resetting his crossbow and he looked at me, tipping his wide-brimmed hat.

I was tempted to spill all of these grisly details to Dad, but I ended up sparing him.

How did you get home? he said.

One of the foot soldiers led the way home, I said.

Only I didn't tell Dad we got lost a few times. The guide was probably a good urban-warfare-type fighter, but he sucked at directions. Hul, that was his name. He wouldn't tell me his superior's name, the one with the white hair and crossbow. We stepped over the bodies of a few Scythians, and a few Avars in white skullcaps. They must have been guarding Ciaran in the night, or trying to. They must have been hiding when I walked with Ciaran to his dwelling.

We got turned around in the marshy alleyways, and came to the confluence of the Missouri and the Mississippi. The Missouri must have migrated south over the last few months. On the other side of the Missouri, I saw a warehouse on fire, and vultures circling the column of smoke. I could see Hul's face in the orange light. It had a lot of scars. I just wanted to get home. Even though my leg got bandaged up, it still hurt to walk.

Shit, he said, more to himself. I think we went the wrong way.

I could tell he wasn't thrilled about taking me home.

It took us a few hours, but we made it. The bandage on my leg kept getting loose so I had to readjust it a couple of times. While I did that, Hul went on little foraging trips in abandoned buildings. Once he came back with a nice bottle of sherry. God knew how. After the third swig he offered me the bottle. He must have been surprised by how quickly I took it from him. We took turns drinking from it, and we had it half down by the time he got me within sight of home.

I can take it from here, I said, passing the bottle back to him one last time. He was no doubt more than happy to let me go. Before I took off, though, he grabbed me by the shoulder and said: Just act like your brother's already dead. That he doesn't exist. Because he doesn't anymore. Trust me, it'll be better that way.

Then he was gone.

The man with the white crossbow hadn't had much sage advice for me after he shot my brother an hour before. He didn't say much after he bound my brother, and whistled for some of his men to take Ciaran, and then gathered *The Children's Book of Heroes* into his arms. Another man picked up the gelcap with the wasp—which hadn't broken—and with a medicine dropper attempted to get what he could from the antidote that had spilled on the floor.

I want this room burned, he said to his men, in twenty minutes.

Then he turned to me and said, Your trials are over, Macy.

But they had only really begun. I wondered whether I should have put it together—that the nameless bounty hunter was looking for my brother all along. I knew that Ciaran was pushing

himself into dangerous territory—but *this* dangerous? Espionage dangerous?

And I wondered whether I would ever be able to forgive Ciaran. I'd been to family therapy with him before, with our whole
family, but that didn't help at all. Ciaran was still Ciaran. We
could have had small group sessions until the cows came
home—and it wouldn't have made any difference. We could
work and work at our relationship, strain to come to the barest
understanding about each other, and it still wouldn't matter.

I stewed about this as I recovered. I kept a lot to myself. Dad
let me crash for a week, until he sprang his plan on me. My leg
healed pretty well, but Dad wouldn't think of having me move
around too much. He didn't want me jostling the chakra, whatever that meant.

I was the only family he had left with him, so I didn't get
angry at him for saying stuff like that. I couldn't. But that didn't
mean I was thrilled about it, either.

And I did try to take Hul's advice to heart. I did try to pretend that Ciaran didn't exist anymore. But it was hard. Most impossible things are hard. I was still too pissed at him to be able to
turn him into some kind of a ghost. In fact, he was less of a ghost
to me than Sophia was. And Sophia was God knew where.

The sky was turning darker earlier and earlier. Dad had a big
party on the darkest day of the year—after which, the world was
supposed to get better. In a spiritual sense at least. Winter solstice
was a big deal for him. He told me he wanted to recognize the
darkness, and face it head on.

In other times, it would have been a Christmas party, but in
this case it was for Mithras, or a god like that. It was hard to tell
the difference when it came down to the details. There was good

food and a yulelike log and something resembling holly boughs, the works. There were a lot of people there—from Dad's neo-hippie circle of course, but also a few Lou politicians. Including the lieutenant governor of Missouri—what was left of it—who in a drunken haze of Everclear proposed marriage to me. He offered me a house and two hundred head of cattle. Luckily I was able to repel him with a promise to think about it.

Other than that, I was festive. The sangria helped. Jeremy danced with me to a small band covering Rihanna and Tom Petty on mandolin, fiddle, and kettle drum.

Dad had tried, valiantly, to keep Ciaran's troubles—and my wounds—quiet to his friends. But people found out, and afforded me a strange mix of warmth, pity, and hero worship. Everyone kept telling me how lucky I was.

I tried not to let it get me down.

Because my dad was happy. Even with all the astrology and loopiness, he was happy. And loved by strangers, or close to strangers. And it was good to see that. He needed that, after everything that had happened with Mother.

I mean, he danced. He *never* danced.

As the party was dying down, and after a kind of group prayer that involved (apparently) Aramaic and the stomping of feet, I started to help pick up the party mess. The house smelled good. Pretty soon Dad and I were alone, though we could hear people singing in the streets, and others telling those people to shut up, did they know what time it was already. But then the singing would start up again.

You don't have to help, Dad said, gesturing at the dishes I was shuttling to the kitchen.

Oh, I said. Not a big deal. I don't feel like sleeping anyway.

You haven't been sleeping much, he said. You need your sleep.
I looked at the floor and shrugged.

So we ended up helping each other out, and we got into a
cleaning rhythm. My first real job—I mean, besides mowing
lawns around the neighborhood—had been the summer before
as a dishwasher at a Shriners banquet hall. It was hard work and
my bosses were crazy. It was the only job I could find that summer and I was sick of hanging around at home. But the job was
miserable. Thousands of scorching, dirty plates, sanitized water,
and Shriner banquets with initiation rites. At times the kitchen
doors would swing open and I would see old men wearing their
funny hats, their underwear, and nothing else, dancing on tables.
They were assholes. Washing dishes after that helped me purge
memories of the Shriners.

I want to talk to you, Dad said, interrupting the silence between us when we were almost done.

Go ahead.

You're not going to like it, he said.

I could see he was choosing his words with care. I set a stack
of plates down. Dad, I said, laughing, I can't tell you whether I'll
like it unless you tell me!

Okay, he said, okay. He sat down. I need you to do me a favor.
But it's a huge favor, and I understand if you don't want to do it.
But I still need you to do it.

Talk about mixed messages.

Does . . . does this have anything to do with Ciaran? I asked,
sitting down.

How did you know?

I'm telepathic, Dad, didn't I tell you? I said.

Truth was, I was shaking. I didn't know what he'd ask me,

but I knew I wouldn't like it, and that it would probably get me angry.

Your brother will be on trial in Nueva Roma, he said. I don't know what that means. I'm not a lawyer. Someone from the capital has contacted me about it through a letter.

Dad, I don't know if lawyers exist anymore.

He ignored me, plowing on. I've asked around here a little but no one is sure what will happen. What the procedure will be. Since the trial is a result of the "interest of the Emperor." It's not part of provincial law.

I kept silent.

Okay, he said. I'm not going to beat around the bush. I need you to go down to Nueva Roma and make sure Ciaran is okay. That nothing happens to him or—

No, I said. I almost told him to fuck off, but held my tongue.

No—no to what?

You can't be serious, I said, crossing my arms. I'm not going down there. I don't even know what to say.

It looks like you want to say *something,* he said to me.

All right, I said. My face was red and hot. You know, Dad, let's leave aside Ciaran for a little bit. Remember how we almost died coming here? That was with a boat full of armed men. How am I supposed to get down there without dying?

God, Macy, do you think I'd ask you to do this if you wouldn't be safe? No, it's much safer from Lou to Nueva Roma. That's the heart of the Empire. Minnesota is on the fringes. There's a passenger ship going south in a few days. It's safe.

I thought about this for a bit. What he said made sense in that regard. That the closer we got to Nueva Roma, the safer it would get. But there was the larger question, the big elephant in our kitchen.

Here's the thing, Dad. Do you consider Ciaran part of the family? I said. After everything he's done?

Of course, he said, blinking. Don't you?

No, I blurted out, thinking of the cut my brother gave me. I couldn't sleep, more than anything, because I would have nightmares about him leering over me with his knife. And when I wasn't sleeping, when I was walking through Lou or doing chores, his image would pounce at me inside my head. I'd try to push it away but it would never leave of its own accord. It was only when I'd give up, exhausted and on the verge of tears, that his image would leave.

I know he did a bad thing, Dad said. But you have to go.

I don't. What, are you going to order me to go? I don't have to listen to this, Dad.

I was considering telling him about how Ciaran had cut me, but I still wanted to spare him. Maybe that was a sign more than anything that I was losing it.

I know you don't, he said. But we don't have much in this world except each other. And I just know that if Ciaran was given a chance to explain himself . . . I don't know. Perhaps there'd be a chance for his release. But I know, whatever history there is between the two of you, he'd be so glad to see you. I'm sure he feels terrible. He's alone, Macy. You'd be all he'd have, until you both come home.

There were too many questions washing over me to answer any of them. I didn't dare ask whether Lou was, in fact, home, or whether that concept could exist anymore.

Dad, he *is* guilty. I saw the antidote. He was taking it to the Scythians.

And the Empire is our great friend? he said in a low voice. And the Scythians aren't dying from the plague, too?

I clenched my jaw. He wasn't getting it. He was dense. That's not the point, Dad, I said. And besides, why don't you come with? Why can't we go together?

He said: I know, I know. That's why I said it wasn't fair. But I can't. The governor won't let me leave. He says I'm too important to the well-being of his district.

I could see the conflict on his face. One second, he was trying to push down his pride about how needed he was. Another second, I could tell that he was feeling guilty about this, not to mention sending me alone.

Also, he said, swallowing, my star charts for the next few months are dire at best. I shouldn't travel. Yours are much more auspicious.

You charted me? I said, snorting. Dad, I know that's important to you, but you can't rely—

I have to, Macy, he said. It's not what I *believe,* it's what I *know.* And what I *know* is that you'll be fine on this trip.

I paused and stared at him. He was dead serious.

Then I started laughing. I didn't know, even then, what had come over me. Except that it was absurd. It was all absurd, and it didn't matter whether I stayed home or went to Nueva Roma. At that point, I didn't care whether Ciaran lived or died—but I also didn't care whether I did, either.

The last few months had caught up to me, crashed over me, and I was too numb to care about what would make me happy.

Fine, I said. I'll go.

Really? he said.

Yeah, I said.

Oh, he said. He looked scared, tentative.

Are you having second thoughts, Dad? I said, smiling. My

voice sounded distant to me, like it was someone else speaking from behind a thick wooden door.

He shook his head and took my hand.

I let him squeeze it.

Three days later I was on the steamer *Victory,* heading south.

In my state, I wasn't sure of much when I started traveling south on the Mississippi again. But there was one thing I knew: I had no idea whether I could keep myself from strangling Ciaran when I found him.

I had no idea whether it was a journey of rescue or revenge.

The Shroud

When news of Ciaran's capture reached Nueva Roma, the Emperor declared a private holiday. The holiday affected about fifty members of his inner circle, as well as several immunologists who were researching the mating of rats and wasps. Word was given to those above. At the pinnacle of the Tower of Justice, an argent flag with a black bear at the center was flown for about two hours. Then the flag was hoisted down, furled, and placed in a glass box for safekeeping. This flag was Ciaran's heraldic standard. Every year, about ten to fifteen enemies of the state were given their own flags. It was considered a great honor. And since most of these criminals came from American families or noncitizen families that didn't have their own standards, there were no conflicts of interest with *The Book of All Heraldries,* which was painstakingly updated every year. The criminals had their own section in the book's appendix.

After Ciaran's execution—in theory, this wasn't a done deal, but nobody in the court considered any other outcome plausible—his severed head would be wrapped in his flag and tied up. Imperial physicians concluded many centuries ago that the human soul wasn't located in the heart, but rather inside the head. The heart's patterings were merely indicators of a false soul, which could not be trusted. Thus, part of Ciaran's soul would be transferred into the silver-embossed threads of the flag, and the outstretched paw of the angry bear. Many indentations of Ciaran's face would be transferred as well: the nose, the brow, the chin. The flag and the head—both property of the state—would be placed again into the glass box and stored for archival purposes. Future generations of Imperial citizens would be able to access the glass boxes during occasional public displays. In museums and churches, people could imagine, underneath the standards, the horror of those heads, and whether there was any contrition for evil deeds when it was too late.

The Empire specialized in arts of forgetfulness and remembrance. But whether a death was forgotten about or remembered, it was, above all else, to be accepted.

Ciaran knew none of these things as he was deported, blindfolded, on a prison ship down the Mississippi, nor would he know these things in his cell in the Tower of Justice. He would never see his flag while he was alive. It would be hidden from him until his spirit opened its eyes, and his soul bled into the cloth.

A secret committee of war widows sewed these flags. They considered it a form of penance, for their bad fortune to have married unlucky husbands. Their gods and saints were not smiling upon them. The woman who sewed Ciaran's standard had two sons, twins, who were about Ciaran's age. They were about to be deployed to the ruins of Atlanta. Her husband died on account of the plague. His body was lost somewhere in Alabama. She was given the flag's intended design by a clerk of the court astrologer—but as she stitched, next to a window overlooking the palms of a pensioner garden, and the waves of the Gulf of Nueva Roma, she tried to make the bear fierce. To give the bear a crazed look. She hoped that the criminal's afterlife proved to be fitful.

CHAPTER 16

Memphis Siege Time

CAN I SEE YOUR MAPS? I ASKED THE CARTOGRAPHER.

Huh, he said, as if he hadn't noticed me. He might not have. He had about a dozen maps spread out on his bottom bunk. Our cabin was one of the few private ones on the cramped, creaking *Victory*. The steamer was Empire made, built from nineteenth-century designs they probably dug out of an old engineering journal. The steam power was haphazard, to say the least; the captain had tried to fire up the engine once, just south of Lou, but I was scared to death from the hissing and screeching from down below when he did. Luckily, they must have decided to cool it, because the weird sounds stopped.

This is great, I said. It was only the first day and I was bored out of my skull. I missed Dad, somewhat. As much as I was able to tell myself I liked being alone, I still had an amazing capacity to feel fragile and sorry for myself one minute, and vicious and angry the next.

There were other passengers from Lou on the boat, but I didn't feel like mingling with anyone. The cartographer—I had no idea what his real name was—must have been in the same mood. We made a great team, eyeing each other.

He had lots of maps, though. And I wanted to see them. I pulled my coat tighter against a chilly breeze that blew under the door. The weather tilted toward balmy the day before, but then a freezing rain had set in. The weather teetered; it couldn't make up its mind. I had looked outside for a while, but didn't recognize the territory much. I didn't think it was part of any America I recognized: red-bark trees and large orange birds with snow on their wings that they shook off as they took flight. I'd never traveled this far south before, so my general expectations of the American countryside were from books and movies and the like. The banks were flooded and marshy, much like Lou tended to be. Mist covered everything at intervals that didn't make any sense. Boating must have been pretty nerve-racking. None of the banks seemed to be developed with docks or strip malls or marinas, but I might have missed them. I only saw a few shitty towns, worse than Fortune City, little slimy log hovels, clusters of houses that seemed ready to collapse into the river. No people to be seen. They were probably hunkering down or planning to leave. I would have. I thought of those families that were holing up in the Red Wing train station, way upriver, and I wondered what happened to them.

So, where are we? I asked him after another ten-minute silence, desperate not to go stir crazy. Why don't you show me where we are on one of the maps?

Papers rustled below me. He sighed. Then a hand shot up with a rolled parchment in it. I took the parchment.

Cool, I said.

What?

Uh, nothing.

I unrolled the parchment and squinted at it, moving closer to the tiny oil lamp that was set in the wall next to my headboard.

There were spiderwebs of rivers colored in a robin's-egg blue. There was a major, wide current depicted, but it snaked and I couldn't follow it with my finger. It looked like a series of ink spills rather than a map. But then I looked at it longer, and the waves of lines, and the dots that I assumed to be towns, came into some kind of focus.

I began to say: I can almost see where we're—

Sorry, the cartographer said. I gave you the wrong one.

His hand jutted up with another parchment, and I traded with him.

Which one was that? I said.

No idea, he said. But it was inaccurate.

I unrolled the new map. I didn't recognize *anything*. The colors were brown on gray. I couldn't distinguish water from land— and there *had* to be water, we were on it—for the life of me.

Where is this? I said.

Here. What we're passing through.

There were small etchings along the corners, and within the map itself, of animals—crocodiles, hippos, pronghorn elk, and lots more. Some seemed to be in battle with one another, or were positioned for battle. I looked closer and saw that the etchings might have been exquisite stamps, like the kind you'd buy—or used to be able to buy—in a scrapbooking store.

The hippos had devil horns I swore I hadn't seen before.

I hopped off the bed with the parchment.

The cartographer was looking at the maps spread on his bunk with a tiny monocle. He was also holding an oil lamp close to the parchment.

Careful, careful, he muttered.

Yeah, yeah, I said. I knelt down next to him and waited until I caught his eye.

Look, I said. This map doesn't make sense. Where's Arkansas? We have to be close to Arkansas, right?

Where? he said, turning back to his own maps.

There used to be a place called Arkansas, I said, pointing to an indiscriminate place on the map. It had the Ozarks. The Ozark Mountains. Arkansas was a state. I don't know. Maybe it's here somewhere?

The cartographer shrugged, and removed his monocle and looked at me, as if for the first time. These maps, he said, come from accounts. I travel to verify the accounts. I have scores of accounts. I have not committed many of these accounts to paper. Maybe I never will. Accounts are from reliable and less-than-reliable people—but they all end up in the morass of their . . . peculiar interpretations. Most accounts are all the same. They're not very helpful.

He cocked his head at me, like a parrot. Does this not frighten you? he asked me.

I guess I hadn't thought about it, I said, though I did think about it—maybe not in those terms—almost every day. And it did frighten me.

It frightens me, he said. And I'm in charge of this shit.

I laughed.

The river, he said, doesn't stop, and it doesn't stop changing. I'd like to see the headwaters, one day.

I'm from there, I said. Well, near there. Trust me, you don't want to go there. It's not very nice anymore.

He took on a bemused expression. Why don't you sketch out your homeland—what was its name again?

Minnesota, I said. That seemed as good an answer as any. I got a pang of homesickness.

Right, he said. For him, it must have been like any other

place name. Then again, we stole the name—and a lot more—
from the Indians. Now the name itself was of little concern to
cartography.

So I described Minnesota for him for about an hour. I told
him about the State Fair, and loons, and the charitable smug
people who I grew up around. And lots of other things. Goose-
berry Falls (where I almost fell and broke my neck when I was
six), the Foshay Tower, Aquatennial—hell, I threw in the record
of the St. Paul Central football team for the last three years. It
ended up being a kind of rant about the life I used to have, and
also about how those things were gone, and never coming back.
But the cartographer took it all in. He might have heard crazier
in other accounts.

When I stammered to a finish, he was quiet for a while, scrib-
bling notes. I wasn't able to see what kind of language or alphabet he used. When he was done, he put down his fine pencil
(graphite stick might have been more accurate) and said: This
will prove most useful, perhaps, at some time.

You're welcome, I said. Do you know much about Nueva
Roma?

You shouldn't be on the river, he said, with a forcefulness that
surprised me. It's very dangerous.

Yeah, well. My brother's in prison there, I said. I have to try
to . . . help him, I guess.

I tried not to let my ambivalence show, but I suspected I
wasn't doing a very good job.

I stand corrected, he said. You *should* be on the river, then.
I'm afraid these maps can't help you, though. Except for this one.

He handed me a small block of wood, no larger than two
notecards taped together. There were grooves that looked like insect burrowings, in intricate patterns that my eye couldn't follow.

What is it? I asked.

Nueva Roma. Or the center of the town. It's quite a detailed representation.

I see, I said, though I didn't.

Why is it a block of wood? I said.

Not all maps are parchment, he said. This one will serve you well. It can float, which is smart. I mean, I'm on a fucking boat full of paper maps, right?

I laughed.

Just hold on to it until you get there, he said. You should sleep.

I will, I said. Thanks.

I disembark in Memphis, he said, but I wish you luck on your journey.

As I tried to sleep that night, I heard him crying below me. I never found out why. I wish I'd known more about him. When I woke in the middle of the night, he was already dead by a stray javelin. I didn't know this at first. I was groggy and stupid when the sound and smell of fire woke me up. I didn't see the fire yet but there was acrid smoke in the air. *Victory* lurched. The cartographer was nowhere to be seen. There were shouts mixed in with the fire. I didn't like the sound of it. I jumped out of my bunk. Maps were scattered everywhere, but I didn't know if I had time to collect them. Which was smart, because I didn't.

Dawn was just beginning to come. I left the cabin and saw Memphis burning.

It was, of course, as much Memphis as Lou was St. Louis. Which was to say, somewhat. Along the river the fog had cleared—replaced with the smoke—and in railway yards and stockyards were broken obelisks of slender granite and schist. All these stones I learned about in geology class. I couldn't see what was written on them. There was a glass pyramid on a hill, where I think they used to play basketball games. Most of the glass was shattered. Winding between the obelisks were men on horseback, without stirrups, wielding bows and shooting into dim corners.

I stood there, dumbstruck. The battle—a battle I didn't know existed until now—had been won by the Scythians. This was the cleanup. A few giraffes also wandered among the obelisks, with plate-armored necks and empty saddles. I had no idea who could have possibly ridden them, and I wondered whether I would see Carl, the giraffe my brother had sold, in the field of battle.

Our boat was steaming into the middle of the cleanup. This had happened to me before, with only slight differences, farther up the river—when the *Nadir* had rescued us. But war, I was beginning to see, was like that. War stuttered, repeated its sentences, forgot its lessons, over and over.

Turn back! I heard someone above me shout. Everyone back to their berths!

But people were jumping overboard, taking their chances with the river and Memphis instead. I turned to face the bow, and I saw why. Ahead of us I saw about six triremes of black wood and black sails blockading the river at its narrowest point. The river made a sharp right turn—this was where the black boats held fast. I had no idea what tribe or nation they were from. I only knew that they were not Scythians, who couldn't build a boat if their lives depended on it.

We were unarmed and doomed, but I decided to stay on the boat. Bailing in Memphis seemed far worse. Even though I told myself I didn't care whether I died or not, I didn't expect to go

out like *this*. But I tried to be brave and cold, ready for whatever
might come.

I kept thinking of my mother, how I was glad she wouldn't
have to see me die like this, or have to be here with me.

I moved closer to the back of the boat, and tripped over the
cartographer's body in the process. He had the aforementioned
javelin in his back. I felt bad for the old guy; it managed to punc-
ture through my numbness. He had been surly, but pretty nice to
me at the end.

I heard shouts and a roar behind the *Victory*. I couldn't see
from my vantage point what the commotion was about.

Move! I heard shouted behind me, farther upriver than our
boat. *You fuckers, move!* Then there was a crash into the aft of our
boat. We were being rammed closer to the black-sailed boats
ahead. This wasn't good. The crunching of the wood was like
bone. I flinched. The boat tipped starboard and took water.

Fuck, I said, louder than I'd wanted to. A group of four men
ran past me. One of those men lurched to a halt once he was past
me, a short guy in a tattered FedEx uniform. I could tell that he
was thinking about hurting me. Maybe he wanted kicks before
dying, or to hurt someone before he got killed.

Do you speak English? he said. He had a Midwestern accent,
southern Illinois or Indiana maybe.

I tried not to shake, and pretended not to hear him. I didn't
want to turn my back on him. He moved closer. I could smell
sour alcohol on him.

Good, he said. Good. Then the boat lurched again and he fell
toward me, to his knees.

Then, trying not to startle him, I yanked the javelin out of the
cartographer. It slid out with ease.

I'm not doing this, I said to myself. *I'm not doing this.*

I spun the tip forward and jabbed the javelin into the man's open mouth.

I'm not doing this.

I had pierced the back of his throat. He stared up at me. He became a delivery driver again. I dropped my end of the javelin and stared at him. As he fell, his jacket broke open; he was using, as a liner, pages from comic books—Spider-Man and X-Men fluttered out.

I thought of Ciaran; I thought of him smiling at me and giving me the thumbs-up sign. I felt like I had to throw up.

Then I tried to run away from the deliveryman, but the *Victory* broke up for good. The last things I saw were the Imperial boatmen behind us on their prow, ramming us. I saw, in the dawn light and smoke light, their unyielding faces in the middle of defeat, their determination to use the *Victory* for cover and keep heading downriver for home.

For the next few hours after I hit the water, there were bits and pieces of memory, but they didn't add up to much. The memories were wet, soaked with what I couldn't see or understand—like how I had managed to hold on to a shattered plank of *Victory* and navigate past a naval battle. It made no sense. The battle had been winding down, but still.

I woke up groggy, holding on to the plank, in the middle of the river. I startled and almost lost my grip. I didn't know if I would have had the strength to tread water on my own, even for a little bit. There was fog all around me, and I couldn't see either bank. I felt like I was in suspension. I couldn't even feel the current moving me downriver.

After I caught my breath, I checked myself over the best I

could. Though the water was cold, it could have been worse, and aside from a few bruises on my arms, I didn't have any other wounds. Nothing horrible, compared at least to the memories of stabbing a man, and maybe killing him, which stuck to me like a leech.

He probably died anyway, I kept telling myself, repeating this over and over. He probably died anyway.

I then said it out loud. I thought it would help. It didn't. My voice died in the fog. This was what I thought the bottom was. Nueva Roma seemed like less than a dream.

I had to get out of the river, but had no idea how far I had to swim to reach either shore. I saw distant green lights on either side of me that would fade after a few seconds, as if there were giant fireflies in the fog. Then I would hear shouts—at first in front of me, and then behind me. I couldn't place them. Or maybe I was imagining them.

At one point in that haze, I saw about a half-dozen corpses float past me a few arm's lengths away, facedown, like a squadron of the dead rushing toward a battle the best way they knew how. I couldn't smell them and I had no idea how they were moving faster than me downriver.

After an amount of time that was hard to pin down, I was about to bite the bullet and try to swim toward one of the shores. But then I saw a large, curved shape in the river ahead of me, looming in the fog. At first I thought it was a whale. It wouldn't have surprised me. But as I drifted closer, I saw what it was, and I almost slipped off the plank then and there.

A submarine. And there could only be one submarine. The *Nadir of the M* was inert and there was no noise coming from it. The hull was bathed in an ethereal glow coming from pilot lights on both ends. There was also a haze of cindered smoke above it. I kicked my legs toward it, and when I reached it I grabbed one of the ladder rungs protruding from it.

Without thinking, I climbed the ladder. I wanted, more than anything, to get out of the river. The rungs were slippery but after a couple of false starts I managed to bound up to the flat platform at the top of the submarine.

When I reached the top, I stopped and tried to catch my breath. I was shivering, but I kind of forgot that I was on a submarine. It was cool. The vantage point still didn't break the endless fog but I did see those corpses keep drifting past the submarine.

It was dumb, but I pounded on the hatch with the flat of my palm. But sometimes dumb ideas work. I heard a lock loosen on the other side.

I pried the hatch open. I scurried in, grabbed a ladder leading below, and closed and bolted the hatch behind me.

Hello? I said. My eyes adjusted to the fluorescent light set into the ceiling; I squinted and saw that it was a kind of dried sea anemone affixed underneath a metal grate. There was only one door leading out. I opened it and found myself in a mahogany-paneled corridor, lit by small lanterns. The floor buckled. The submarine was submerging. I closed the door and bolted it shut. The paintings along each wall of the corridor were all creepy portraits of old people. They also didn't seem to be from one single time period—some were Roman-looking and some were even photographs.

Then I heard a dog barking somewhere ahead of me. I took a few steps forward. At the end of the hall, a dog turned the corner and faced me.

A rangy mutt with a lumpy head.

I squinted and stopped cold.

It was Xerxes. His head wasn't wounded, but it had ridges that I hadn't noticed before.

Then Xerxes started running right at me. I took a few steps back.

Stay away! I said.

He stopped halfway down the hall and lifted his head.

Macy! he shouted, in a wrenching voice that was not quite a dog's, yet entirely a dog's as well.

I swallowed hard. I knew at once what was going on, what had happened, even though it was crazy.

It wasn't Xerxes. It was William. My baby brother, William.

It was nuts, almost beyond belief, but after everything that had happened in Pig's Eye and beyond, not quite beyond belief.

William? I said in a soft voice.

Macy, oh Macy, he said. His tail was wagging. And then: Hi.

I couldn't help thinking of what Xerxes did to my mother. Was it his fault? Could a dog have a fault? But what happened afterward was anyone's guess—tossed into the river by my father, left to survive or drown, wandering starved for more than a month with all of those . . . changes. Ciaran had a gut feeling that Mother's plague had done something to the baby—accelerating his growth, for one. It wasn't much more of a stretch to think that William had somehow gotten *into* Xerxes. Crazier shit was happening all around me all the time.

Hey William, I said, getting down on one knee, still a little tentative. Come here.

He ran and pretty much pounced on me. I tensed, but he only licked my face, wagging his tail like mad.

I wanted to cry, because no matter how fucked up it was, I had family with me.

So sorry, he said.

No, no, it's okay, I said, scratching behind his ear. God, you smell.

I knew then that I had to protect my baby brother at all costs. If I could do that one thing, I reasoned, then maybe I wouldn't be such a colossal fuckup after all.

Then William tensed. He turned around and started barking at something farther down the hallway. It was a confused bark, like a person trying to bark and sound menacing at the same time. He bounded down the hall before I could say anything, but then stopped and waited for me where the hall branched in a T.

When I caught up with him, William looked dazed, like he forgot what he was barking about in the first place.

Look, he said.

I looked to where he was pointing with his head, to the left. At the end of a short corridor was a porthole made of thick glass. We were underwater, getting deeper every second. The view was lit only by a bluish light—from searchlights, I guess. The sub kept going down. I knew that the Mississippi was deep, but I was getting vertigo from our plummet.

At last, it leveled.

I heard footsteps behind us and had no idea whether we were saved or in even greater shit.

It was hard to turn away from the porthole. I gave myself a few seconds of serene, aquarium murk before I turned around.

William's Window

William's early life was full of calamity. He didn't remember being pitched off the *Prairie Chicken*. He woke up on a rocky beach north of Lou, after dreaming about a womb. He hurt! He hurt in lots of places, and missed the womb. In the womb were other voices—his brother, his sister. And most important the womb's owner. His mother! There was also his body that was protecting him. His body had four legs with paws. When it came time, William entered the body and had to get away! Others wanted to get away from him, too, but he still wanted to get away. What was happening to him!

There were only dreams of his first moments. William knew that his body had a life before William, but he couldn't say anything about it. His leg was broken, and he missed his mother. He vomited up a lot of blood. There were times, those first few nights, when he thought that he would never ever see his family again. He had to heal. He had a voice! He tried telling this farm lady about his voice, but she ran away. But he was still able to take some chickens from her. Then the farm lady's boy came. Late coming home from the Jesus place a few miles away. William decided not to talk! And he rolled over and the boy bandaged his leg. Then the farm lady came with a few men with knives and that wasn't so nice so William had to run away.

He ran to Lou and saw his brother from a distance. He barked and barked but Ciaran was being taken away! Ciaran might not have known that he was William instead of just a four-pawed body! Ciaran was in "chains." William knew about words like chains but wasn't sure how. He learned a lot of words just by wandering around and begging for food. He listened. It was a wonder that he didn't die lots of times. He decided to follow his brother because his brother needed him! So he followed him but then a funny thing happened because his sister passed by him on a boat! And he picked up her scent and then started following her through these swamps. He was about to burst with happiness thinking of her, until he lost her again. How was he going to keep track of his siblings; they were all over the place! He tried to follow but lots of men were fighting in a city and they were hurting these horses with long necks and that was not fun. He thought he was never going to get help but when the men were killing each other he saw a submarine in the river and he went inside! To ask directions!

CHAPTER 17

Fencing Lessons

It was Em. It had to have been.

You have a talking dog, she said. Her voice was deep but also lilting.

Yeah, I said. He's . . . he's my brother.

William craned his head back and forth between us, as if he wasn't sure we were talking about him. But then he figured it out and said: Hello!

Hmm, she said, crossing her arms. She was tall, that was for sure. But she had one of those chameleon-like faces that—at different angles, in different light—was hard to pin down.

She was also very pregnant.

Hello, William said, in a smaller voice.

Em bent down and scratched behind his ear and became more like a human being to me. William wagged his tail.

How did . . . how did you find him? I said.

Em smiled. He came swimming toward my craft farther upstream, she said, and I couldn't allow such a curiosity to drown, or die in the middle of a senseless battle. It appears that the two of you are of a feather, gravitating toward submarines like you do. So strange.

Yeah, it's pretty weird, I said, feeling awkward.

Although not *terribly* strange, she said.

You know many talking dogs? I blurted out.

I really expected to get my throat cut or something else dastardly. Instead, she laughed and said: A few, a few. An ex-boyfriend or two. Tell me, why should I keep you and your brother on board my craft?

It was a brilliant question, and I couldn't think of anything *practical* that would appeal to anything besides her sense of altruism or justice. And I wasn't even sure if she had either of those senses.

Please? William said.

We don't want to die, I said, we're just trying to get to Nueva Roma because my . . . other brother—

Is he a dog, too? she said. Perhaps a cat? Tell me, how can I know that you—

She pointed a finger at me.

—that you were once not a dog, and got transformed into a human being?

That pretty much stumped me. At first glance, it was an easy question to answer, but with another glance, it wasn't.

Well, never mind, she said. Even if both of you are dogs. In which case, you're lucky dogs. Because I have to go to Nueva Roma myself.

My brother's on trial for treason, I said.

She raised an eyebrow at me.

Are you going to rescue him? she asked.

No . . . no. Just to be there for him, and find out if I can help him.

It was a pretty halfhearted answer. I figured she was seeing right through me.

That's too bad, she said.

I didn't ask what she meant, whether she had any quick and easy rescue plans in mind.

At any rate, she said, clearing her throat, even though you're passengers, you'll have to work for your passage. Like a wooder. Do you know what a wooder is on a steamship?

Yeah. They feed the furnaces on the ships.

Right. And you're in the same boat. Since I don't expect dogs to work, I expect you to work double. And from the look of you, maybe harder than you've ever worked before in your life.

Where's the rest of your crew? I asked.

You *are* the rest of my crew, she said. For a few days. This is a solo operation, except for when I have . . . friends aboard.

I was going to ask her about the story of her old lover and ex-captain, whether it was true or not, but I bit my tongue.

What, I said, trying not to let my exhaustion show, do you want me to do?

Do you read? Can you count and do figures?

I nodded.

Good, good, she said. Come with me. She started down the opposite corner.

Wait, what about my brother?

What about your brother? He can sleep in the midshipmen's quarters, starboard and down the stairs. Of course, no one's there now. Food will be served twice—noon and midnight. I'm sure you'll see to that on your own?

I nodded. It turned out to be sealed peanut butter and jelly sandwiches and old cases of Crystal Pepsi that by some miracle survived the apocalypse. Still, I didn't mind, since I hadn't had a PB&J in ages. I could have eaten those five days a week in the best of times.

Good, she said. As for you, I doubt you'll be sleeping much. Now, like I said, come with me. You have a lot to do.

It would be difficult to describe the submarine without a lot of graceless bullshit. Part of me didn't want to describe it at all—not out of a prohibition, but rather clumsiness on my part. But I'll try. In a lot of ways, walking around with Em, or by myself, it didn't feel like a submarine at all. I never felt submerged—except for the times when I would stumble upon a porthole and see dark water, or else a sudden flash from a taillight illuminating startled gars and long sharks and giant angelfish. Or else the light would come from the fish themselves, like floating blue lanterns. I never found out how this Mississippi ecosystem developed. Once or twice I'd see ruins under the water, cast in that dim light—a gas station encrusted in coral, or a radio tower broken in two and pinned inside a crevice. It was pretty cool, and also sad.

Also cool was the galley with its hand-cranked ice-cream maker—not that I got to use it—and the exercise room that had a dozen medicine balls as its only equipment. The smallest was as large as my thumbnail (though it was still pretty heavy), and the largest was twice my size.

There were a lot of other wonders. The submarine contained more rooms than I could count. There *had* to have been a finite number of them, but I never seemed to reach the end of them.

Not wondrous was my job. It was hard work, and required me to use the math part of my brain, which hadn't gotten too much practice since Central High. I worked at a roll-away desk in a storage closet near the boiler room. Well, I thought of it as the boiler room since it was warm on that lower deck—and I tried not to think that actual nuclear energy was coursing through my body.

At any rate, I had boxes and boxes of records: a mix of parchment, sheepskin, stone tablets (small ones), papyrus reeds, and 3-Subject notebooks from Medea Paper, Cincinnati, the Ohio Territories. I had to look for the English language, and transcribe numbers next to the said English-language fragments onto a giant sheet of egg-white paper that fell over the edges of the desk. This was what the captain called the "proof."

What am I transcribing on the proof? I asked during my ten-minute orientation session.

Kill counts, she said. Be neat and be quick.

Most of them were in regards to the Upper Midwest. The sub must have had long-range capabilities beyond the pale. I wondered whether I would have recognized any of the names, like Jim Merwrus, who used to sit next to me in chemistry class, and always used to try to crib answers from me during pop quizzes. Not that I was any good at chemistry, so I had no clue what he was doing. He was a gung-ho type, and could have been conscripted. But I didn't see his name. There were too many to keep track of.

There were lots of town names as well. EPIPHANY, ILL., THEDELPHIA, ARK./LOUIS.; MEN, VIS. I didn't know whether MEN, VIS. was an abbreviation or typo. Lots of names, like I said. Male names and female names. Concentrating on this work meant I didn't have the time or energy to dwell on my own problems.

Once during one of her infrequent checkups I asked the captain whether she felt okay with all of this.

That stopped her. Felt? she said. Okay? What are you talking about?

All those people you killed.

I didn't kill them, she said. Missiles killed them. I just pressed the right buttons.

Those were . . . ordinary people, I said, not able to believe that I was willing, or stupid enough, to argue with her. Would she jettison me out, keeping my brother as a weird pet?

You're wrong, she said. No person is ordinary. You're more than welcome not to like the kill counts, as long as you do your job—and you're more than welcome to leave anytime. But if you don't intend on leaving, get back to work.

I got back to work. Trying not to feel like a prisoner. I wondered what Ciaran would have thought about being on the submarine. He probably would have tried to hijack it, which I had fantasies about as well.

I hate her, I told William a few hours later. It was during one of my breaks and sleep sessions. More like a power nap.

William raised his eyebrows. He was resting on the floor next to my cot.

I said: I mean, I know we're at war, or rather there are these fights everywhere, warlike activity. And maybe the people she killed would have killed *me,* or people like me. Oh hell, William, I don't know.

This is a sub, he said.

Right, we're on a fucking submarine, so it doesn't matter anyway, I said. I petted him. It was good to spend a little time with William. I had no trouble thinking of William as William and not Xerxes, which never ceased to surprise me. I took it as a gift and didn't delve too deeply into the matter.

The work cramped my hands. The transcribing of names was nonstop hell. She would always wake me just when I thought I was drifting into an actual deep sleep. She would tug at my sleeve.

Swing shift, she would whisper.

Every shift was a swing shift. After two days of this, I *was* ready to jump out of the hatch, sleep with the fishes and the algae-encrusted octopi.

Then she surprised me, when I was almost falling asleep while working, but too aching to sleep.

Put that pen down, she said, tapping my shoulder. That's enough of that.

As if it was my idea to write down an endless stream of names and I just couldn't stop.

I could have screamed. Instead, I set the pen down.

Good, she said. Now, let's work on your swordplay.

Excuse me? I said.

Come on, she said. We went through a new diagonal corridor on one of the upper decks that I hadn't noticed before. Set into the walls on both sides were glass cases with fish skeletons—some as large as my hand and some as large as my body. There were sharks, pikes, fish with fangs. The corridor smelled like a natural history museum.

She said: All those names are fake, by the way.

I was so surprised that I almost stopped, but I was also relieved in a way that I couldn't explain. I was probably just slaphappy.

No, she said, well, those people no doubt exist somewhere, and their cities and pathetic towns exist. But I didn't kill them. It was, how do you call it, busy work for you.

Just like study hall! I didn't say this out loud. I also didn't say anything about her "pathetic towns" comment, though I wanted to. My dad lived in one of those towns, and Sophia in all likelihood did, too.

I wanted to see, she said, if you would persevere with a ridiculous task set in front of you. But more important, I wanted to see how well you held a pen. The motion of your wrist.

Um, all right, I said.

We reached the end of a corridor and went down a set of steps. William was napping somewhere, no doubt. At the bottom of the stairs was a room with swords lining the walls, and a halogen lamp that hummed, giving the room a meat-locker ambiance. The swords were rapiers, scimitars, katanas . . . pretty much everything. She took a slender blade off the wall and handed it to me. I handled it as if it were a snake.

Now I can teach you to properly kill people, she said.

No . . . what? No, I said. That's not what I want at all.

Are you sure? she said. You've killed before, right?

It was hard to look her in the eye. I have, I said. I'm pretty sure. But he was trying to kill me.

That's all it ever is, she said. On one level or another. And if you were trying to kill him, it's the same difference.

She grabbed another sword off the wall similar to mine, and pointed it at me. She leaned toward me.

Now defend yourself, she said.

At that moment, I thought she was crazy all this time and the whole reason she took me onto the submarine was to run me through. And also steal William away.

I held my sword out in a certain way, leaning forward. I knew this much about swords.

Good, she said. She was graceful and lithe, even while pregnant. So different from my own mother, who had trouble walking while pregnant with Ciaran.

I . . . I don't know what I'm doing, I said.

Her sword's tip rattled the edge of mine, and her blade danced away.

I bit my lip and waited for her to attack again. She lunged forward and I parried, metal scraping on metal.

That is quite nice, she said. Spread your feet a little.

I spread my feet a little. She nodded and then said, Come at me, then.

I didn't hesitate. Something in me snapped; I was like a guard dog given a command to attack. An unskilled guard dog, but still. I didn't think. I slashed, whipped my sword arm around, and did my best to hurt her. She parried everything I threw at her, and she had a smile on her face as she countered me.

Good, she said. You need the fire first. The rest can be taught.

I slashed at her again and soon was panting hard.

Wait, control your breathing, she said. Take a break.

I put my hands on my knees. When I had caught my breath, she got into her fighting stance.

Now attack me again, she said.

I stared at her and then dropped my sword. It rattled on the hard floor.

Fuck you, I said. Fuck you and your swordplay. I really don't care about it, or any lessons after your bullshit fake names and bullshit kill counts. I don't want to learn . . . this. Kill me, or throw me off the submarine. I don't fucking care. But whatever you do . . . leave me . . . the fuck . . . alone.

She lowered her sword. A little embarrassed, I picked up the sword off the floor, put it back in its place on the wall, and left, hoping I wouldn't get lost. I was shaking. I figured Em wouldn't lance a defenseless woman in the back. So I had that going for me. I ran up the stairs and then through corridors with no rhyme or reason. In case it wasn't clear already, the *Nadir of the M* was a lot bigger on the inside than it was on the outside. I could lie, pretend that it only *appeared* that way, but I knew it wasn't true. I passed a room full of broken musical instruments—pianos, oboes, strings attached to oval stones. I moved on, trying to find my way back to my room and William. Not happening. I ended up collapsing in a rather small room that had a low ceiling and piles of newspapers. U.S. military newspapers from before the invasions, a few decades ago—with smiling soldiers and sailors, maps and timetables of deployments to minor and major wars across the world, christenings of nuclear submarines and battle-ships. I crouched and leafed through them, hoping I wouldn't get killed by Em.

I didn't cry while I idled there. I let the silence ease into me, and I realized with a start why I left my lesson with such a spec-tacular tirade: I didn't want to be like Ciaran. More than that, I was afraid I already was, and that nothing could stop me from sliding deeper into numbness and violence.

After a few minutes I heard footsteps. I didn't look up until Em started talking. She crouched next to me.

You know, she said, when I was your age, I would *not* have done what you did. I would have found a way to kill. I ended up hurting most of my teachers. I mean, they'd lose fingers. It ended up hurting me in the end. I never learned weakness as a virtue. I still haven't. But, as you can see, in a way I'm having that forced upon me.

It's not weakness. And it's not going to be like this forever, I managed to say, looking at her belly.

Will it? I'm not sure. I'm not sure how it's going to change me. Whether I'll want to continue my work after I have the baby. That scares me.

Is your work that important to you? I asked.

She didn't answer that question exactly. There was this boy I loved when I was your age, she said. This is making me sound old.

She stood up and stretched.

Well, I am old, she continued. Older than you. It's hard to think about how young I was then. We had a castle on the edge of the sea. Well, not really a castle. That was what my father called it. I entered the navy. . . .

I think I've heard this story before, I said, thinking back to that night of storytelling on the *Prairie Chicken* by old men I never saw again. That seemed like a long time ago.

Really? I've never told anyone this.

Why now?

Because I'm not sure what I make of you. I want you to be able to defend yourself. There are monsters out there, Macy, with two arms and two legs that live and breathe like you or me. People love them—parents, spouses, and friends. And they wouldn't hesitate to maim or murder you.

I know, I said.

But the swordplay . . . well. She coughed. I need to find a way for you to protect yourself that suits you, not me and my ego. And I need you, she said. I need you to do something for me.

This surprised me. What? I said, standing up, too.

First let me finish, and you can decide whether to accept or not. Anyway, I followed a captain. This wasn't good for me in the military, a good career move, but I didn't care. We were on the same vessel. I knew him when I was growing up. He was an ex-slave, his mother an Avar. He was never kind to me, but he considered me part of himself. It's beyond kindness and compassion, that consideration. You don't feel empathy about your own leg, or heart. That's what it's like with another who is yours.

I wouldn't know, I muttered.

You will. One day you will. But the important thing to remember is: not to act until you feel like this person is part of you. Until you're sure. You can move too quickly. That was my mistake.

She paused and I said: Was this vessel his? I looked around me to indicate the submarine.

She crossed her arms. You catch on. Yes, it was his. He lost his command because of me. He hasn't been the same since. And then the people who commanded us left, and soon enough there was just . . . me.

Sighing, she said: He isn't well. He's a bounty hunter and spy for multiple factions. The Avars, for one. But also the Empire. He gathers contracts like children collect butterflies or frogs.

And you think you can save him?

She nodded. It's about saving myself, remember? And once he knows about the baby . . . well, I'm hoping for the best. Let me describe him for you. It won't be hard to find him.

Holy crap find who? William said. He had found his way to us, God only knew how.

Can this . . . friend of yours help my brother? I said. I mean Ciaran. The one in prison.

I don't know, she said. Do you want him to? Do you want your brother to have help?

I didn't say anything for way too long.

Exactly, she said. You don't know if your brother deserves help. Which is fine. You need to figure that out before you start asking for help. Now listen: He is tall, spindly. An albino, or close enough to one. His name is Wye. He carries a crossbow. . . .

She went on a little longer, but my mind froze, and I couldn't concentrate on individual words. I didn't want to tell her that I knew him, that this was the man who had captured my brother.

It wasn't fair for Em or me.

When she was done, I managed to lift my head. If she saw my—what? Pure shock? Fear? Was I afraid of him?—she didn't notice. I asked her what the message was.

She squinted at me. I'll write a letter, she said. But it should be obvious, shouldn't it? Now come. We have an observation deck. We are almost to Nueva Roma. I want you to see the city as we come upon it.

William wagged his tail and bounded after her. It took me a few seconds to put my body in motion again, wondering what made a friend, what made an enemy, and which I would be to Wye.

The old Mississippi Delta was the last obstacle before the shining city of Nueva Roma—and although it made commerce difficult, it proved to be an almost impenetrable barrier against the barbarian tribes, who couldn't navigate the Delta if their lives depended on it. In the changes that had been wrought in the world, the Delta had lost its cities, towns, people, and animals. There were a few plants—lichens, mostly, and ferns. And deeper underwater, there were the freshwater dolphins and freshwater vampire squid and freshwater whales as large as the *Nadir of the M*. But the Delta, for the most part, was sludge and blight—shit-colored corals and ichor fogs, petrochemical refineries turned to slime domes. It was a half-day journey to navigate the crooked byways of the Delta, and it was not easy, even for experienced captains. Safety, for the Empire, was even more important than gold, although gold ran a close second.

The dead Delta made Nueva Roma, the island city in the Gulf, that much more desirable. That was the Empire's plan. Lafayette was the last town before Nueva Roma—named after a compatriot of George Washington, a friend of Americans and liberty long forgotten. Those who lived in Lafayette had no past, present, or future—only mud. Near the docks there were about three dozen trailers that used to be white. But the vinyl siding had been corroded and pockmarked, with every inch covered in indecipherable graffiti: eyes, devil tails, stars-and-stripes, shout-outs, fleurs-de-lis, thumbs-up signs. No one lived in those trailers; no one liked to walk by them alone at night.

At first, the Empire wanted to build Nueva Roma right at the foot of the Delta. But the military surveyors were too plagued with ghosts to even begin their work. Most of the ghosts were sounds—odd and faint strands of brass music that were a few bars off-key, as if out of deliberate neglect.

Let us leave, the surveyors told one another, this land is accursed.

They had left a few surveying instruments and a Mithraic sun obelisk, as tall as two men and encrusted with tourmaline and garnets, which they had used for prebuilding consecrations of the area. Within a few weeks, after several horrible rainstorms, the obelisk had tilted and sunk into the mud and waste.

CHAPTER 18

A Thousand Years of Peace

THE *Nadir* SUBMERGED JUST OFF THE SECRET DOCK WHERE I WAS standing. When the sub was gone, William said: That's air-affirming. I feel relieved!

Then William took a dump. I wonder if he had been holding it on the sub, which wasn't a dog-friendly place, to say the least.

I burst out laughing. Yeah, um, it feels good to be on land again, doesn't it? I said. My legs feel wobbly, though.

That got a canine *huh* sound out of William.

It was around noon. The air was hot and humid and I already felt gross. All around me were the towers and high-rises of Nueva Roma. I couldn't believe that I was, at last, here. I was caught between Em's generosity and the difficult, rather shitty task she gave me. William and I were in a small courtyard with yellow-vined walls. A raised, wooden sidewalk led to an open gate, which led to the rest of the city. It was deathly quiet, except for the breeze and gulls squawking here and there. I expected bustle.

Em was right to have shown me the approach to Nueva Roma. I'll never forget it, ever. The first sight of the island city's towers was almost worth all the trials and heartache that led me to the city in the first place. Maybe I'm romanticizing an imaginary feeling. But it was still pretty wild. The high-rises jutted up everywhere, leaving little space between them. They were all made of stone, not steel and concrete, but were almost all at least fifty stories tall. I should clarify a bit—it wasn't as if they were made of Empire State Building stone, but rather Chartres Cathedral stone, castle stone, even Pantheon stone. That is to say, dozens and dozens of skyscrapers built by people who had never seen a modern skyscraper before, or at least didn't care about modern architecture. I didn't know how they were freestanding, but they were. They all had teeny-tiny windows on each story. There were shapes between the towers that I couldn't quite make out. I had asked Em about them. I wished she had a telescope, like my dad had.

Drawbridges, she said. They can be put up in case of attack from another building. Most people don't use the streets; they use the skyways and drawbridges.

I liked to think at the time that she was sorry to see us leave, even though she needed me to go. And I wasn't sure how I felt about her. What do you do when a brutal person kind of likes you? It's scary but also kind of flattering. And we were tied together, however much my pacifist routine was an attempt to distance myself from her.

The dusty, cobblestone street on the other side of the gate was pretty much empty. There was a wicker cart at the end of the street that didn't have anyone attending to it. A couple of guys passed me, wearing turquoise scarves, looking at me funny. They were tall, and had raven-black hair. I turned my head. The streets were all narrow alleyways, the tall buildings creating deep shadows. Em had told me Ciaran would be held in the tallest high-rise in Nueva Roma—the Tower of Justice, how stu-

pid was that name. I'm sure it was a least-common-denominator
type of translation.

I had memorized the name of the ad agency Lydia's father
ran, and wondered whether to drop in on Lydia or not. I had lost
the wooden chip with the numbers she had given me during the
Victory crash, but I didn't know how much that would have
helped me anyways. I wanted to catch my bearings, in other
words, before I barged into the Tower of Justice. And moreover,
how much did Lydia and her family really know Wye? He had
traveled with them, looking for Ciaran. Surely there was a connection there, of some sort?

This is fucked-up crazy, depending on where we're going?
William said.

Yeah, pretty much, I said. Now, be sure to keep quiet.

Why?

So people . . . don't find out that you're a talking dog.

Why?

So . . . I don't know. So we don't get burned as witches.

I turned onto another street. None of them were marked.
Some of the building fronts had animal emblems carved into
them—a griffin here, a manticore there. Once again, Warcraft
came in handy.

This is hella hard, he said.

I gave him a dirty look and he simmered down. Where did
he get such a potty mouth?

I heard many hooves rumbling behind me. William barked.
Okay, that was doglike. I thought that the rumbling would pass,
but the sound grew louder, then the sound turned the corner and
I saw two chariots bearing down on me. Heads popped out of
lower-story windows like Whack-A-Moles, and people started
babbling, even exchanging little tusks and coins between win-

dows. Each of the chariots was pulled by two horses. I had no idea how they fit into the cramped street. Their wheels jostled. I heard the iron screech. And the horses weren't quite horses. They were smaller, but not ponylike at all. Not like the Scythian horses, either. Meaner, even. They were sorrels and had nubs, the beginnings of horns or antlers, on their foreheads. Their mouths were all frothing like they were rabid.

All of the detailed description, of course, was from a few seconds' observation in the middle of trying to get my brother and myself the fuck out of the way so we wouldn't get trampled by the demon horses. I dived toward the eaves of a griffin door. There was a guard there; he thought about pushing me back into the street, I could tell, but he saw my terrified look and let me stand there. Or maybe he had a bet on the race and didn't want to deal with me. Cool air hit my back. William sat, serene and picture-perfect.

In no time, the chariots blew past us in a wave of spittle, iron, and horseshit sounds and smells jumbled together. The two charioteers, neck and neck, were whipping each other, not the horses. Past them, almost right on their heels, came a crowd of spectators. Or rioters. It was hard to tell. Most of them wore turquoise scarves, like the ones I saw on the two guys before, but a sizable minority wore teal scarves. I was glad they were ignoring me and my brother. Except for one guy, near the back, who was a little pudgy and out of shape, wearing one of those teal scarves. He had a nasty gash on his forehead and blood was streaming from it. He was like eighteen or something.

You nearly got killed! he said, standing in front of me and shaking the dust off his breechings. Yeah, they wore breechings. And sandals.

He knelt to pet William. Hey, boy! he said.

William wagged his tail. I hoped to God that he wouldn't use any of his "dog boy on acid" slang.

What *was* that? I said, hoping that he'd wipe his forehead or something, because it was gross.

Wow, you're really not from around here, are you?

I shook my head. I'm from . . . up north, I said. The guard to the building coughed and I stepped out of the doorway. The boy gave the guard a crude hand signal that looked like a cross between a shadow puppet duck and a shadow puppet bunny.

Aren't your friends getting away from you? I said.

Oh, them? Well . . . I won't be much use in the fight. He pointed at his forehead and laughed. So the north? he continued. He started walking and William started following him, so I followed, too. I figured that I could do a lot worse than this guy, and he seemed pretty harmless.

Yeah, I said. I tore off a little corner of my shirt—one of Em's spares—and handed it to him. He smiled at me and put the cloth on his bleeding forehead.

Thanks. Did you see any fighting up there? he said.

The stupid guy I killed flashed in my mind again. He was stuck there. I wanted to exorcise him.

A little, I said. I couldn't look him in the eye.

That's insane! he said, not noticing my discomfort. I hear they're coming for us. That they'll be invading Nueva Roma any month now. Or at least try to, as if! The Teals will be there, no doubt!

He made an elaborate gesture near his scarf with his free hand.

Listen, I said, stopping him. Do you think you could help me find a friend?

I told him the name of the ad agency, Advance-Net Jackal or something. I hoped I got it right.

He looked at me with wide eyes. Those are your friends?

Well, kind of.

Those people are friends to Teals forever! Yeah yeah, I know where they're at, come on.

He started running, although rather slowly, since he was already out of breath and bloodied. It was easy enough to keep up with him.

He cut through the streets like he knew where he was going, so that was good. When he stopped for breath the second time, I asked him: So what's with the colors and the scarves and the races?

Well, the Teals are only *the best* charioteers in the city. Sure, we don't have as many members as the Turquoises, and we haven't been around as long as the Aquamarines, *but* we're much stronger than the Beryls, who are total pussies.

So you just . . . race? I said.

Race, and fight to keep the peace, and run for city council! We run the streets! Well, all of the four colors combined run the streets. The Teals run about a fifth of the streets. Come on, we're almost to one of our buildings. And we can get to your friend from there.

Sure enough, in a minute or two we ducked into the lobby of one of the high-rises, this one made of sandstone and granite, and about sixty stories high. Above the main doors was an elaborate mosaic of a teal kraken tearing into some boats on the high seas. The lobby wasn't quite as comfortable as the other building earlier, but there was still plenty of cool air. The vestibule had a small fountain and something resembling an elevator platform.

I think we can get across from the twelfth floor, he muttered, going to the platform.

How do these run? I said, stepping onto the platform uneasily.

I don't know, he said. Hydraulics or slaves or something.

What? I said.

Hydraulics or—

I heard you, I said. I'm just a little shocked—

The platform shuddered and we clanked upward. It was terrifying, more terrifying even than the riverboats or whatever else backassward gear passed for technology anymore. I lost the capacity for speech. The elevator platform lurched to a halt on each floor, but only for a second or two.

Get ready to jump, he said near the twelfth floor.

William looked ready to jump a few floors early, but he held himself.

We made our jump and our Teal guide looked determined to get us to the right place. Which was endearing. We found ourselves in a narrow hallway decorated with potted, violet-leaved palms, and a grill, on which small, ratlike bodies were sizzling.

Like I said, we run the streets, he said. But we don't run the upper floors. When the city floods, we try to fight our way up to live. It's not easy.

That would be a nightmare, I said.

He just scrunched his face at me and turned away.

The public corridors were narrow and more crowded with people than the streets were. I realized this was where most of the city's action was. Everyone was shoulder to shoulder, from all parts of the Empire: Nueva Roma, of course, but also Thracian expats in goat-hair tunics, long-haired hayseeds from Texas (or at least wearing Don't Mess with Texas shirts), and many

many other people from places I couldn't place, from lands I didn't even know existed. I almost tripped on two discarded fish heads that were tied together with a piece of string.

We reached the drawbridge connecting two towers. The drawbridge was open-aired, made of thick iron and planks, manned on each side by guards in black armor. I hesitated before the drawbridge, but our guide took my hand, which was warm and shaking.

It's okay, he said. Everyone's scared the first time.

But I wasn't scared of falling. I was more scared of the soldiers. I was paranoid that they would somehow know that I was Ciaran's sister. That his mark was on me somehow. But they didn't give me a single glance.

I didn't let go of his hand until we crossed. What's your name? I said.

Oxna, he said.

That is, I thought, the worst name anyone could name their child.

What does it mean, I said.

That surprised him, and he stopped this time. A thousand years of peace, he said.

And then I understood. That's cool, I said. One of the guards squinted at our stopping, but we were soon off again.

One more stretch of jostling skyway, a cramped elevator with a woman delivering something resembling spinach pizzas piled high on wooden trays, and a last flight of stairs.

Then we found ourselves in front of a stone archway on the thirteenth floor that said: ADVANCE-NET JACKAL INSECT, with an elaborate bas-relief carving of, well, a jackal insect. An Anubis scarab.

William was panting. He needed water pretty bad; it had

been a long haul. I knocked with the heavy metal knocker set
into the thick oak door. After a few seconds, a middle-aged
woman opened the door up a sliver, and peeked out. She was
bleary-eyed, and had her hair in a peach bow.

Yes? she said.

Hi. Is, uh, Lydia here? I asked.

Who are you?

Well, I'm one of her friends from . . . from the river tour.
And I'm with my dog and, um, another friend.

Smooth, I thought.

She opened the door a little wider. Are you Macy? she said.

Yeah, I said, surprised. That's me.

She put her shoulder against the door and heaved it open.
Oh, this fucking door, she said. She was in a yellow kimono and
boozed up. Lydia's mentioned you, she said. It's so wonderful
you could join us. Come in, come in.

We stepped in. The room was giant, and was decked out in
all manner of knickknacks and plunder. A lot of it no doubt was
acquired on their tour, bartering poor people down for fun and
authenticity, and also taking what they could when no one was
guarding it. Rugs, paintings of an Ibis-like Elvis and Osiris-like
Carl Perkins, gold bowls, amethyst goblets, spangled electric
guitars, an autographed photo of a random monk, the works. In
the midst of all this mess were the vestiges of an office, no doubt
the "creative" space, set with a huge worktable strewn with colored pencils, rolls of parchment, and more trinkets.

Introductions were made. Oxna was wide-eyed. The woman
was Lydia's stepmom, Crystal, who used to coach soccer and
teach marketing at Bloomington Jefferson High School, back in
Minnesota.

It's so good to have someone else here from Minnesota, she

said. She clapped and a woman from a shadowed corner of the room came and presented a bowl at William's paws, and then glass bottles of water for Oxna and me. I thanked her, but she ignored me. We drank up. The woman retreated to the corner, but not before fetching Crystal a fresh Manhattan. I tried not to be creeped out.

Where's Minnesota? Oxna asked.

Up north. Way up north, I said. It's our homeland, sort of.

No, it *is* our homeland, Crystal said, and we should be proud of it, the values it stood for.

I didn't say, though I wanted to, that Minnesota was broken and ravaged.

Crystal touched the edge of Oxna's teal scarf. We designed these, she said. Oxna gave her a goofy smile.

You really are in the Teals' corner, he said. It's been huge—

The stepmother laughed, and it was cutting. No, no, she said. Our brand-identity team designed the logos and apparel for *all* the colors. The street campaigns are designed so that each color thinks they're the unique target—that no one else "gets" them, their unique needs.

Crystal made the quote mark sign with her hands, which I'm positive Oxna didn't get. She squeezed Oxna's shoulder and said: Our little secret, okay?

Oxna's shoulders sank.

Oh, blessed! William said after he was done with the water, but it came out as a sloppy cough, and no one registered that William was saying something. You know, dogs sometimes sound like they're trying to say something, isn't that funny?

So, uh, Lydia is here, right? I asked.

Oh, stupid me, Crystal said. She's in her room. She's probably dying to see you.

She took a swig of her Manhattan and called out, Lydia! Lydia!

No answer.

Well, Crystal sighed, rolling her eyes. She's in her room with one of her friends. Macy, feel free to barge in and haul her out here. And Julia—Julia, can you come here?

Julia, the woman who was in the corner, stepped forward. She was about twenty, and dressed in some outfit that was supposed to look maidlike but had more of an "I'm dressing up like the Amish for Halloween" look. She was blond and pretty and the first thing I looked for were bruises or marks on her wrists. Red grooves were there.

Julia is *not* a slave, Crystal said, out of nowhere. She's from Wabasha. We're keeping her until she has the money to pay off her debts to us. I just want to make that clear.

She pointed her drink at me. Just so you don't get any weird ideas about what type of people we are.

Sure, I said, taking a couple of steps back from her. Okay. I'm . . . going to see Lydia now.

Crystal put on one of her crystalline smiles. It scared me that it seemed genuinely warm and not psychotic.

I went in the general direction that Crystal pointed to, and passed a kitchen that was as large as the living room in our old house in St. Paul, hearing the trickle of running water and the cawing of unknown birds from a nearby open window. I caught a glimpse of the sun. The light striking the other towers was something to be seen. I heard a flute playing from the end of the corridor, what I took to be Lydia's room. The door was a thick black curtain with a white skull painted on it. I was nervous— what should I say to her?—as I pulled back the curtain.

It took a couple of seconds to adjust to the dim light. When I did, I saw that Lydia was in bed with a man, a man who was kissing her neck. A pale man with long locks of white hair.

They didn't notice me at first, but when they did, they froze.

Macy? Lydia said. Oh my God, Macy?

I took Em's letter from my back pocket, not quite believing that I already had the chance to deliver it. This is for you, I said to Wye, thrusting it out to him, doing everything I could not to throw it at him.

Time, and motion, then rushed in.

Jesus, Macy, what are you doing here? Lydia said. Why did you barge in like that? What the hell are you doing in town?

She straightened out her shirt and looked embarrassed. Wye, however, didn't. He stood up and cracked his back. I wanted to growl at him. I eyed his crossbow in the corner of the room. The flute playing kept going—it was jaunty and absurd. It reminded me of the Jethro Tull records my dad used to play, which I would try not to laugh at.

But the music was no less absurd than finding good old Lydia in bed with Wye, the man who had hunted down Ciaran and had who knew what other star-crossed fates on his conscience. If he had one. Not to mention Em. Em loved him. Maybe it was a character flaw of Em's all along. Maybe her letter admitted as much.

Wye then noticed what I was holding out for him.

A letter? he said, yawning. Who is this from? Have you come all this way to give me this? Is this from that governor of Missouriland?

No, I said. I came for my brother. But someone wanted to give you this.

Even though I still wasn't sure whether I was going to help Ciaran or not.

He saw that I wasn't fucking around. Lydia looked around at both of us.

What the *fuck* is going on? she asked. Wye?

Wye ignored her. He took the letter. I tried not to take a peek at Lydia.

When Wye saw the seal, his eyes widened, and then he wasn't fucking around, either.

Where did you get this? he said, jabbing the letter toward me, as if I'd stolen it.

You know where I got this, I said. Isn't it obvious?

You were on my . . . her craft?

Of course I was. I think you should read it.

I'll read it when I want to.

Your choice, I said. I guess. But it's pretty important. She wouldn't resort to using me if it wasn't.

Lydia burst out: Who's *she*?

Wye stared at her, as if he'd never seen her before in his life. Then Lydia leaped off the bed and ran out of her bedroom, crying.

That stupid flute was still going strong.

Would you *please* stop playing? Wye shouted to the walls. Maybe Lydia bribed the house musician for an hour's time off the clock. The whole thing was freaking me out, but all the same, I almost felt jealous of the two of them. No, jealous of everybody, except maybe Ciaran and other unhappy people of the world. Pent-up people, like me.

At last Wye opened the seal. He glared at me but I was in no mood to move. He sighed and read the letter, which was on old stationery of a navy that didn't exist anymore. After he read the letter, he dropped it.

When? he said. When will it . . . happen?

I'd say a week or two, at most?

And how does she look? Is she okay?

She's fine. Moving around well.

He looked up, staring at the ceiling.

I need to go, he said, more to himself.

I can't believe you were fucking around with Lydia, I said.

He laughed. Do you realize it's none of your business?

I was scared but kept pressing on. It is, I said, because I'll be more than happy to tell Em about it, unless you help me.

He stood up, laughed, and went to the corner to retrieve his crossbow, which wasn't a good sign. But he slung it over his shoulder and said: You wouldn't.

I would, I said.

This was dangerous shit. I had no idea if he would be so tied to Em, in the end, that he wouldn't want her to know about any impropriety. That in his mind—and hers—they were still together. If it took playing to his soft spot, well, he deserved it. Not all of it added up, of course. After all, he caught Ciaran, who was a liar and a thief and tried to kill me.

What do you need? he said, exasperated. What could you possibly need?

I need to speak with Ciaran, I said.

You're joking, right?

That's why I'm here in Nueva Roma. To meet him and help him if I can.

Oh, please, he said. Your brother's a menace. He doesn't have a soul.

I kept staring at him.

He bit his lip, and squinted at me.

All right, he said. Fine. I can *try* to get you an audience with your brother, if you want it. His trial starts next week; after that, you won't have much chance. Meet me tomorrow at noon on the twenty-fifth floor of the Tower of Justice. He handed me a gold tusk from his pocket, carved with serpentine grooves. This will get you in, he said. I should be going.

Thanks, I said.

The letter . . . he said, trailing off. It's good news, isn't it?

He didn't seem too sure. His doubt softened his features for a moment, made him look haggard.

I think so, I said. Yeah.

He nodded. It seemed the news in the letter was only then beginning to sink in. He left. A few minutes later, Crystal came in the room and almost fell onto the bed. There's a *parrot* loose in the *kitchen,* she said. I have no idea how it got there. We never *bought* a parrot. Where's Lydia and her friend?

I shrugged. So much for parental oversight.

Where are you staying in the city? she asked. With your parents? Are they settled someplace nice?

No . . . I'm just here by myself. With my dog.

Oxna and William must have still been in the vestibule. I hoped they weren't bored out of their minds, or scared out of their minds by Crystal.

Well, you must stay here, Crystal said.

Well . . .

No. You must stay here. It's so hard for young people to get a start on their own two feet, especially these days . . .

I managed an okay. I asked about Oxna, but he had left. Which was fine with her, the snob, but it made me a little sad. I doubt she offered him anything for his forehead. That was the last time I ever saw Oxna. I had half-expected that we would have future adventures together, that our lives would intertwine more. But life doesn't work like that all of the time.

Crystal showed me to a massive, quiet bedroom with white and coral walls, a wide window letting in sea breezes. Ships were as small as june bugs or water-skimmers from this height. William came into the room with me, carrying a large turkey drumstick, which Crystal found hilarious. Then she left, to freshen up for a party.

William started chewing on the bone. I collapsed on the bed.

Do you mind if I sleep? I said. I was ready to collapse.

I have a giant mind, William said. Ciaran? The baby brother is next?

Ciaran *was* the baby brother, to all of us. Regardless of age. He always seemed the strongest and toughest, but it was only a way to cover up his weakness. And he had fooled everyone, including himself, for a long time.

I crashed with the first real good sleep I had had since Lou. When I woke up, it was just before dawn. Lydia was sitting at the foot of my bed. She was wearing a pink headband and sweatpants and big sunglasses and I just wanted to laugh.

Hi, she said.

Hey, I said, still groggy. I craned my head to see if William was around, but he was off gallivanting.

Look, I'm sorry— I began.

She leaned down and kissed my forehead. It's okay, she said. It's really okay. It's not your fault. I should have posted a guard or something. So you wouldn't have had to have seen that.

Um . . . okay, I said. Do you know what any of this is about?

I love him, Macy. I really do. He doesn't understand that yet. But he has to.

Look, I said, it's a little more complicated than that—

You're meeting him, aren't you?

Well, yeah, but just because—

I *have* to come with you, Macy. I have to, to explain where I'm coming from, how much he means to me. I mean, I know he has a checkered past, but who doesn't these days? Sure, that letter might have been from some old flame—but it doesn't *mean* anything anymore, does it?

I sank back down on the bed and covered my face with my hands. You're fucking hopeless, I thought. Love—or your crush, whatever—has made you fucking hopeless. I said: His lover is pregnant, Lydia. The baby is due this month. And he's going to go with her. Look, I'm sorry—

You're making this up! she shouted. You want him for yourself!

You're fucking hopeless, I said.

At last, saying what I actually thought!

You know that? I continued. Fucking hopeless. Yeah, I want to bang the guy who hunted down my brother. Uh-huh. That *turns me on,* Lydia.

She sat there in stunned silence and then started crying. I let her cry. After about a minute, she said: I'm sorry, Macy. I don't have any friends. You're right, about all of this, but I still love him.

I grabbed her hand. Try not to think about it, I said, at least for a little while.

William came into the room and bounded onto the bed. I let go of Lydia's hand. She gave a little jolt of a laugh as William curled up on the bed between us.

Too much unmoored, he said.

Lydia looked at William, and then at me, with no small measure of surprise.

Uh, cat's out of the bag? I said.

We sat and talked for a couple of hours, and it was good. I

tried to explain where I had come from—literally and figuratively—the best I could, and where I had to go. It was hard to explain the talking dog, and the submarine, and my mother dying, but I did the best I could. I also tried to talk about a few good things, wonderful unreal sights, sharp pangs of joy in the middle of chaos. And how my dad actually seemed at peace. Just to make my life seem less of a total downer. Lydia talked about her life, too, how much she hated her stepmom, and was numb about her father (which was even worse than hatred).

She also said that I needed to take it easier on myself. I asked her what she meant.

You've been through a lot, Macy, she said. You've, like, been in shit that would have turned me into a complete wreck. So it's okay to be a little bit nicer to yourself, and not think that you're doing a horrible job with everything. Because you're not. Right?

I guess not, I said, blushing a little.

You might have to forgive your brother at some point—maybe you will, maybe you won't. But you have to forgive your-self, too, for all the bad stuff you think you did.

I told her that I would take that to heart, even though I only had the slightest idea how to go about that. Just saying to myself *Hey, I forgive you!* wasn't going to cut it. There had to be some-thing deeper, something I couldn't see yet.

Then, she expressed her hope I would punch Wye in the lip for her when I saw him.

I didn't do that, though I was tempted. I didn't know what the hell he was thinking fooling around with her. She had known him for a while, at least in passing, from the river tour. She must have thought he was dangerous, and he was.

But was that all it took to fall head over heels for someone? That and white hair and a wicked-sweet crossbow?

A Case History

Things began to fall apart for the Palmers when Ciaran was born. It was a difficult birth for Grace and almost killed her. The doctor was a glad-handing misogynist, which didn't help matters, and when Grace was almost dead, the doctor didn't notice until Carson shook his shoulders hard. Like: *wake up, wake up*. And so Grace didn't die, though the labor took more than forty hours, and she was in the hospital for three weeks, and Ciaran had to use a respirator. Macy was too young to know what was going on, but Sophia wasn't, and she spent a lot of time in the hospital with one of those hospital gowns and shower caps. When Carson had to teach, she would play crossword puzzles with her mother and watch *Hollywood Squares* with her. When Ciaran was well enough to be removed from the respirator, Grace would let Sophia hold her brother. Carson wanted to sue the doctor but Grace wouldn't allow it. She had had enough and wanted to rest. Painkillers helped her rest.

Ciaran was both fragile and fierce, even from a very early age. He didn't change much throughout the years. In some ways he would never change. He always drained his immediate family, and also his aunts and uncles, visiting from Columbus, who seemed to regret the trips west almost immediately after setting foot in the Palmer house. Ciaran would set things on fire, like his hair. He didn't care. Their pediatrician told his family that the boy was far less sensitive to pain than anyone else he'd ever seen. He ripped books in two, shat in books, spat in books. At the same time his parents knew that he wanted love. But it wasn't love they were able to give him, or—best case—fully give him. He was like an addict, but no one knew what would satiate him, what he was hooked on. Except perhaps fire—but how can you cut out fire from the world?

Grace and Carson weren't parents to coddle Ciaran with material things, nor with sports-lifestyle choices and overregulated stimulation. They sent him, instead, to incompetent professionals. Their incompetence was luck of the draw, like the obstetrician. The professionals who had been referred to the Palmers had fallen through the competence net, and sought, in Ciaran, to purge their own demons. All psychotherapy of that era would have an element of that, a tense dialogue between two adversarial personalities, or parts of personalities. A prisoner and a negotiator. But well-meaning directives to Ciaran—given, of course, in the nicest tones possible—turned more shrill, session after session. Ciaran broke therapists like toys. The state revoked one license on account of him, after one counselor threw back a toy tractor that Ciaran had thrown at him.

For a few years, after Ciaran entered kindergarten, Grace tried to take him head on. She read books on discipline and tried with all of her might to implement rules. Disciplining Ciaran became her hobby—her life pursuit. But Ciaran won. Ciaran was impulsive but also had everlasting patience. The state, almost by default, ended up investigating the Palmers for signs of abuse, but found nothing. Even at seven and eight, Ciaran would tell his therapists that his parents loved him, and never hurt him. What's mine is mine, he would say. Grace was never the same after she lost. She became drained, and struggled to regain her energy for the rest of her life.

Ciaran almost welcomed pharmacological solutions. The incompetent talk therapy gave way to paint-by-numbers psychiatrists who would talk to Ciaran for ten minutes about school and football and write out a prescription before returning to the gated community in Eden Prairie along the golf course. Ciaran took the drugs, but they did little to affect him in a positive fashion. At times the drugs would make him sleep for two days straight, and at other times he'd trash his room with great thoroughness. HMO-approved psychiatrists would try different drug cocktails with him. They treated him like a dog testing different types of dog food. Grace and Carson hated this. The drugs seemed to have no consistent bearing on his behavior. Then there would be times he seemed to grow tolerant to a drug that seemed to be working okay for a few months, and they'd have to start all over again. When Ciaran entered eighth grade his parents stopped the drugs altogether and started acquiring brochures for military and boarding schools for the troubled.

And then the Scythians rode upon St. Paul.

Despite his troubles, and the troubles he caused, Ciaran was capable of great love. He loved his mother a great deal, and his father almost as much. Sophia, too, and William later. And Xerxes, until Xerxes turned on him. He loved his family—except for Macy, and he only stopped loving her when she turned on him. He wanted to become something larger than he was. When the war began, and the Scythian agents approached him in Lowertown about smuggling a package—an antidote that could save thousands upon thousands of lives—he took it upon himself to love his mission. He wanted to save lives. He didn't want anyone hurt—he just wanted stupid people hurt, and people who would hurt him hurt. He would dream about Scythian babies dying of the plague just like his mother, and he couldn't stand it.

After he was caught, he imagined what his trip up the Missouri River would have been like, with many adventures of his own involving more daring escapes and more strange animals and sights, and in the end being greeted by the Scythian king (one of them, anyway) on a white horse, wearing dazzling gold armor. The king would thank him profusely, and would give him the people's love. And he would love them back. Then he would be able to pick a horse of his own, and he would pick a white one, just like the king's.

These loves, these desires for good, could not be extricated from the demons.

They *were* the demons.

CHAPTER 19
Justice League of Nueva Roma

THE NEXT DAY, I GAVE MYSELF PLENTY OF TIME TO REACH THE Tower of Justice. It turned out that I needed it. I brought William along. His sense of direction was distracted by the bustle of the city's skyways, but I needed a familiar face to get me through this ordeal. And besides, I figured Ciaran would want to see William alive and well.

I didn't want to chance the street level again. I didn't want to get caught in any more hooligan chariot races. The sky had clouded up and threatened rain. A couple of times, backtracking, I got weird stares from passersby, but I ignored them. This wasn't my city; it was natural for people to stare at a girl like me in a place like that. A few times closer to the Tower I was stopped by drawbridge guards, but I showed them the gold tusk Wye had given me and they hurried me along. I took stairs, not trusting those hand-cranked elevators.

All my traveling had kept my mind off seeing Ciaran again, but it hit me as I was walking—I had no idea what Ciaran would be like. It seemed entirely possible that he would be more damaged. Prison and treason charges tended to do that to people. And I had no idea what I would say to him. Did I come all this way to extract an *apology* from him? No. I didn't know if he would be capable of it. But what, then? With each step closer to him, I got more and more edgy, because I didn't know.

When I crossed the final skyway onto the twenty-fifth floor of the Tower of Justice, I found Wye sitting next to a fountain that was encrusted with various jewels. There were small gold tusks in the water. It didn't seem that many children would make it up to the twenty-fifth floor to throw in money and make wishes. Wye stood up when he saw me.

Macy, he said. And Macy's dog.

William, mercifully, didn't say anything. It was strange, but the most sane member of my family, including myself, was a dog. I never had a problem with him—never.

An uncomplicated relationship floored me.

Do you want this back? I said, holding out the gold tusk. I straightened my spine, trying to appear tall and somewhat confident.

No, you keep it, he said. You might need it later. Come on, it's on this floor.

He led me down a side corridor that got darker, less illuminated by funky birthstones. I noticed faint writing carved on all of the walls. It was an alphabet I didn't recognize, wavy in places, blocky in others. I asked Wye about it.

All the laws and codes of the Empire, he said, are written on these walls. The oldest regulations are on the lowest floors, and they get newer the farther up you go. That's why they keep adding floors to the Tower, because they keep writing and reinterpreting laws. This script here—he ran his fingers along the walls—is a few hundred years old. It's readable, but barely. Only a few scholars can read the script on the lowest floors.

The walls had been closing in on us. Then the corridor

widened a bit and after a few turns we came to a jailer's desk. I heard screams. I listened for Ciaran's voice in those screams but didn't hear him. The jailer was doing a search-the-word puzzle with a marker and a piece of butcher paper. The corridor smelled like vinegar.

Ciaran Palmer, Wye said to him. The jailer sighed and looked up from his puzzle.

Him? he said. He's not supposed to receive visitors.

Consider that countermanded, Wye said, launching into about a ten-digit number, and ending with the word "falcon." The jailer grunted and got up from his desk. He saw the dog, and appeared ready to say, No dogs, but Wye's magic number must have blown past any no-dog regulations. He led us through a thick, wooden door that had a hive of small, stone cells on the other side, arranged in hexagonal fashion. The cells were all empty except for one.

Ciaran was sleeping, huddled in the corner, so I got a good ten seconds to observe him before he woke up. He was thin—I mean, he was already thin before, on the river, but now he was skeletal. He had a purplish scar on his forehead. He looked taller, too, even though I knew he couldn't have grown that much in less than a month. When you watch people sleep—especially when they are dreaming—their faces sag or sharpen in ways that make them look like different people. It's like watching clouds change. And just at that instant, Ciaran was like a broken old man.

William jolted forward and his paws scraped on the rusty iron of the cell bars. He barked and Ciaran stirred. I rushed to the gate, too. The jailer muttered something and left. Wye, I could tell, was standing at the wooden door, watching Ciaran wake up with a coughing fit. Then Ciaran noticed William, and stumbled to the door, too.

Xerxes? Xerxes? he said, croaking, as if he hadn't used his voice in weeks. He probably hadn't.

William was beside himself. Oh God, this is Ciaran! he said. Brace me!

Ciaran fell back.

Hi, Ciaran, I said, coming closer.

And his face just broke. He wasn't acting like a hardened smuggler anymore (although he still was that); he was a fourteen-year-old kid in a prison who was scared out of his mind. I was floored—I had expected something tougher off the bat.

Macy, he said. Oh shit, Macy, you've got to get me out of here. Please, Macy. Please.

He started crying. I hesitated for one second, and then reached through the bars and touched his hand, which was grimy and clammy. I thought to myself: I have to help him. Screw the past. I'm here now, whether he expected me or not. I'm going to try to make this right between us.

He must have blanked out on William's talking, but it came back to him when William licked the hand that I was holding on to.

What's going on? he said. Where's Xerxes? All of the good memories with Xerxes must have crowded out the bad, in his state, but some of the nasty, vicious memories must have been inching back to the forefront.

This . . . this is William, I said.

What the fuck are you talking about? he said. And then: You mean, William?

It's true, I managed to say.

He accepted it, more or less. But he let go of my hand. That was okay. It would take time. William whined but settled down again after a few seconds.

Listen, Ciaran, I'm going to do everything I can to help you.

Do you have an escape plan? he said.

Funny, Em had asked the same thing. I wondered whether they had drugged him, blindfolded him, the whole nine yards, before bringing him to the twenty-fifth floor.

No, Ciaran, I said. I don't have an escape plan. It doesn't work like that. You stand trial in three days—

Get me out of this! I can't stand trial! Can't you declare me unfit for trial?

Well—

His voice was raising. Can't you hire a good lawyer?

My head was getting hot. I don't have the money for—

Goddamn it, Macy, then why are you here? What good are you?

The vulnerability was gone. Did it matter that it was there for a few seconds? Could I have held on to that? I was doing everything possible not to have our relationship back to that moment when he called me a cunt and we tried to do as much harm to each other as possible. After all that happened, I didn't want to go back there. I would have lost something essential.

I mean, besides my mind.

I tried to tell him this.

Listen, I said. Listen good. I traveled through *wars* to get to you. Not because I wanted to, but because Dad wanted me to. But do you know what, Ciaran? Until you started—I don't know—talking, I was glad to see you. Because you're my brother.

Am I your brother? William said.

Yes, you are, William, I said. And I wish you could see Ciaran differently. Because . . .

Here I had no idea what to say, how I could compliment Ciaran.

. . . because he's a good kid, I lied.

Ciaran stared at me for a little while.

Look, I'm sorry, he said. I panicked. And I've been stupid.

He stepped away from the bars, into the corner, and crossed his arms. It's just this prison, he said. I haven't been able to sleep, they keep waking me up at odd hours of the night. . . .

Have they tortured you? I said. I'm not sure what I meant by that—sleep deprivation was torture, too. I guess I wanted to know if they had taken hot irons to his skin, or pried off his fingernails.

No, though they threaten it every day. Please, Macy. I'm sorry.

He started crying again. I heard Wye sigh behind me in exasperation, but I didn't turn around, because I didn't want Ciaran to know that his captor was in the room. That would have been bad.

I sighed. I was still guarded, but was trying to accept his situation as much as I could.

Ciaran, I said, I'll try to do whatever I can to help you.

Is that really William? he said between sobs.

It *is* William! William said.

Okay, Ciaran said, trying to compose himself. And I'm sorry for, you know, saying what I said to you. And attacking you. Earlier in Lou.

Thank you, I said, exhaling. I mean, his insult had hurt me at the time, and in a way it hurt more than the actual knife wound that he gave me in the leg. It had lingered and festered. Ciaran could very well be executed. I was glad I was able to forgive him for at least one of the shitty things he did.

Listen, Macy, he said. There's something else.

What? I said.

He opened his mouth to say something, and then closed it, crossing his arms. No, he said. No, never mind.

Seriously, Ciaran, what? I said. I thought at first he was playing another one of his mind games with me, but then I saw how serious he looked. He shook his head.

It's okay, Macy. I might talk to you about it next time. Not now, though.

We left him soon after. As we were walking out of the prison corridors, I asked Wye: So why were you fooling around with Lydia? I just want to know.

He laughed. I was glad he didn't say anything about my re-union with Ciaran, try to make any cracks about it.

You know, you're a lot like Em in that way, I said. Laughing at inopportune moments.

He laughed again.

See what I mean? I said.

You are . . . what did they used to call them? Wye said. A psychologist. You are psychological.

Um, I said, just tell me why you were seducing Lydia and leave psychology out of this.

She was seducing *me,* he said. You've got it all wrong. I had traveled with her family—and even then, you know, when I was looking for your brother, she had an eye on me.

You need to talk to her, I said. She needs to hear *no* from you. In your own words.

I think you should worry more about your brother, he said, cracking his knuckles. Oh, and your talking dog—

William, I said. My other brother.

Hi! William said.

Wye laughed again. I wondered what it would take to get a rise out of people about William's capacity for speech.

You have a strange family, he said. You are a strange girl.

I guess I'll take that as a compliment, I said.

He stopped and turned around. The amused look was gone. I'm going to tell Em, he said. I'm going to tell her everything. I just want you to know that.

Then he kept walking, not giving me the chance to respond. I wondered if this would be the last time I'd ever see him—I was positive that Em had killed for far, far less.

We came to the courtyard and the fountain.

Say, he said. Do you know any midwives?

What, do you think that just because I'm a girl I have this *secret connection* to some kind of midwifing cabal?

He shrugged. I don't know, he said. I'm just asking.

Well, I said. I do. But it's not going to be much help to you. My sister was training to be a midwife, but she's . . . I don't know where she is. I wish I could tell you.

Em had mentioned it in the letter, he said. It said, If you love me, find me a good midwife.

You'd better get on that, I said.

He nodded and left without another word. I stood there for a minute, staring into the fountain. Earlier, I had ignored his comment about worrying more about my brother, because he was right. I thought about what Lydia had told me, about not being so hard on myself, and forgiving myself every once in a while. I had done a good thing, to see Ciaran and not rip him to shreds.

I pulled out the golden tusk Wye had given me. I made a wish and tossed it into the fountain. I knew then why the fountain was there, why it was so full of money.

Then I swore to myself and fished it out, thinking that maybe I would need it again. I was glad no one was watching me. They would have thought I was a common thief.

I wasn't sure if my wish still counted, though.

I went back to Lydia's place. She let me stay there. Her invitation was much more important than her stepmom's. Lydia was trying to forget about Wye, though she was still in pain. I wondered whether he was trying to make his way back to Em. I assumed so; he seemed sincere, but who knew. More than anything I was protective of Em—not that she needed protecting.

I only went to the street level a few times, to get air and exercise with Lydia. Walking around Nueva Roma always made me miss St. Paul: jogging around Lake Como with my sister and then going to the conservatory to walk around the tropical plants, going to the Cinco de Mayo parade on the West Side, hanging out at Nina's Coffee with my friends and watching all the college students doing their homework with their boyfriends and girlfriends and wanting to be like them. Nueva Roma just wasn't the same, but exploring the city with Lydia and talking about Minnesota with her made things a little easier.

Lydia hated the different scarf gangs. Once, we were on street level, trying to find this band from up north that was supposed to be playing in a courtyard—we never found it—and she went off on this rant.

It's all manipulated by my stepmom and dad, she said. They keep pretending to give people something authentic, but it all turns out to be force-fed lies. Look at this.

She was drinking some kind of papaya rum concoction from a Dixie cup. She pointed at some graffiti of a unicorn sparring with a gladiator. The unicorn had a cup in one of its front hooves. The cup was overflowing with a green liquid. PAPAYA-OVERLORD! it said in English, and there was demotic script below it. The same slogan, I assumed.

They use "street teams," Lydia said. These freelance art-school dropouts from up north pretend to be actual graffiti artists and tag the city with these *stupid* ads.

The Romans used to do the same thing, I said. I mean, the graffiti, not the street teams.

Really? she said, not believing me. She probably thought I was making a dumb joke, but sometimes history sounded like a dumb joke. History was either a dumb joke or a cruel joke.

Anyway, she continued, taking a sip of the very same papaya drink that the unicorn was touting, sometimes the street teams—when they don't get paid on time, or just get bored—go on a tear and put up their graffiti in unauthorized areas, or rob people and graffiti *them*—sometimes with tar and paint, or sometimes with knives.

Crazy, I said, a little shaken up.

Yeah. Anyway, it doesn't matter in the long run anyway. Aren't we all going to die of, like, plague or something? Or the Scythians will learn to build boats and invade?

Well, we are going to die, I said. Just in general.

Yeah, she said, looking thoughtful. I guess you're right.

We smoked kef together in her room. Not a lot, but some. It made us edgy, but we'd drink shots of vodka to take off the edge. Julia, the indentured servant who no one wanted to call a slave, followed Lydia around everywhere in the apartment, attending to her every need, real or imaginary. Mostly imaginary.

Two nights before Ciaran's trial was supposed to start, it was storming outside, with curtains of warm rain. Lydia and I were sitting around smoking, and Julia was standing by the door. I offered kef to Julia.

No way, Lydia said, trying to swat the kef out of my hand. Don't give it to her. Don't!

But I was able to dodge her slow blow with great effectiveness.

Why not? I said.

Crystal . . .

I snorted. Crystal, I said, is passed out in the bathtub. Come on, Julia.

Julia was hesitant and looked to Lydia, who sank back down on the bed.

Oh, *whatever,* Lydia said. I don't care.

I passed the kef to Julia. Have you tried it before? I asked her. She shook her head.

The first time, I said, you don't want to take it in all at once. You need to let it take notice of its surroundings. I picked up the bottle of vodka.

This might help, too, I said.

In fifteen minutes, high in that jangled kind of way that kef gets you, we were all plotting ways to free Julia. And doing shots. Julia was quite talkative and had a lot of ideas about what she wanted to do with her life when freed. She had been in vet tech school before the invasions, but decided that she now wanted to be a dentist. Less training would be required to become a dentist in Nueva Roma.

I think about murdering your stepmom, she said, all the time.

Lydia gave Julia a dirty look, but then we all burst out laughing.

How about an electric eel in the bathtub? I said.

I didn't really want her dead. Kef made people laugh about death, which was why it was such a popular drug. But if I were Crystal's indentured servant, I might not have been kidding around at all.

We all paid for it the next morning with killer hangovers, and on balance, we overdid it *a bit*. But those moments—with actual friends—kept sharp to me in hindsight. I was able to forget my wounds for a few hours at a time, and not in some fucked-up way that did more harm than good in the long run. Rather, it was like forgetting to scratch at a scab—I could let the healing process do its own work, under the surface, without having to bloody myself up and start the whole thing over again.

And anyway, I needed a bit of space and time to think through my last encounter with Ciaran, its mixed signals and blessings. I didn't want to fuck up our relationship any more than it had to be. I wanted my brother to be free, of course—but it didn't seem likely.

The rain had stopped outside. My head pounding, I couldn't settle down. I paced. I concocted schemes to free Ciaran. Nothing seemed to fit together.

You okay? Lydia asked me, a few hours past sunrise.

What? I said.

You've just been staring out the window.

I was. Even though it wasn't storming, the sea was choppy with gray waves, and there weren't a lot of boats on the water.

I shook my head, trying to clear it. I said: I need to take a walk.

By yourself?

Yes, by myself. I'll be okay.

I think she was a little stung, but I didn't want to be a complete drag on her. I *thought* I was being generous, but not keeping everything pent up was selfish on my part.

William, as I was leaving the apartment, indicated that he wanted to come along.

I have to pee, he said. Don't like litter boxes!

All right, all right, I said, trying not to get exasperated. He couldn't help himself.

We bounded down the slick steps. There must have been a water break somewhere. In the middle of our way down, William tried to drink out of a brackish puddle that had mosquito eggs in it. Or something worse than mosquito eggs.

Stop that, I said.

By the time we got down to the street, I wondered why we bothered. The towers made you want to stay put, not venture too far out, making it exhausting to do so. Maybe that's why they were built. Everyone wanted to be alone with their privacy. The streets were canyons of shadows.

After William did his business on a building's corner, he bounded down a street we hadn't been on before. The air was muggy, threatening another thunderstorm. The people who were out on the streets congregated under awnings at corners, where they served beer and seaweed tacolike snacks, and other food sundries. They watched me, smoking long, ivory pipes that gave off a whiff of kef. I felt a little lost, not quite in my own body, as if my life was just an interlude between rainstorms. And so what did the rainstorms mean, then? Anyone's guess.

In front of one of those rickety awnings we passed, someone had strewn cut flowers in a ring. Soggy red petals were everywhere. The awnings provided an opening to a small courtyard. I happened to turn my head as I passed, because I heard a familiar laugh, and that was when I saw her.

It *couldn't* have been her, but it was. Sophia was pouring beer into a wooden pitcher. Men crowded around her, holding out mugs. She looked older and more tired than when I had seen her last, when I had the plague. Her hair was longer and she looked like she belonged there—not serving drunk assholes who didn't want to get wet, but rather in Nueva Roma. She looked Nueva Roman. And it was clear that the laugh I heard was only to humor those men, because she settled into an exhausted silence again.

Sophia! I said, moving toward her, underneath the awnings and into the courtyard. All the men turned to stare at me. Sophia met my eyes in a glint of shock, and turned back to her pour.

Oh my God, *Sophia*! I said. I didn't give a flying shit about the guys who were still looking at me weird. I pushed past them. They stank in more than one way. William growled—he could be as tough as Xerxes when he wanted to, which made sense, since he had Xerxes' body—as I moved forward and stood next to her.

Hey, she said. Her hands were shaking bad. I yanked the pitcher away from her and set it down. The men—Turquoises, I saw, just great—grumbled. I had no clue at all what was going on. If Sophia was working, why would it be a problem to see her long-lost sister?

I put my arms around her neck and gave her a hug. I'm not letting go until you hug back, I said, desperate to get any kind of emotion out of her. Jesus, Sophia.

She broke and then was crying and hugging me. Oh God, she said, I'm so glad to see you. But you can't stay here. You need to get out of here.

Is someone hurting you? I said.

William jumped up on us.

Oh God, Xerxes? she said, pulling away. She had a distaste for Xerxes to begin with, and it had festered all this time.

Decidedly not Xerxes! William said.

She screamed and put a hand over her mouth.

Everything happened fast after that. Someone put a hand on my shoulder and spun me around hard. My elbow tipped the pitcher over. A man with tiger tattoos up and down his arms leaned toward me. He was handsome probably about ten years ago. Who the fuck are you, he spat at me. And why are you fucking with what's mine?

What's yours? I said.

Oh God.

She's not *yours,* I said, pointing a finger at him. She's my sister.

Everyone laughed, except for Sophia and me. The man grabbed her arm. She tried to pull away but fell down. I could see, attached to her arm, that there was a black disk with red circles around the edges. Like something you'd get at the Olive Garden or Red Lobster while waiting for a table that would let you know that you were ready to be seated.

Righteousness wasn't going to work this time. Righteousness was going to get me killed. I started panicking, wondering how I was going to save myself, much less my sister. I was still in shock that she was right here, in flesh and blood.

Aha, then, he said. Who's *yours,* then? Have you run away?

With Sophia on the ground, he turned around and tried to grab my wrist. He almost succeeded; I just managed to slip away. He liked grabbing people. I'm sure he got away with it a lot. That was when William bit him in the crotch. And William didn't let go as the man fell back against one of the awnings, making the whole thing collapse.

When I fell, I fell right next to Sophia. Come on, I said.

I can't, she said.

What? Come *on*.

My ankle is chained, she said.

She bit her lip in pain. I looked at her ankle. It was twisted at a funny angle and there was a plastic cord around it.

Fuck, I said. One of the Turquoise beer-swillers almost fell on me in the confusion.

And I owe, like, five thousand tusks, she said.

I don't care, I said, about to lose it. I'm going to get you out of this. I promise.

Then she was wrenched away from me.

I shouted her name. I wanted to follow her, but I had to get out of there. There was no way I could have saved Sophia at that moment. I was no good to her dead or captured. I rolled toward a hole I saw in the tangled canvas and whistled for William. My head popped out of the fallen awning and I saw, running down the street toward us, a group of about a dozen Teals, much younger than the Turquoises under the tent. The Teals were ready to strike when the iron was hot.

Someone grabbed my ankle. I kicked back, using the contours of a fat man's face to propel myself out of the fallen tent. The Teals ignored me as they pounced. They had shovels and clubs and started beating the jumble of bodies under the tarp, on the half closest to the street and away from my sister. But still too close.

Don't hurt my sister! I shrieked. I had thought she had gotten away from the worst of the fight in time, but I couldn't be sure. I looked for William. He was already running back down where we had come. I stumbled after him. I didn't know what else to do. Some of the Turquoises managed to find their way out of the tarp, cutting at it with knives they had, knives they were all too ready to use on the Teals. I looked for Oxna in that crowd of Teals, but he wasn't there. No one would have cared if Sophia died, except maybe the man with the tiger tattoos, since he would have lost a chunk of change on her.

I didn't feel safe until I had caught up to William, who was waiting for me at the elevator, wagging his tail.

That was our sister! he said.

Yeah, I said, collapsing next to him, and setting the crank for Lydia's floor.

I tried to catch my breath. I was desperate, beside myself as to how fucked up my family situation was. One brother a dog, the other in prison, my sister an indentured servant. And I hated being sorry for myself, because their problems were a hell of a lot worse than mine. The worst problem I had was not understanding myself one lick, and I could at least hobble along with that. It wouldn't kill me.

One thing I did understand, at that moment, was that I was sick of holing up, waiting around for things to happen to me, waiting for forces to conspire against me. Sick of it. Sick of trying less than I should have, and congratulating myself when I managed to do something, anything, even when it wasn't nearly enough.

I knew I needed to change that. Being angry helped. The anger made me want to do things.

What are you thinking? William said, as we clinked onto our floor and we jumped off. You're cooking, he said.

I patted William on the head. You saved my life, William. And Sophia loves you. She just doesn't know it yet.

Then maybe it wouldn't hurt as bad, he said, as I started walking with him toward Lydia's door. My foot was in a lot of pain, and the rest of my body hurt only a little less than that. But I didn't care. I knocked on the door with my good foot. When Lydia let me in, I walked right past her, through the living room, and into her room. I didn't want to stop among her family's ill-begotten plunder. I didn't trust myself to keep from breaking and trashing any of that shit. As calmly as I could, I sat down at the foot of Lydia's bed.

Macy? Lydia said. What happened to your face?

I met her eyes and didn't say anything for a few seconds. Then I looked up at her. I had no idea whether I could rely on her for support. But I couldn't keep myself bottled up about it.

My sister's a slave, I said. And I'm going to free her.

She sank down to the floor, stunned. Oh my God, she said. But how are you going to do that?

I have no idea, I said. I suppose if I was playing with this god-forsaken place's rules, I should pay off her debt or something. That would be the right way to free her.

I stood up and looked out the window at the gray swells on the water, and the white kingfishers skittering between the sky-scrapers.

But *fuck that,* I said.

The Benefits of a Price

Sophia didn't realize she was indentured at first. When she did, she felt fooled and ashamed. It didn't take her long, after leaving the *Prairie Chicken,* to sign a contract. After reaching the shore, she had found a muddy, narrow trail, crowded with prickly brambles. She only had to walk about a half an hour inland before she came upon a larger trail, and a slave trader. Of course he didn't call himself that. He wore a black tie, and a blue vest, and also chinos. That attire was in itself striking in the midst of the wilderness. Plus, he rode a horse, and behind him were transport wagons. He was shipping people to their new jobs. The mules pulling the wagons wore blue shawls and the wagons were also painted blue. The slaver offered Sophia water. Sophia was both flattered and cautious. The water was in an Evian bottle but was a little murky. She drank it anyway. Water was scarce on the *Prairie Chicken* and she told him this. He smiled and told her about opportunities, and that she had a face and countenance that indicated she would be a great member of the team. A winning smile. Only later when she was being taken into one of the wagons did she notice that the mules' eyes, all of them, were bloodshot. This was more of an omen to her than any of the slaver's words. His name was Gary and he used to live in Texarkana. He was a marketing district manager for the name of a chain she couldn't remember. But then he had found new opportunities in the world. His responsibilities were even greater in current times. She was light-headed and went into the recruitment wagon, which was near the back of the caravan.

Gary's human resources assistant, dressed much like him, was there. He was blonder, though. She remembered that. He smiled and described the benefits of team membership. The benefits were almost too numerous to behold. There was security in the opportunities provided to Sophia, and provided that she worked hard—and it was clear, he said, that she was a good worker—the sky was really the limit. She must have felt it fortuitous, the recruiter had told her, to have come upon their caravan. He presented several papers for her to sign, and gave her a pen. She squinted at the papers. They were hard to read and there were a lot of misspellings, worse than any stereo instructions she'd ever seen. She wished that her dad was there with her to walk her through the process, just to get a second opinion. She asked what *kinds* of opportunities, what specific jobs, she was interested in midwifery as a career eventually, but she would be open to other forms of child care if the chance arose. All she wanted was a foot in the door. The man smiled and straightened his tie. He said that the positions that needed to be filled were based on flexibility of the team members, and that the strength of his company was that no single opportunity could be pinpointed to any single person. There had to be a certain amount of trial and error with one's talents.

She signed the papers. Giving the pen and papers back to the man, his countenance changed in a subtle fashion. He told her to go to Wagon C, and once she arrived at one of the company's regional base camps, she would be given a uniform and dental exam.

Dental exam? But he didn't say anything more on this matter. When she jumped out of the back of the wagon, she landed awkwardly and toppled over a little.

Don't hurt yourself, the recruiter said. It sounded more like a command than a show of compassion. The mules brayed and the wagons rolled again. Gary swung by on his horse as Sophia ran to Wagon C, which was painted with a C.

Wagon C, he said.

Yes. I know, thanks.

Someone with giant hands in Wagon C hoisted her up. She had no idea she had been drugged. The wagon train was heading to Lou, with a few stops in nameless company towns in between. Gary received most of his workers from contract enticements and commodity trading with the Empire, but also from strays who had washed up on the river. STRAY, he wrote on the bottom of Sophia's contract, under the heading that said: FOR OFFICIAL USE ONLY. The wagon had about six or eight others inside. No one made eye contact with her. The youngest person there was a fifteen-year-old girl and the oldest was a sixty-five-year-old man. The man who helped her up looked Neanderthal, and he wore a blue vest as well, and also a name tag that said SECURITY. He had a short sword, strapped to his belt, that looked good for jabbing. Sophia found a place to sit in the back of the wagon. SECURITY crossed his werewolflike arms and spent the rest of the next few hours glaring at everyone. Sophia was tired and she thought it was from all the stress of leaving the *Prairie Chicken,* and the sudden changes. She missed her family, and felt bad for abandoning Macy and Grace in their hours of need. But, she thought as she fell asleep, they would understand—she had her hour of need, too.

The wagon train stopped overnight in a shantytown called Independent Spirit. A doctor, or med-tech of some sort, measured Sophia's teeth, and asked about cavities and crowns. The exam took place in an abandoned Best Buy, in the home-theater section. Every high-definition television screen was shattered. Then the med-tech told her to take off her clothes, and he measured her breasts, and then her jaw length, with a tape measure. She asked about this, the necessity of this procedure, but the med-tech said this was part of the contract, and to shut up.

During her voyage down the river to Nueva Roma in the converted hold of an oil tanker, she began to realize how fucking stupid she was, and how, for the time being, she couldn't do anything about it. Her name meant wisdom but never before did she feel so improperly named. They gave her a name tag—misspelling her name as SOPHA—and a training manual for her to read on the voyage. The manual had few words, but a lot of pictures showing proper ways to serve people. At the end of the manual was a disclaimer and a ledger, which told her that the name tag, the manual, the uniform she would receive, room and board, and her training would require an investment of five thousand gold tusks, which would be taken out of her future earnings.

She closed the manual and dry-heaved.

The tanker still smelled like a smoldering gasoline fire. The servants on this voyage were fed well enough—they were coded HOSPITALITY, and had a higher caloric mandate than LABORERS—but it was still miserable. Sophia wanted to escape more than anything, but she had no idea how she would get away with it, and none of the other people in her hold seemed enthused about such a thing. Many vomited blood on the trip and a few died from dysentery. The training manual had key hospitality phrases in several different languages common in the Empire's capital:

WOULD YOU LIKE ANOTHER?
THANK YOU, AND PLEASE COME AGAIN.
WOULD YOU LIKE TO SPEAK TO MY TEAM MASTER?

IT WAS ON. I WAS ON. I DIDN'T HAVE MUCH TIME. I WANTED TO FREE her right away, but I needed to cover my tracks, make sure she could have a clean break. I had so much to ask her—like how she got to Nueva Roma in the first place. It probably wasn't pretty—looking for minimum-wage work on the river, not knowing what she was getting into, lured by promises no one had any intention of keeping. Something like that.

It could have been me, and that kept me up at night.

I wondered if I would ever tell Dad about Sophia's captivity.

But the first person I needed to talk to was Ciaran. Wye had made it sound like it would be a major problem to get back to Ciaran's cell, but I was surprised that, with the golden tusk, I had no problems getting to him. The jailor even deferred to me. Ciaran seemed surprised and relieved to see me and William.

Hey, he said. His voice was hoarse. He was growing a beard, but it looked wispy and pathetic. But this in itself was a part of growing up.

I didn't waste any time.

I've found Sophia, I said.

He put his hands against the bars and leaned forward. Are you serious? he said.

I nodded and told him how I had run into her, and how I was almost captured myself. I spared nothing.

Shit, Macy, he said. You have to free her.

I know. I will. I'll do anything. I . . . just am not quite sure how.

He laughed; it came out like a cough. Are you asking me for advice? he said.

A little, yeah, I said.

And I was. I needed to talk to him. He was good with dastardly plans, even if they didn't always quite work out for him.

I have an idea . . . he said, trailing off. But . . . well . . .

What? I said.

I need you to do something for me, too. I'm begging you, actually.

I expected the worst. What is it? I said, my hands shaking.

He took a deep breath. Okay, he said. I was going to ask you last time, but it didn't seem right then. I was still, well, figuring things out.

He certainly looked desperate.

Tell me, Ciaran, I said.

He pressed his face against the bars. There are Scythians in town who have been in contact with me, he whispered. They've managed to smuggle a new vaccine to the plague out of the Emperor's palace.

Go on, I said in a quiet voice. I felt my body tensing up.

This would be their last chance to mass-produce the vaccine and distribute it everywhere. But they need someone who *no one* would suspect—

You want me to smuggle the antidote up the river to the Scythian camp? I said.

This hit me between the eyes, as they say.

Well, only up to Lou, he said. They've recruited someone new to take it up to the Scythian camp. But yeah. So . . . seriously? What do you think?

I could see the longing and desperation on Ciaran's face. More than that, he was trusting me. He was trusting me with something *huge*. That trust in itself was huge.

I took a deep breath.

I'll do it, I said. I want to.

And I did. I wanted to complete what he had started. It hit me then: I would do anything for him. Because I loved him. I loved my brother. It took that moment for me to know I loved him. Not as an abstract proposition, but as an unquestionable truth like gravity.

Okay, Macy, he said, exhaling. I don't know what to say. I was worried that you'd say no. I'd screwed up so much with all of you.

Well, I said, if you hadn't forged that letter, we probably all would have died in the refugee camp.

I guess you're right, he said. So listen. This is what the Scythians told me. The person who will take it up to the Scythian camp from Lou—she'll be at the confluence of the Mississippi and the Missouri at the first Tuesday of every month. She'll have a red cloak on. You can trust her.

Okay, I said. We'll get out of this, Ciaran.

He shook his head. He looked afraid and also resigned. Not me, Macy. Not me. Let's be realistic.

But I'll be here for your trial—

Then I stopped.

No, Macy. You won't be able to come back to the city for a long while. It would be too dangerous for you. If they even suspected you had anything to do with the vaccine leaving Nueva Roma, they would hunt you down and kill you.

I knew that he was right. I wouldn't be able to come back, and I would be in the dark about his sentence.

But anything could happen to you during your trial, I said.

He nodded. There wasn't any comfort in going ahead with the smuggling operation.

All right, I said. These Scythians, would they be able to help free Sophia?

I'm sure of it, he said. So listen. There are Scythians who live in the northeastern tip of the city, in the ravines.

I had no idea Scythians were in the city, I said.

They're all displaced. Ex-slaves. Or fleeing from something or someone. Or working in the city for part of the year. Look for a place called the Black Sun. The man with the vaccine is named Ren. You can find him there.

He then started to tear up, though he wiped the tears away.

Sophia's going to be safe, I told him. So don't worry. I want you to know that. I'll take care of her.

He closed his eyes. Tell her that I'll miss her, he said.

I will, I said. I will.

He grabbed my arm and opened his eyes. And don't let anyone else know, he said. No one. You and I are the only ones who can know about the vaccine. Okay?

I promise, I said.

And William, William said.

And William, of course, Ciaran said. Come here, William.

William was scared, seeing Ciaran so fragile, but he approached him and squeezed his nose through the bars.

Ciaran stroked William's ear. Ciaran had a faraway look in his eyes, as if wondering how the hell he had reached this particular moment in time, from being a troublemaking kid to a smuggler to a prisoner. I was wondering the same thing.

It was almost too much. Almost. But I had to keep going.

You should go, he said. You don't have any time to waste.

He was trying to be brave, I could tell. But he was only fourteen, and he could die alone in a few weeks. The pain made him sound old and wise.

But he was just a kid.

Okay, I said. You hang in there, all right?

Yeah, he said.

I couldn't take any more, so I squeezed his hand and turned around.

Macy? he said.

Yeah? I said, not quite looking at him.

Wait, he said. Do you remember those pills you took when you had the plague?

I half-laughed, not sure where he was going with this. What about them? I said.

Well, you couldn't find the bottle when you woke up, right? he said.

That seemed like half a lifetime ago. Yeah, I said. I remember.

Well . . . He stopped and coughed. I was the one who took the bottle, he said. I tried to sell it to those people from the gladiator ship—the dad of that girl you were talking to. He said they were just vitamins. He had the same vitamins in his pack and showed me.

I turned around all the way. William looked up at me, trying to figure out what was happening.

Go on, I said.

Anyway, I just wanted you to know that—that I gave you shit earlier about not giving those pills to Mom. You'd thought they were antibiotics. But they weren't. And they didn't cure you, either. You . . . you were just lucky, Macy.

He wiped his face with his sleeve. So don't feel bad about Mom, he said. It's not your fault.

Thanks, I managed to whisper. I mean it, Ciaran. Thanks.

It was pretty much the most decent thing Ciaran, or anyone else for that matter, had ever said to me.

Then I left with William without another word. I didn't want him to see me crying. I wanted him to think that I was strong, and wasn't going to screw anything up.

I was morose, edgy, and determined as I bounded back to Lydia's apartment. I needed to let her know that I would be going—I owed her that much—and to pick up my meager possessions. I kept my head down. The duration of the walk back was a blur for me. I took the elevator and reached the apartment. It was silent. I went to Lydia's room and slowly opened the door. She was curled up in bed with her back to me, and she was crying.

Lydia? I whispered.

Leave me alone, she sobbed.

What's wrong, Lydia? I said. I took a step toward her.

Please, she said, a little louder. Please.

Lydia, I need to go, I said.

Whatever, she said. Go, then.

No, you don't understand— I started to say. But then I decided I didn't have time to say any more. I backtracked, shaken up. I went to my room, gathered my little bag of things, and went to the living room again. No one else was around. Julia had left a note that she was out vegetable shopping. I was desperate to meet the Scythians and get the ball rolling.

But when I was just about to leave with William in tow, I heard someone shuffling behind me.

It was Dave, Lydia's father. I waved to him, but he motioned me closer.

Hi! he said. Have a seat.

I was just leaving, I said. I have a lot to do today.

I'm sure, I'm sure, he said, laughing. But, still . . . just for a minute. I promise I won't bite.

He looked at me with the dead eyes of a vampire. But cheerful. Always cheerful.

Um, okay, I said, sitting down at the central table. The clutter seemed to be spawning on its surface: a mixing bowl begetting a Thracian doll, an emerald kitchen magnet begetting a cubist brooch, a pearlescent acoustic guitar with hieroglyphs imprinted on it. It was endless excess. William huffed but lay down by my feet.

Okay, he said, sitting down, too. Great. This is great. I'm glad we're able to spend some time together.

You are? I said.

Of course! Lydia's friends are my friends.

He stretched his arms up and yawned.

That's good to hear, I said. Is Lydia okay? She seemed a little . . . down.

Of course she is! he said.

I wasn't sure if he was responding to my question or my observation. He smiled again. With each smile, I could tell more and more something was going on underneath the pristine surface of his face, but what it was, I couldn't say, except that it wasn't good.

You have a lot of pride, he said. I can tell that, Macy. And I know you don't want to reveal your origins or lack of money too much.

Excuse me? I said.

You're clever, he said, as if I hadn't responded at all. You don't want to give your hand away. I know you're just an outcast, a castaway, and you're trying to survive.

I should go, I said.

He slapped the table with his fist so hard that it shook. William's head perked up.

Stay, he said.

I froze, afraid. William growled a little bit.

And tell that dog of yours to shut up, Dave said.

I scratched William's ear. It's okay boy, I told him in a low, soothing voice. He settled down again.

You know Julia ran away? he said.

No, I said, startled. But I'm glad.

I'm sure you are, he said. She was getting ideas from you.

What, like not being treated like chattel? I said.

I wasn't afraid of him anymore. After his spite toward Julia, I wanted to put him in his place.

You want to apply the rules of our old life to our new life, Macy, he said. But it doesn't work that way anymore. That's just being nostalgic for its own sake.

I don't know how Lydia lives with you, I said.

That cut him for the first time, or seemed to.

Lydia . . . he said, taking a deep breath. Well, she's not going to like it. She misses Julia, but for all the wrong reasons. It's going to be hard for her to make the adjustment, but the good news is that you'll be there for her through the worst of it.

I paused. What are you talking about? I said.

He smiled. Well, a repayment of sorts. You'll be taking Julia's place.

Oh, fuck no, I said.

He pulled a slender chain with a handcuff out of his jacket pocket and in a swift lunge—faster than I thought he was capable of—he reached over the table and tried to grab my arm.

I pushed my chair backwards, feeling his hand brush against mine as he tried to snatch me. William was on full alert through this whole exchange, despite his silence, and he leaped up and started barking. I took the hieroglyphic guitar on the table with my other hand and smashed it against his arm like a club. It was as light as balsa wood but it shattered against his hand like glass, sounding like a dozen wind chimes being knocked together. His arm bled from lots of little cuts. I tossed the ruined guitar at him. He ducked. The guitar crashed behind him. He yanked a spiked cricket bat off the wall and growled and tried to move around the table.

William! I said, turning around. William was already by my side. I didn't look back. I didn't want to see the look on Dave's face or, worse yet, the look on Lydia's face. I just ran, out the door, down the short corridor, down the stairs, taking three steps at a time, not knowing how far I'd have to run to escape the man who thought he had the right to capture me.

I heard the elevator clunk downward—Dave must have been trying to beat me that way—and then I heard Lydia at the top of the steps when I was about halfway down running for my life.

Macy! she screamed. Macy!

I had no idea what she wanted, and I didn't care at that point.

Shut up! William shouted back.

We reached the bottom of the stairs. Though we were both panting and almost out of breath, we burst past the fountain in the empty vestibule and out the archway into the street. Right as I did, a man grabbed my shoulder and pulled me toward him.

No! I shouted, struggling to get free. William was barking like crazy, and was ready to pounce on my captor. But the man loosened his grip a little and turned toward me.

It was Wye. He had a black eye.

Macy, he said. What's going on?

I was still struggling, though, since my mind had leaped to the natural conclusion that he was working in conjunction with Dave. William, I was sure, would have been all over him if I wasn't so close to him.

Macy, Macy, easy, Wye said.

I'm not going to let you take me back to Dave! I said, struggling to get free.

He gave a confused laugh, and said: No, no, Macy, I've been looking for you but—what?

I eased up for a second. That asshole tried to enslave me, I said. I need to get out of here. I need to save my sister.

He let go of me. I started running again. William huffed, gave Wye a dirty look, and started running alongside me again. Then Wye was, too.

He tried to do *what*? Wye said when I told him what Dave had done. Come here, follow me, I can show you a hiding place.

He took off in a diagonal direction from where I was heading—though I didn't know where I was heading. I sighed, and decided to trust him.

Hey, wait up, I said, trying to catch up to him.

He slowed down a hair, and led me through a few alleyways that I was sure were dead ends, until we reached a square with a life-size stone statue, its features defaced by age. The statue was of a man with a large, pointed crown who was pointing off into the distance. I couldn't tell if he was pointing at anything significant. There were a few pedestrians lingering near the foot of the statue. The shadows from the skyscrapers put the square in a twilight. I saw no sign of Dave, though I kept expecting to see him bounding toward us.

We took a minute to catch our collective breaths.

I pointed at his face. What happened to your face? I said.

Yes, well . . . he said, touching his cheek. Em and I are working things through. We're patching up our relationship. And I still need to find a midwife.

My mind was racing forward. I thought about my embryonic plan to save Sophia, and the vaccine that I had to traffic. I gave Wye a long, hard look, and then told him that I knew where my sister was.

Are you serious? he said.

I nodded.

We must free her, immediately!

I'm working on it.

Because Em is about to give birth.

I had a brief vision of her cussing out the walls of the submarine and the fishes outside, in pain that she couldn't control.

Is she in labor? I said.

He took a deep breath. No, he said. But it's close. She's also paranoid. She wants someone on the sub who she can trust. I was about to find any midwife to bring to the *Nadir*—anyone that would be able to help her. But now . . .

All right, I said, still peering around, hoping we weren't followed. But I'm going to have to have some people help me. She's chained, and the beer garden where she works is swarming with Turquoises. You and I aren't going to cut it by ourselves.

He cocked his head. All right, he said. Who?

I took a deep breath and told him.

He wasn't thrilled about the possibility of working with

Scythians, to say the least. No, not so much. I could tell that from the look on his face.

But he nodded and said: Whatever it takes.

The plan was simmering in my head as we left the fountain square. After a winding block or two, I stopped under the eaves of a narrow skyscraper that looked like the Imperial equivalent of one of those payday check-cashing places, with thick glass windows and lots of tusks being taken on and off scales by clerks. I realized that I had to steel myself for a little heart-to-heart between William and me. In order for the plan to work, William could not be seen.

William, I said. You need to wait for us at the sub. Do you remember where we came in? You need to go there.

No! he said.

Please, William—

No! he said, louder.

Wye eyed William and shuffled his feet.

I sighed. You need to guard the sub, I said. It's a very important job. Em will be counting on you.

It is, she is?

Yes. I can't do this without you doing this, William.

He agreed, and darted off to the secret pier without another word. He seemed to know where he was going. All the same, when he left it was like I lost one of my limbs. I worried more than anything that he would be trampled by a chariot race or picked up by a freelance dogcatcher.

We need to keep hurrying, Wye said. We started walking toward the northeast section of town, on dirt avenues, on causeways, over canals that led nowhere, and underneath gangplanks. Wye kept quiet. I had no idea whether Wye was having a change of heart about working with the Scythians, or was just desperate. Either way, it was a good sign. It was good that he was desperate enough to do anything for Em.

But all the same, there was more he needed to know, if the plan was going to work with a clean conscience on my part. I stopped him underneath a vined archway. I needed to take a breather anyway. I was exhausted.

There's something else, I said, realizing at that moment that I was breaking a promise that I had made to Ciaran. I hoped he would understand, if I ever saw him again.

What? he said.

Well . . . I shuffled my feet. You need to know up front, I said. I'm going to be brutally honest with you.

I told him about the vaccine. I told him pretty much everything—that Ciaran was the one who gave me the names of the Scythians, that I would be taking the vaccine up the river to the Scythians, and what was Wye going to do about it. Anything? He couldn't do anything. At least that was what I had hoped.

Of course, he could have had a complete turn of heart and thrown me into jail, then and there. That possibility only hit me after I started telling him all of this. I'm sure he saw right through my bravado.

Hmm, he said. Hmm. Well. You know . . .

He was going to say something else, but then stopped. I had never seen him this flustered before.

What? I said.

I get it, he said at last. I understand what you have to do. And—how do I put this? I had been feeling some . . . remorse over what had happened to your brother.

That I hadn't expected. Really? I said.

Your brother . . . reminds me of me, when I was his age. So consider this my chance to redeem myself, at least a little bit.

But the Empire— I began to say.

The Empire is— It's just an empire. It doesn't matter to me. It doesn't have any pull on me. It doesn't even have any pull on itself. And it will go on, no matter what I do or you do or your brother does. Until it dies, and another one takes its place.

All right, I said. Well, I'm glad we have that settled. That went better than I thought.

He laughed, and we started walking again. The skyscrapers started having fewer stories, and the streets themselves became more ramshackle. When we turned down an alley with several wooden skyways above us, the ground started getting muddier. Then, on the other side of the alleyway, we came to the crest of a long, sloping hill dotted with campfires. There was a mix of hide tents and cottages made out of scrap lumber, all the way down to the sea. This section of the city, ravine after ravine, was a catchall for refugees. Not just Scythians, but displaced people from the edges of the Empire—and outside of it—who were too poor to live in the towers. I saw a train of white mules inching forward from halfway up a ravine on a narrow trail. I saw a couple of kids throwing around a deflated football on the slope. I saw a man selling dove sculptures out of bars of Ivory soap, and right next to him a woman selling T-shirts emblazoned in the Scythian language. The air smelled like manure and clove cigarettes.

Where are we supposed to meet them? Wye said.

A place called the Black Sun? I said, crossing my arms.

Ah, he said. I've been there. I know the way.

I then worried whether I was putting Wye in mortal danger by bringing him to the Scythian part of town. I supposed it depended on what kind of reputation he had.

I hoped to God it didn't precede him.

Ancient Desires Seek Bodies of Insects

The Emperor and his court lived underneath the Tower of Justice. To those few who lived in its enclosures and later told their accounts of the place (such as the wildly popular *A Kansan in the Secret Court,* a Jack Anubis publication), it seemed more of a prison than the cells of the Tower above.

One of the prized conquests from the Empire's counterinsurgency was the laboratory of an immunology lab from the Centers for Disease Control, and five immunologists. The lab was a small one, in relative terms, and some of its sanitary nature was compromised by its transport and final internment. The Emperor didn't want anyone to see the lab, or take credit for its potential future accomplishments. Science was dead—he had declared this. On the other hand, science, being a lost art, needed to be recovered to a point, and then reconfigured into something else more useful and unnameable.

The immunologists were allowed to continue their work in the palace. They were allowed one hour of sunlight a week— which was *much more* than many of the Emperor's closest confidants received. Did they know, their handlers told them, how deadly the barbarians were? Did they know how lucky they were?

The scientists were allowed to dine with the Emperor, who

could never tell them apart. He could never tell Americans apart. Two were married to each other, he knew, and were from a place called Nashville. All of the immunologists were converted, with a small amount of persuasion, to the Empire's state religion and took proxy ancestors and celestial patrons upon themselves. When the whale oil was in a state of shortage, they would work by candlelight: reconfiguring their knowledge to what they had to know about the world in order to survive.

And also what they knew about insects.

The Emperor had a great deal of fear about the plague, and the Scythians. They were intertwined entities for him. By extension, his family was haunted by the Emperor's fear, especially the Emperor's son. On more than a few occasions, his only son, the young heir, would awaken shrieking from dreams of dead faces. The faces were always lumpy and surprised. They were surprised at coming so close to a living boy, and the heir of a large empire at that.

What are you doing here? the faces would cry out to the boy. Can't you tell we're trying to sleep?

The heir's screams would wake the guards, who would go down from their barracks to the governess, telling her that the heir needed her attendance. She would waken and take the iron spiral stairs down to the heir's room and hush him back to sleep. The air in his room, which was an entire floor of the palace, smelled like rust and earth, with charcoal urns every thirty paces that burned with blue fire.

The Emperor himself rarely slept. He would pray to his ancestors and conduct experiments, both in poetry and the natural histories that were written upon the body by age and disease.

The island floated toward what it desired— he would begin.

But the rhythms weren't right. He wanted to be remembered and right.

At last the Empire found its quarry—

He put that line aside for future reference, rolling up the Post-it into a little scroll and giving the Paper Mate to one of the attendants in his study.

The heir stayed away from the floor of sciences. His governess protested, many times, that an underground environment was not healthy for a child, especially one who would become the Ruler of the Agreeable Lands.

This is why he must stay under the earth, the Emperor himself corresponded to her. *He must stay for his realizations and dreams of sunshine.* A courier gave her this message on a Post-it, with an imprint of the Imperial seal on the corner, large as a thumbnail.

The Emperor had a Post-it addiction. His study's walls were lined with thousands of them. He postulated that America had something to teach his Empire, at least in small measures, and that the Scythians couldn't comprehend the treasures in front of them. Natural resources such as adhesive paper were precious, and could revolutionize—given proper study and spiritual guidance, of course—whole archives of knowledge. He impressed upon his immunologists that they should record their findings on Post-its. And so their labs had candles and statuettes on one side, and walls covered with Post-its on the other. Their lab also had an apiary, many loose rats—it was hard to tell which rats were part of their studies and which were merely passing through—and fruits and flowers in various stages of decay and spoilage, along with the usual conglomeration of microscopes, test tubes, and the like.

They induced wasps to sting apples. The apples would turn to rough, gray paper.

They also had to work with certain prescriptions: *A rat must find a home in the soul and identity of a wasp. The wasp must have fur on two-fifths of its carapace for a successful and blessed endeavor.*

The ideal wasp must be fecund.

CHAPTER 21

Live from the Invasion of Nueva Roma

Wye and I kept walking through the warren of shacks, and came to a black shipping container, the kind that used to be stacked on a giant ship and carried useless crap from China to America and back again. The end toward us was open. There was the smell of frying meats and peppers. Inside was a counter, and a few tables and chairs. A man was standing at the counter, leaning toward us. He was wearing a black skullcap.

Hello, he said. What would you like?

I noticed that above him was a blackboard with chalk outlines of a chicken, a sheep, and a cow. They were all crossed out, and there was an outline of a fish next to each. Behind him was an empty kitchen with cauldrons, a wood stove, and a grill.

Slow? Wye said.

The man shrugged.

Are you Ren? I asked.

He pointed at the name tag on his leather vest. It said REN.

All right, he said. And you must be Macy.

I startled. Yeah, I said. That's me.

Wye took a half-step back.

This is my friend, I said, pointing at Wye. He's a little shy.

I remember you, Ren said, squinting at Wye.

That's very possible, Wye said, tensing up.

But maybe not, Ren said.

I explained to Ren that my sister needed to be freed, and that I'd be able to take the vaccine up the river with great speed afterward, without spelling out that I would be using a submarine.

That's fine, he said. Whatever you need.

I wondered what it would take to rile him up.

That's great, I said. Really appreciate it.

So how do you propose doing this? Ren said.

Yes Macy, Wye said, crossing his arms. What do you say?

I told them my plan. It had seemed ridiculous when I had first thought of it as we were walking over, but the line between crazy and plausible was a little blurry. It had been for a while.

They agreed, and after an hour, Ren had marshalled a good dozen other Scythians. Night had come. The horses were led from secret stables—beach coves, Ren said—to our launching point. In the back of the Black Sun, where Ren kept his own horses, Wye and I dressed in our costumes. Or rather, they were costumes for us but not for the Scythians. I had to wear the Scythian battle armor of one of Ren's nephews, and it didn't fit great.

The Scythians didn't have much of a chance to wear their battle gear in Nueva Roma anymore. For ceremonial purposes and special occasions, perhaps, or to bring out to tell stories to their sons and daughters. Or when they managed to go north to visit long-lost family, threading the shifting battle fronts.

It was fun watching Wye struggle with his own Scythian armor, and almost fall over once after putting on leggings.

You doing okay there? I said.

He snorted. Anyway, it kept me distracted from my own fear. He helped me tie the back of my breastplate. I fitted the helmet over the hood, then pulled on the leggings lined with gray fur.

When we were done, Wye looked me over.

You look menacing, he said.

I look like a hobbit, I said. But *you* look like a Scythian.

Eh, don't remind me, he said.

But he did.

Oh, he said. Wait. I almost forgot.

Wye took a dagger out of his bag and held it out for me. It didn't have fancy jewels on it, any crazy bling. But it had my name engraved on the hilt. And a dedication. *To Macy. From Em.*

She has an automatic engraver on the sub, he said.

I can't, I started to say. But then I thought, screw it, and took the dagger. Wye handed me the sheath on a belt and I tied it around my waist.

Thanks, I said. Then I blurted out: I'm scared.

Who isn't? he said.

We walked to where the horses were, milling in front of the Black Sun. The rest of the posse was congregating. Some were men and women only a few years older than me, and some could have been grandfathers and grandmothers. Everyone looked eager, but I was nervous more than anything. Ren told me that I would be riding with him. I would have to tell him where to go.

I don't want anyone killed, I said after we mounted. Remember?

Yeah, yeah, Ren said. It's okay. Here, we should drink.

What? I said.

It's customary.

He pulled out a flask from a pouch and started passing it around. No one looked askance when it came to me. I hesitated for a second and took a few swallows. It tasted like milk, whiskey, and a little bit of cinnamon. I kept myself from coughing and handed it back to Ren. My vision blurred for a second and my skin felt flushed.

At midnight we rode. I had never been on the streets this late at night before. They were deserted; we were a blur winding between the towers. Hawks and bats darted above us, like dolphins following in a ship's wake. Or maybe that was my imagination. I held on to Ren as his horse charged forward. My ears ached from the wind. When the horse got to a full gallop, I was terrified. I felt that, at any minute, someone would run out into the middle of the street and the horse would collide with the pedestrian and I'd sail over the horse to the ground, breaking my neck. But Ren had complete control. I got the sense that Ren was like a centaur, and that when I had seen him in the Black Sun, walking around on two legs, he was only half a creature. He leaned forward. I leaned forward. I wondered what my brother would have thought of me on a horse—whether he would have been jealous of me.

Did Imperial troops impede us? Any watchmen? I didn't see any. They weren't worried about disturbances in the street.

We got to Sophia fast. Almost everyone in Nueva Roma lived in buildings that climbed up and up, but it surprised me how small the island was after shooting from one end to the other on a swift horse. I tapped on Ren's shoulder when we reached the beer courtyard. Everyone pulled up and trotted into the archway. Business was slow. The lights were dim and the shadows were long. The proprietor of the beer garden, the one with the tiger tattoos, had his back to us. There were about a half-dozen other patrons, Turquoises all, finishing their mugs, and they were drunk enough that it took them a few seconds to realize that there were, in fact, a dozen Scythian raiders on horseback inside the open-aired tavern.

I saw Sophia off in the corner under a small but high awning, washing mugs in a tub. Her eyes widened as she saw us. She was likely the only sober one in the place—and that included Scythians and pretend Scythians like me. I wasn't drunk, but had a hot buzz. I wanted to jump off Ren's horse then and there and rescue her, but I needed the masquerade to play out in order to be able to escape alive.

We're closed, the tiger-tattooed man said, his back to us. He was counting tusks and separating the copper and the silver into separate cloth bags.

Ren pulled out his short sword. He didn't say anything. Did he need to say anything?

The other patrons took a few steps back, and the owner turned around with a scowl. But then he saw us and the anger was mixed with shock, which he did his best to hide.

The proprietor was about to say something, but Ren put a finger to his lips. He was theatrical.

The owner kept quiet.

Then Ren pointed to the bag of tusks, and then Sophia.

The owner was trembling, and a coward, that much was clear. But cowards could still be dangerous.

Fuck . . . fuck you, he said.

Sophia was trying to squirm away, trying to slip the plastic cord from her ankle. My heart broke.

One of the Scythians took his horse closer to Sophia and held out his hands, motioning for her to stop.

The other Turquoises looked at the tiger-tattooed man, as if he were supposed to lead them. But he was no leader—he only ran a tavern.

Fuck you, he said again.

I pulled out my dagger. I was ready for anything, in my own limited way.

Shit, it's happening, one of the Turquoises said. I knew it!

I don't hear anything else in the city, another said.

It's an *invasion,* the first said. It's a *surprise raid.*

Those aren't the same things!

The first Turquoise shook his head and then growled. He pulled out a long sword. The others had a mix of daggers, clubs, and swords. Soon the weapons were in their hands and they charged us. The tiger-tattooed man stumbled behind them with a long dagger.

If history is a tragedy at first and farce the second time around—I forgot who said that—then I didn't know what number the world was up to when I was trying to free my sister. Maybe it was a refined blend of tragedy and farce, like in a silent movie. The Scythians didn't say a word as Ren whistled. The horses moved in a tight box formation, and the Scythians had their own swords out. Those on the edges parried everything that the Turquoises threw at them. The horses danced in syncopation as the Turquoises tried to get a good angle. The tiger-tattooed man swooped around the edges, cursing, but he wouldn't get any closer to the action. Then Ren whistled again and several of the horses on the edges darted forward and pivoted, so the Turquoises were surrounded. Hooves kicked at them and a couple of the drunkards fell over.

The silence was unnerving the Turquoises, I could tell. The Scythians were like ghosts or hallucinations. After a couple of minutes of this, the Turquoises ran through a narrow opening in the formation, shouting. The proprietor looked around, surrounded on all sides, and then Ren leaped off his horse, taking him by surprise. The taverner took a swipe at Ren, who dodged with ease. Ren lunged toward him with the hilt of his sword and smashed it against his temple. He fell to the ground, onto his back. Sophia remained frozen. Ren motioned to me and I slid off the horse with a couple of hops.

The owner was out cold, eyes closed, with a half-smile. As if he were dreaming. He almost looked peaceful.

Do you want to kill him? Ren said to me, tracing a line on his own throat. I knelt down next to the unconscious man and took a deep breath.

For a second I pretended that I had a choice.

No, I'm good, I said. Let's leave him.

Ren smiled and sheathed his sword, and then gathered up the bags of tusks.

Then I felt something hit my head. It stung. Another of the Scythians got pelted by something. I looked up. From high windows surrounding the courtyard, people were hanging out and shouting at us, throwing rocks and broken bottles. Men and women, young and old. A heavy bell started ringing above us.

Shit, I said.

I could hear shouting a few streets away.

Don't worry, Ren said, but I could tell he was getting nervous for the first time. The horses were beginning to get edgy in the enclosed space. A sharp rock beamed one of the Scythians and he fell off his horse, and staggered up.

We need to leave, Wye said. Now.

I nodded and ran to my sister in the dim corner, my heart racing. Not as much as hers, no doubt.

Oh God! she screamed. Please, no.

She started to cry. I still had my dagger out. I knelt next to her and cut her cord. Then I took off my helmet.

Sophia, I said. Hey. It's me. And my friends.

It didn't register with her right away that it was me.

It's a long story, I said, answering a protest she didn't make. There's not a lot of time. Come on.

I took her hand and lifted her up. She wobbled.

I'm not going to let go, I said.

We took a step forward toward the center of the courtyard. A bottle crashed at her feet and we stopped. She didn't have any armor. Out in the open, she was an easy target.

One of the Scythians dashed out of the courtyard to the street and came back after a few seconds.

About fifty, coming toward us, she said.

I wondered if my plan was turning into a fiasco. The din of the bell was making my ears hurt.

Listen, Wye said, we should split into two groups. One to lead the gang on a wild-goose chase and the other to make a break for the submarine.

He circled the courtyard with his horse and kept a nervous eye on every conceivable angle from where we could get attacked. I could tell he expected people to be bursting through nooks and crannies at any second. The noise of the crowd approaching us got louder.

Okay, I said, having to raise my voice. Ren?

Ren nodded. Macy, you and your sister can come with me.

But no one else knows the streets well enough to keep from getting caught, I said.

I do, Wye said.

Wye, don't, I said. Em needs you.

She needs your sister more, he said, pulling out a second sword that he had hidden God knew where. Trust me, he said.

Okay, okay, I said, and at last I saw what Em must have seen in him for many years.

But if you get killed . . . well, I don't know what I'd do with myself, I said.

Don't worry, he said. A sharp stone bounced off his shoulder. He winced and brushed his armor where the stone hit. The Scythians divided into two groups. Sophia and I sprinted across the courtyard as the horses cantered into the street. I squeezed her hand tight. We got dinged a couple of times, and I had glass shatter on my arm, but we kept moving. At the other end of the street, I could see the mob from the light of their own torches, and their homemade black-and-turquoise banners, which were also aflame. I couldn't tell whether they thought an invasion was in full force, or whether we were Teals in disguise, or what. They were already throwing stones at us, and though their aim fell short, it wasn't comforting.

I helped Sophia onto a Scythian's horse, and then Ren helped me onto his. Wye wasn't wasting any time. With six other Scythians right behind him, he charged right toward the mob of Nueva Romans. Then when he was a stone's throw away from them, he pivoted his horse sharply left into an alley. The throng roared and sprinted after them. I could hear the rumble of chariots intermixed in the crowd. It would be a long night.

Who *is* he? Sophia whispered, pointing at Wye before he disappeared around the corner.

That's another long story, I said.

Ren whistled and the other half of the Scythians, with Sophia and me, had their horses galloping in the other direction. I clenched Ren, trying to remember how to retrace my steps back to the secret pier. While we were riding, I looked over at my sister, who was holding on to her Scythian rider for dear life. Her brown hair was streaming behind her. Her face had been cut by a stray shard of glass, and her cheek was bleeding, but she didn't care. She couldn't care less. Her eyes were closed, and she was laughing, like she had never been that free before in her entire life.

A Birth During Wartime

At 8:02 p.m., on the seventh day of the egret's month, 120 yards below sea level, two miles northeast of Nueva Roma, Macy [last name redacted] was born to Em [last name redacted] and Wye [last name redacted].

Her weight at birth: 5 pounds, 4 ounces.

She is of no nationality, no country. She is of the sea, and her parents.

The birth proceeded without incident.

Macy is a name from Old French, which means "weapon."

(log of Sophia Palmer, midwife)

EPILOGUE

EVERYTHING ELSE IS A LOOSE END, AN ONGOING PART OF ONE struggle or another. Maybe that's the way it's always been.

The first group made it back to the *Nadir* with none the warier. William was waiting for us at the secret pier, the model of composure—until he caught sight of Sophia and almost bowled her over. Which I had warned her about, so she was ready. She wasn't ready for the news of our mother's death, and how she died. But how could she have been? I told her later in a quiet part of the submarine. It was hard. Really hard.

I had offered to load up all the Scythians on the sub, but Ren had told me they were better off with their families in Nueva Roma. And besides, they knew tons of hiding places in the tunnels underneath the city. Ren then gave me the vaccine vial and the rest of the cinnamon whiskey, and told me not to get them confused.

Wye and the other Scythians made it to the sub a few hours later. It wasn't pretty, but they all lived. There was a hand-to-hand skirmish in one of the skyways—God only knew how they got up there and back down again—but they all lived, though a couple of the Scythians were barely conscious, propped up in their saddles. And these Scythians Em did shuttle to the north-east part of Nueva Roma, where they were taken to safety by Scythian refugees hiding in the beach coves.

Then Em's water broke, and Sophia had her chance to shine.

All in all, the rescue had enough contradictory signs and rumors surrounding it—including whether it had even happened at all, according to official channels—that the Scythians in Nueva Roma were able to keep safe. A lot of the other gangs thought it was a stunt pulled by the Turquoises themselves to garner sympathy and glory.

I didn't find out about all of this until much, much later. After little Macy was born—a birth and choice of name that left me speechless with joy—Em and Wye took us Palmers up the river, away from Nueva Roma and its false invasions, to our home. Which meant Dad. Dad was rather surprised to see us knocking on his door one crystal-clear but cold afternoon. He was wearing an apron, and was cooking enough stew to feed an army. He broke down. We all broke down. I had to tell him about Ciaran, which was fucking hard. That I had no idea what would happen to him—but I also got to tell Dad about how brave and valiant and kind Ciaran was, too. I got to gush. I think he appreciated hearing that from me.

It's pointless to try to separate the happiness and sadness of my time in Nueva Roma. I tried to follow the advice given to me earlier in Lou, though for a different reason than intended: *assume that Ciaran's dead*. And I did assume the worst, because I couldn't bear any stupid false hope.

But I also had a promise to keep, for Ciaran's sake. On the first Tuesday of the next month, I made my trek to the confluence of the two big rivers. It made me think of our time up north, on Pike Island, seeing the rivers coming together like that. I saw her right away—she was hard to miss in her striking scarlet cloak. It looked like she had been waiting for me for a long time. She had that look about her. It was Mari, the fisherwoman who had rescued my family after we were kicked off the *Prairie Chicken,* and who I'd see around town here and there.

She waved. I waved back and then took the vial out of my pocket.

Thank you, she said. Thank you.

I wanted to tell her all about Ciaran then and there, and his sacrifice, but I supposed I would be able to tell her another time. She took the vial from me, wrapped it in a white cloth, and then put it in a pouch that was slung around her shoulder. We hugged each other, and then she got in her rowboat, and started rowing up the Missouri, slow and steady. I watched her until she was just a speck, and then I sighed—both out of relief and from feeling a little more complete than I had when I woke up that morning. I watched a few kingfishers skitter along the surface of the water for a few minutes, letting the solitude seep into me. Then I started my walk home.

It took a while for Sophia and Dad to get used to William, but they did. Our family had been scattered to the winds, and yet I felt closer to all of them than I ever did. And I think everyone felt the same way. Which meant a great deal, after all the shit we went through.

I think Mother would have been happy.

It wasn't until months later that I heard any word about Ciaran's fate. Wye had tried to keep tabs on him, but the Imperial court was secretive. At last, he had heard glimmers of rumors, and then more concrete information. He broke the news to us on one of his monthly visits to Lou, with Em and little Macy: Ciaran was alive.

Regarding his sentence. A funny thing happened. Three months after Ciaran's trial, the Emperor died. Choked on a peacock bone, which had been misplaced in his meal. No one could prove anything. At any rate, the new Emperor, a boy of thirteen, sued for peace with the Scythians, no doubt under the influence of his half-Scythian aunt, exchequer of the Empire. His mother had fled to Florida. That was how things worked. Though there was a truce to the north, the pirate archipelagos to the south were beginning to get antsy.

There would always be a front.

Anyway, the Emperor ceded Minnesota and the Dakotas to the Scythians and fourteen other affiliated tribes, and commuted the sentences of about thirty traitors such as Ciaran to five-year sentences. Five years. He could have a life. I could be there when he got out.

One day at a time. I had to keep up being patient. It was hard.

In that light, I settled in. Dad had been trying, in our absence, to set up a college of some sort in Lou, and he was close to succeeding. I figured I would end up taking some classes, though God only knew what I wanted to do with my life. What opportunities were open to me in the first place. Em also taught me proper fencing when she came up for air and visited us every month. I sparred for self-defense. And exercise. And because it was like yoga with edged weapons. And there was nothing wrong with that.

It wasn't all rainbows and unicorns. I still had a lot to learn and I still had more pains than I could count. I missed my mother and brother tons. I missed Lydia and wondered if she would ever forgive me for abandoning her to the hands of her psychotic father and stepmother. And at the same time, the final incident with her really freaked me out, and I couldn't say with absolute certainty that she wasn't, deep down, as crazy as her father. The vaccine distribution was slow as hell, and the plague flared up again in late spring. Since I had contracted it already, I volunteered for graveyard duty, and buried teenagers, old people, kids. People I knew. It was awful. We got through it.

And it went without saying that our family still had its fights and stresses. But all in all, it was a wonderful thing to have Sophia and William and Dad close by, and I promised myself to never take it for granted, ever.

Because the river never left me. It kept gushing into me, even when I was on dry land. My sleep kept getting interrupted by the river—sometimes it would be a beautiful dream about peaceful mermaid-crocodiles welcoming me into their underwater kingdom, and sometimes it would be nightmares about submerged and violent battles, bayoneted refugees being dumped into a slow current.

The river was both.

While on the river and under it, I would feel the water open in my mind, and unfurl, flowing down from Minnesota like a slow explosion—but to what end? And what purpose waited for me at that end? Total oblivion, more or less. Though too young and dumb to read all the tea leaves of life with my family—its small triumphs and somewhat larger tragedies—I could nevertheless see on the edge of my sight, even then, that all the weirdness on the river paled in comparison to the phantom byways in our heads—cold clear wellsprings and dead bogs alike. We were, each of us, alone, and yet bound together in ways that none of us understood. In fact, any attempt at wisdom almost always led to disaster.

I understand that now. I understand love a little bit more—and what it can cost. But it's a cost I'm more than willing to pay.

Mother taught me that. Ciaran taught me that. My living, breathing family is still teaching me that. I don't pretend to be wise anymore, and I don't try to stop being afraid when I'm afraid, or angry when I'm angry. It sounds so easy but it's the hardest thing in the world.

Because you have to roll with the punches, the good and the bad. You have to keep moving forward. It's like the river—even after all the crazy things that have happened, the river's not running backwards anytime soon.

ACKNOWLEDGMENTS

Throughout the writing of this novel, the information and narratives in *Voices on the River* by Walter Havighurst (1964, reprinted by University of Minnesota Press, 2003) proved to be indispensable. Any inaccuracies and vagrant geographies in this novel, of course, are mine alone. Thanks go out to: Richard Butner, Lena DeTar, Haddayr Copley-Woods, and Dave Schwartz, who read the book in one stage or another and provided invaluable advice; Chris Barzak for the unending encouragement; my agent Colleen Lindsay for her tireless support; Juliet Ulman, for bringing it halfway around the bases; and Noah Eaker, for bringing it to home plate. Thanks also goes out to my family and wife's family, without whose love and support none of this would be possible. And lastly, thanks goes out to my wife, Kristin, for all of this and everything else.

ALAN DeNIRO was born in Erie, Pennsylvania. He graduated from the College of Wooster and received an MFA in poetry writing from the University of Virginia. His collection of short stories, *Skinny Dipping in the Lake of the Dead,* was published by Small Beer Press. It was longlisted for the Frank O'Connor International Short Story Award and a finalist for the Crawford Award. His short fiction has appeared in *One Story, Crowd, Interfictions 2, Strange Horizons,* and elsewhere. He lives outside St. Paul, Minnesota, with his wife, Kristin, a dog, and three cats.